John Howard Marsden

Philomorus

Notes on the Latin Poems of Sir Thomas More

John Howard Marsden

Philomorus
Notes on the Latin Poems of Sir Thomas More

ISBN/EAN: 9783337407155

Printed in Europe, USA, Canada, Australia, Japan

Cover: Foto ©Andreas Hilbeck / pixelio.de

More available books at **www.hansebooks.com**

Philomorus.

NOTES ON THE LATIN POEMS OF

SIR THOMAS MORE.

--- Φιλέμωρον se declarabat.
ERASMI EPIST.

SECOND EDITION.

LONDON:

LONGMANS, GREEN, READER, AND DYER.

1878.

CONTENTS.

CHAPTER I.

THE Epigrammata of Sir Thomas More, v. in 1518. Page 1. Recent additions to the first edition of the present work, 2. So the M noble character, 3. All trifles relative to him are worth preserving, 4. Sharon Turner quotes Cranmer the weak points of More's character, 5. Cannot seem p The Latin epigramma of the 16th century always from the modern epigram, 6. More's wit and playfulness, 7. The steeple, 8. His jocular remark upon one of the works of Erasmus Lord Herbert upon More's inopportune jests, 10. Jests 11. More's reputation as a poet, 12. His English verse, 12. So ideas in Shakespeare's 'Seven Ages' and in one of tory's and His 'Merry Jest on a Serjeant,' 14. Elegy on the Queen. R on More's poetry by Erasmus, Tyndale, and others, 15. M poetry in the Epigrammata, 16. More himself the sole topic of y, Of tragedy also, 17. His writings in general almost forg Excepting the Utopia, 19.

CHAPTER II.

General use at this time of the Latin language, 20. Er use no other, 20. A fashion of writing Latin verses, 21. In every form and by scholars in all grades, 22. British poetry at 22. Not yet discontinued, 23. Latin of Henry VIII., of bishop of Cologne, the Emperor Charles V., and Pope Leo X And of Don Ferdinand, 25. Interest excited by More's Epigrammata, 25. Erasmian Latin, 26. More's epi f

English language, 27.   Erasmus ridicules the Ciceronians, 27.   Also the
overfondness for classical mythology, 28.   More's Epigrammata are con-
versant with real life, 28.   Some of them are autobiographical sketches, 28.
A charm in their naturalness, 29.   More began by translating Greek
Epigrammata from the Anthologia, 30.   In a sort of competition with
William Lily, 30.   A favourite occupation with Dr. Johnson and others,
30.   Early translators,—and modern, 31.   One remarkable Epigramma, 31.
Quoted by Sir Walter Raleigh, 32.   Adopted by Lord Brougham, 32.
More begins to write original Epigrammata, 33.   He writes on the
accession and coronation of Henry VIII., 33.   Flodden field, 33.   The
Novum Instrumentum of Erasmus, 33.   More's activity and versatility of
mind shown in this collection, 34.   From lively to grave, 35.   Satire
upon vices, follies, and foibles, 35.   Finds the need of caution, 35.   His
love of verse in early life,—and at life's close, 36.

Chapter III.

Learning acquired under difficulties, 37.   In England at a low ebb, 37.
Compulsory education of gentlemen's sons in Scotland.   An Eton boy's
verses, 38.   More's diligence in study, 38.   Assisted by Lily and
Erasmus, 39.   He might have rivalled the verse-writers of Italy, 40.
But his compositions though unpolished are to us more valuable, 40.
Vigour in them and also tenderness, 40.   More a patron of literature, 41.
His reply to a scholastic divine who condemned the New Learning as
heretical, 41.   Erasmus composed his Epigrammata extempore, 41.   Sometimes on horse-back, 43.   More composed an epistle to his children when
on horse-back, 43.   Frequent journeys of Erasmus, 44.   His friends supply
him with horses, 45.   His horse-exercise at Cambridge, 45.   More
thought meanly of his own Latin verses, 46.   His experience of critics,
47.   The opinions respecting these pieces expressed by Rhenanus,
Leland, Huet, Pecke, Dr. Johnson, Landor, 48.   Other writers of Epigrammata in Britain at that time, 49.   Owen in 1606, 49.   Landor in
our own times, 49.   Sundry English translations introduced,—by Sir
Nicholas Bacon, Kendall, Thynne, Pecke, and Archdeacon Wrangham,
50.   More's age and position when the volume was published, 50.

Chapter IV.

Verses commemorative of a boyish attachment, 52.   Wrangham's
translation, 53.   A similar passage in one of Milton's elegies, 54.   More's
two marriages, 56.   Character of his second wife, 56.   Her discourtesy
to her guest Erasmus, 56.   Harsh remark made by Anthony Wood, 57.

CONTENTS.

More's epitaph on hi ... ... wife, 5 ... W
Certain Epigrammata ...ritten before
Kendall's translation, 59. ... Ad...s ... ...
The nation's joy, 61. ... A... ... of Hen... VIII ... ...
young King, 63. ... W ... ...
Henry's marriage, 64. ... Hi... ...
coronation, 66. ... M...a! ... ...
of Queen Anne Boleyn, 67. ... W... ... M...
pieces on the acce...ion, 68. ... B ...
Norham castle, 69. ... Epitaph... IV
by Buchanan, 71. ... War with Fra...7 ... \
Lampoons by the Frenc, 72. ... A... w... ...
and Tournay taken by the En...li h, 73. ... (
74. ... De Brie a...ails the En...lish in h...(... 7...
ridicules in these Epigrammata, 75. ... De B...
in his Antimorus, 75. ... Era... ...ttempts to ...
late, 76. ... His advice to More, 77. ... M...r...
Disputes of modern statesme upon points of L...

CHAPTER V.

More's embassies to Flanders, 80. ... ... W
...n epistle in Latin verse to his children ... ... H
...rder affection, 82. ... Directs their atten...o ...
83. ... Colet's love of children, 83. ... Harsh ... ... S... M...
with regard to priests being sent out as ... ... S...
formed while in Flanders. ... Bu...leiden, ... L... ...
den's library and coins, 86. ... Works of an... ... ...87 ... M
an extra reward for his embassies, 87. ... H... ...
18. ... Is gradually drawn... ... ...ag... ...st his w... ...88. ... ...
of a Prince's favour, 89. ... ...ines on... ...
clown's first view of the King, 90. ... O...
Flanders, 90. ... Others upon the ...a...
different forms of government, 9... ... P... ...s
sentiments reproduced in a public ... ...9... ...
courtiers, 93. ... The Court at th's time... ...h
among foreigners, 94. ... Henry's d... ... ... N...
him, 95. ... More expresses to Colet ... ...
passage in Johnson's London, 96. ... T... ...
written in early life, 96. ... Intent of ... ...o...97. ... \
to print it in England or to transla e it ... ... F...
years, 97.

CHAPTER VI.

More acts as Secretary to the King, 99. Informs Pace of his appointment to the Archdeaconry of Colchester, 99. Writes to conciliate the Earl of Arundel, 100. Approves a letter written by Wolsey to the Queen of Scotland, 100. Conversation with the King respecting an ambassador from Francis I., 101. Wolsey advises that the army in France should remain stationary, 102. On further thought he advises that it should advance. 102. More writes to express the King's approval of Wolsey's out-spokenness, 102. Wolsey advises the King to place confidence in More, 103. Charles V. visits England, 103. More Treasurer of the Exchequer, 103. Addresses the Emperor in a Latin speech. 104. His rapid advancement, 104. For which he states that he is indebted to his love of learning, 105. Speaker of the House of Commons, 105. Cromwell's eulogy of him in that character, 106. 'A 'sordido lucro alienissimus,' 107. Public officers ill-paid, 107. Sir Thomas Elyot complains of straitness in means, 108. Grants made to More, 108. Appointed Chancellor of Duchy of Lancaster. 109. In high favour with the King, 109. The King writes against Luther, 109. Luther replies and is assailed by Rossæus, supposed to be More, 110. More writes a Dialogue against Luther and Tyndale, 110. Is made Chancellor, 110. The speech which he is reported to have delivered, 110. No record of cases decided by him, 110. His custom to kneel in public for his father's blessing, 111. Lord Ellesmere, Lord Bacon, and Lord Somers compared with Sir Thomas More, 112, 113.

CHAPTER VII.

More brought up in the household of Cardinal Morton, 114. When yet a youth gave lectures upon St. Augustine, 114. Inclination to a monastic life and afterwards to the priesthood, 115. Dean Colet his spiritual adviser, 115. Colet's sermons, 116. Colet and More admirers of Savonarola, 116. Erasmus furthers the Reformation, 117. Warm friendship between More and Erasmus, 117. Similar points in their character and sentiments, 117. A monk endeavours to put More on his guard against Erasmus, 119. More writes in defence of Erasmus, 119. He argues against Mariolatry, 119. Roper at the time of his marriage with More's daughter was a Lutheran, 122. Scandals among the clergy, 122. Denounced by Colet and satirized by More, 123. Holy Orders obtained by artifice, 124. Degraded condition of some of the clergy, 124. Preferment given for the training of hawks, 125. And for money, 125. More's lines upon Candidus a priest, 126. Upon

CONTENTS.

the priest of his own parish. 147. I
fessing to a priest. 147. La
expose the Sc... 149. L.
'Occidit littera' ... Bi...
pretended brother, 151. ...
'didus et perpe sen. 152. I
bishop. 153. ... ...
Henry VII. 151. Sup... ...
have applied t. Er...
age and circumst... 155. C
Baker could use ... 155. ... A
Baker's word. 150. M

CHAPTER VIII.

About this time ... ...
description we content ...
142. The eyes of t... ...
hitherto sensuous. I...
things are listened to. 114. Sir T.
church at Chelsea. 145. He ... w.
a splendid ritual. 146. Aver...
pompous funerals. 146. Fi...
of his daughter-in-law and ...7.
in purgatory. 148. Dean C...
priestly pomp in the Utopia. 148. A...
a part. 149. The Sub-dean ... 150. ...
ceremonials. 150. The ritual to C...
attractive. 151. Riv... an...
Cardinal, and the King. 151. M...
153. He writes a secon. 153. A...
Erasmus. 153. Much unduly exalt...
to this effect. Cardinal Pole's opin...
outcry against musical service... I
plains that they run to exce... l...
reasonable footing. 156. A ch...
the Puritans they are entirely put...
excess and meagreness is the res...

CHAPTER IX

Unsettled state of the religious w
clergy ignorant and inefficient. 159. ...

Fox to correct abuses, 159. Monasteries purified; colleges founded; churches built, 159. The Lutheran party nevertheless make progress, 160. In Germany much tumult and outrage, 161. More's great reverence for authority, 161. He is disinclined to a separation, 161. He finally resolves to maintain the Pope's supremacy, 162. According to Cardinal Pole he was reclaimed from former doubts by a miracle, 162. As Chancellor he was bound to suppress heresy, 162. Wolsey had been lenient, 162. How far More was a persecutor, 163. Allowance to be made for circumstances, 163. The King and the Court opposed to Lutheranism, 164. More desirous to conciliate the clergy, 164. Plausible arguments for persecution, 165. Heresy classed with theft and murder, 166. More's own statement, 166. Luther accused of teaching simulation, 167. Lutheranism said to be sedition and anarchy, 167. More styles himself 'hereticis molestus,' 168. States to Erasmus why he was so, 168. Less of a persecutor than many others would have been. 169. He alludes to his former writings, 170. He would burn them rather than that they should harm any one, 171. His polemical writings are violent and coarse, 171. The root of the whole matter according to Burnet and Froude, 172. Frightful outrages reported in Germany, and More feared the like in England, 173. He knew that a reformation was needed, but did not trust the Reformers, 173. A similar dereliction of early principles in Edmund Burke, 174. More's forecast of the future, 174. Yet he preferred to remain on the losing side, 175. Southey's opinion that if a younger man he would have joined the Reformers, 176. Also that he would have pronounced the Anglican Church to be the best the world had ever seen, 176. The author of the work called 'Morus' assumes that he was a faithful son of the Romish Church throughout, 176. On the other side he is claimed as one of the 'Oxford Reformers,' 177. Thus the Greeks and the Trojans fought for the body of Patroclus. 177. Regret that one of those descendants of his who were Protestants did not write his life, 178.

Chapter X.

Pieces indicative of More's habits and daily line of thought, 179. Fondness for animals, 179. Marmoset painted by Holbein, 180. Dogs sent to Budæus, 180. Cat and mouse, 180. Spider and fly, 180. Denounces wanton cruelty, 181. Couplet by Sir William Jones quoted, 182. Frequent allusions to death, 182. Addison's remark, 183. Public life full of vicissitudes, 184. Lines upon Fortune, 184. Holbein's picture of Fortune, 185. Allusion made by the Earl of Arundel, 186.

CONTENTS.

Wear and tear in public life, 186. More' pr..., 187. ... on prayer, 187. Inward prayer, 188. An inst..., 189. Similar sentiment in Milton's Comus, 189. Exp... applause, 189. Vanity of earthly things, 190. On the f... by preceding writers. Chaucer, Gower, Lydgate, 191. Go...y Sidney, 192. More's satirical lines on women, 192. El... More's daughters, 193. Their report of sermons, 193. M... to a remark of Erasmus, 194. Severe remarks on wedd..., 195. The like by Sir John More his father, 195. Erasmus on the E... ladies, 196. Offerings made by wives to St. Uncumber, 196. M... ingenious defence, 197. The King chooses a wife for Mr. B..., 197. And a husband for a certain widow, 197. An English epig... to More by Warton, 198. More's description of a mines... His apology for an act of apparent discourtesy, 202.

CHAPTER XI.

Notices of contemporary literature, 204. The Novum Instru... of Erasmus, 204. Which aided in furthering the Reformation, 205. Approved by Pope Leo X, Cardinal Ximenes, Archbishop Warham, and Bishop Fox, 205. At Cambridge anathematized, 206. Opposed by the Scotists and defended by Sir Thomas More, 206. Attacked in a sermon at Court and again defended by More, 207. The preacher rebuked, 208. A copy presented to the Bishop of Liege, 208. Humorous remark on its reception, 208. More's lines address to the reader of the work, 209. To Wolsey, 209. To Warham, 210. Opposite characters of Warham and Wolsey, 211. How Erasmus was treated by each, 212. Wolsey now at the height of his greatness, 212. More on the way to advancement, 212. Vicissitudes in the life of each, 213. Subsequent intercourse between More and Wolsey, 213. Wolsey's overbearance, 213. Retort made by More, 214. More's speech in Parliament, 214. Invective on Wolsey, 214. Compositions of Busleiden, 215. Hymns 'De Divis,' 215. Two sonnets translated, 216. Poetasters criticized, 216. More's love of art: Holbein, Quintin Matsys, 217. Matsys paints Erasmus and Ægidius in one picture, 217. Allusion to St. Luke as a painter, 218. Head of John the Baptist, 218. Approval of a faithful likeness, 219. Interview between More and Holbein, 219. Engraved portraits of More, 219. Original drawings of More by Holbein, 220. Large picture of the More family, 220. More's collection of Roman coins, 221.

Chapter XII.

Lines on the imitators of French fashions, 222. Attack upon this Epigramma by Germain de Brie, 224. More's defence of it, 224. More an abstemious man, 224. His lines upon wine-bibbers, 224. Lines on a wine-bibber by Erasmus, 225. More's lines on the spendthrift and the miser, 225. On sleep the universal equalizer, 226. More's constitution delicate, 227. An ague, 227. Galen quoted by Margaret Gige, 227. Satirical lines upon the medical profession, 228. The like by Sir John Harington, 228. Others by More, 229. Bishop Fisher's physician applies to the Lord Privy Seal for his fee, 230. On the military profession, 230. Colet preached against war, 231. Erasmus wrote against it, 231. Henry's designs upon France, 231. More's gentle monition in favour of peace, 232. Wolsey promises conquest, 232. Jests upon soldiers, 232. Astrology at that time held in repute, 233. More's ridicule of the astrologers, 234. Lines addressed to one Tyndale a slippery debtor, 235. Probability that the creditor and the debtor were Humphrey Monmouth and Tyndale the Reformer, 236. The city feasts, 237. Lines on a compact between two beggars, 237. On a waiting-maid, 237. Jests upon personal peculiarities, 238. Idle stories relating to the practice of auricular confession, 238. Contrast between these and the more reverent compositions of More's favourite, John Picus of Mirandola, 239.

Chapter XIII.

Sir Thomas More's rapid downfall, 240. He appears as a suppliant to Cromwell, 241. Addresses a touching letter to the King, 241. Refuses to take the oaths and is committed to the Tower, 243. Is visited in the Tower by the Law officers of the Crown, 243. A refusal to answer questions is set down as guilt, 243. What the King will gain by superseding the Pope, 244. Report of this by a Spanish official residing in England at the time. Two obstructions in the King's way, Fisher and More, 245. His attempt to intimidate them, 245. His final resolve to remove them both, 245. Difficulty in concocting a capital charge against them, 245. The King's Solicitor alleges that More made to him a certain admission, 246. More's books taken from him, 246. A devotional book sent to him by Fisher, 246. Trial of Sir Thomas More, 247. The charge being that of High Treason, 247. Sentence pronounced, 247. A singular entry in Cromwell's private list of agenda, 248. Novel account of the execution given by the Spanish journalist, 249. Also of More's address to the peers, and an interview with King Henry in the Tower, 250. More on his trial compared to Socrates, 251. Estimate of his public character by the Emperor Charles V. Accounts of the execution in manuscript circulated at the time, 252. A singular illumination in one of these which belonged to the late Mr. Corser, 252. Sundry dirges and elegies, 253.

CHAPTER XIV.

The abolition of the Pope's supremacy declared over the land by proclamation, 254. Gainsayers in Holderness and in Cheshire committed to prison, 254. It is pronounced treasonable to say that Sir Thomas More was a martyr, 255. Extract from a sermon on the subject preached before the King by the Bishop of Durham, 255. The Pope claimed the power of deposing the King, 256. Canon Croke's sermons on the same subject, 256. Archbishop Lee charged with having been remiss, 257. His protestation, 257. He pleads the incapacity of his clergy, 257. Latin verses on Sir Thomas More's execution, 258. Holland:—Hervetus:—Joannes Secundus, 258. Latomus:—Bishop White:—John Fowler, 259. Alan Cope:—John Owen:—a serio-comic epitaph, 260. Borbonius a writer of Latin verses, 261. Patronized by Queen Anne Boleyn, 261. His scurrilous lines on Sir Thomas More, 262. Imputation of low birth, 262. Many of More's descendants became Protestants, 263. A long interval before his life was written, and longer still before it was published, 264. His English works printed in 1557, 264. 'Il Moro,' 264. Roper's Life when written, 264. Harpsfield's, 264. Stapleton's, 265. Life by B. R., 266. Roper's Life printed, 266. Cresacre More's, 267. Modern Lives, 267. Mackintosh, 267. Lord Campbell, 268.

APPENDIX.

Pirckheimer and Rhenanus, 269. Translations from Amaltheus and Politian, 270. From Melancthon, 270. One of More's Epigrammata translated by Sir Nicholas Bacon, 271. One of his 'witty sayings' versified by the same, 273. 'Merry tale' of a visit paid by John Skelton to Bishop Nix, 273. A ludicrous scene arranged by Skelton at which Sir Thomas More was present, 274.

PHILOMORUS

ERRATA.

Page 48, line 12.   *For* Peake *read* Pecke.

Page 92, line 11.   *After* when *insert*—it was alleged.

Epigrammata of that most illustrious and eloquent
man Thomas More, citizen and Under-sheriff of the
renowned city of London.[1]   In the Epistle dedicatory
Pirckheimer is addressed as holding an office of trust
under the Emperor corresponding in dignity and importance to the office held by Sir Thomas More under

---

[1] "Clarissimi disertissimique viri Thomæ Mori inclytæ civitatis Lon-
"dinensis Civis et Vice-comitis."—On Rhenanus and Pirckheimer see
Appendix, No. i.

B

PHILOMORUS.

CHAPTER I.

HE Latin poems of Sir Thomas More, having been collected by his friend Erasmus from detached and scattered copies handed about in manuscript, were printed at Basle in 1518 by the celebrated and learned Froben, under the supervision of another learned man known among the scholars of the day as Beatus Rhenanus. They are inscribed by him to Bilibald Pirckheimer, a Senator of Nuremberg and a favourite Councillor of the Emperors Maximilian and Charles V.; being set forth in the title-page as the Epigrammata of that most illustrious and eloquent man Thomas More, citizen and Under-sheriff of the renowned city of London.[1] In the Epistle dedicatory Pirckheimer is addressed as holding an office of trust under the Emperor corresponding in dignity and importance to the office held by Sir Thomas More under

CHAP. I.
A.D. 1518.

When and where the Epigrammata were first published.

---

[1] "Clarissimi disertissimique viri Thomæ Mori inclytæ civitatis Lou-"dinensis Civis et Vice-comitis."—On Rhenanus and Pirckheimer see Appendix, No. i.

Henry VIII., and as being, like More, a humourist as
well as a scholar [1] and a statesman. His daughters,
styled by Erasmus ' Bilibaldicæ,' are mentioned by
him as German ladies of high degree who rival the
other sex in point of scholarship; and he classes
them with Sir Thomas More's daughters, ' Moricæ,'
who had attained a like distinction in England.

The former
edition of this
work.

Since the former edition of the present work was
laid before the public, nearly forty years have now
elapsed. It was the growth of an early summer, and
at the creeping on of chill October the revision of it
has been taken in hand, there being added also sundry memoranda which had been jotted down in the
interval. In that original edition the author attempted
to call the attention of persons interested in the life
and character of Sir Thomas More to these minor productions, or Epigrammata, which in his lifetime were
much extolled, and in later times have been much
neglected. It was shown that they in some measure
illustrate and confirm the statements made in the
various Lives of More, down from Roper's original
and simple narrative to the more comprehensive
and elaborate biographies of modern times: such
occasional recapitulation of the events of More's life
being added as might appear convenient for the re-
freshing of the reader's memory. The labour was
not altogether in vain. Lord Campbell, in his Life
of Sir Thomas More, makes frequent reference to
"Philomorus," introducing also copious extracts

[1] Pirckheimer's valuable library eventually came into the possession
of the great collector Thomas twentieth Earl of Arundel; and by his
grandson, the eighth Duke of Norfolk, it was presented to the Royal
Society.

from it.[1] Subsequent writers have done the same.
In the present edition, which is much enlarged, the
author has availed himself of a few incidental and
previously unpublished memoranda notified by Mr.
Brewer in his valuable "Calendar of Letters and
"Papers of the Reign of Henry VIII.," and he
acknowledges with pleasure the advantage derived
from some of Mr. Brewer's able and appropriate
remarks. He has also introduced a few subsidiary
facts gleaned in other quarters, which do not appear
in the ordinary Lives of Sir Thomas More, avoiding
at the same time the drawing upon the ordinary
Lives for a larger amount of material than was
required in order to carry out the intention of so
placing the Lives and the Epigrammata that each of
them may illustrate the other.

Among the original thinkers of the past, and in   Sir Thomas
the list of those great names which have become   More's charac-
                                                   ter such as is
household words in our history, a very distinguished   seldom met
place has been allotted by common consent to Sir   with.
Thomas More. It is generally allowed that his plain-
spoken integrity, his shrewd and sagacious intellect,
his unbending tenacity of purpose, his dislike of all
vain pomp and pretension, his sober-mindedness in
an exalted position, his fortitude in adversity, the
union so rarely to be met with of perfect simplicity
with moral grandeur, and the calm spirit of resolution with which he faced the horrors of the block, all
combine to produce such a character as it is seldom
our privilege to contemplate. No man knew him
more intimately than Erasmus, who had lived for   The testimony
months together as an inmate in his house, and Eras-   of Erasmus.

---

[1] Lives of the Lord Chancellors. Second edition.

CHAP. I.

mus bears testimony to his moral and intellectual pre-eminence in these words: 'Cui pectus erat omni 'nive candidius; ingenium autem quale nemo An- 'glus vel habuit vel sit habiturus.'

The testimony of Richard Pace.

Pace, the King's secretary, described him as a man of unrivalled genius, of universal knowledge, and of incomparable eloquence. He seems to be the earliest instance in our history of a man raising himself to political importance in some degree by his public speaking; and as a scholar he was one of the very few persons in England who had any pretensions to classical scholarship at all. It is very forcibly re-Mr. Brewer's remark.marked by Mr. Brewer that round no man in this great reign do our sympathies gather so strongly, in no man is humanity in its various modes, its sun and shadow, its gentleness and kindliness, its sorrows and misgivings, presented so attractively, as in Sir Thomas More. And with no less truth another writer has summed up his remarks, by stating the fact that in the next generation it was deemed an honour to an Englishman throughout Europe to be the countryman of Sir Thomas More.

Those readers who have learned thus to appreciate the character of Sir Thomas More, following him from his early domicile, when a lively-witted boy in the house of Cardinal Morton the Archbishop of Canterbury, down to the bloody scene on the scaffold on All trifles are worth preserving.Tower Hill, will admit that in dealing with the sayings and doings of such a man, the veriest gleanings are too precious to be thrown aside or lost.

In the case of most of the distinguished men of our country down to the time of Sir Thomas More, the Lives that we possess are generally both interesting

and instructive, but in many cases they do not afford
us much insight into the real character of the individual. And in those cases where we do become a
little acquainted with the real character, we are dis-
appointed to find it rather common-place. But there
is nothing common-place in Sir Thomas More's character. And if any traits in that character can be
learned or illustrated, either by the traditionary
anecdotes of his family, or by his own expression of
a passing thought in Latin verse, they will add much
to the interest with which we read his life.

The failings in Sir Thomas More's character have
been more specially pointed out by the historian
Sharon Turner, in his history of the reign of Henry
VIII., than by his professed biographers. Cranmer
is there quoted as having thought him ' somewhat
' too conceited, and too fond of laying himself out to
' gain the approval and admiration of those around
' him; never willing to vary from anything which
' he had once expressed, whether wrong or right, lest
' he should damage his reputation thereby.' This
delineation of the weaker parts of More's character
must of course be referred to that later period of
More's life during which Cranmer was high in favour
with the King, and at which time he and More would
be occasionally brought together.

On the other hand it is allowed by Turner that Sir
Thomas More was warm in his friendships, and of
' easy urbanity ' at the time when he had attained to
high rank. And he remarks that More's private
prayers which are extant, and which were never expected to meet the eye of any person but himself,
evince a feeling of deep and unmistakeable piety.

Turner allows also that he died, pitied, loved, and passionately lamented by his numerous literary, social, and ecclesiastical friends; and regretted by every one on account of his high reputation and distinguished moral virtues.

These Latin compositions of Sir Thomas More are styled Epigrammata. The term Epigramma as used by scholars in the time of Erasmus was of a more comprehensive character than our modern word Epigram. Like the Epigram it was a fugitive composition springing out of the more salient topics of everyday life, terse in diction, and steady in its pursuit of one subject. But it was frequently of greater length than our modern Epigram. A few lines more or less were seldom taken account of provided that they followed up the one leading thought. Many of the Epigrammata might be classed under the modern designation of *vers de société*. A man of lively imagination committing to paper the result of his thought and observation was accustomed to embody it in Latin verse: condensing it so as to require less space and bulk if he chose to print it, which was not unfrequently the case; and at the same time giving proof to those around him of his scholarship.

The fashion of writing Epigrammata prevailed among the literati of Europe during the fifteenth and sixteenth century to a marvellous extent, and every collection of Latin poetry published at that period teems with them. They were written upon every imaginable subject, personal or public. Whether

eulogy was intended or satire, they were equally available. A writer could flatter the more adroitly and also satirize the more bitingly than if he used the vernacular language of the country. Sannazarius wrote six lines in praise of the city of Venice, for which he was rewarded with an honorarium of 600 golden crowns. Ulrich von Hutten consoled himself under the troubles of life by attacking his personal enemies, and by writing during the war vigorous Epigrammata against Venice and Pope Julius II. As a specimen of an Epigramma from the pen of royalty we have the following, which is said by Clerk, the Dean of the King's chapel, to have been ‘devised and ‘made’ by Henry VIII. himself, and written by his own hand in the volume of his ‘Assertio’ against Luther which he presented to the Pope. By others it has been attributed to Wolsey, and we may leave the Cardinal and the King to share the distinction between them :—

> “ Anglorum rex Henricus—Leo Decime—mittit
> “ Hoc opus, et fidei testem et amicitiæ.”

It is stated by all Sir Thomas More's biographers that he had a remarkable vivacity and facetiousness of temper, and that he was much given to jesting and pleasantry. And it appears rather singular that while in the various Lives of Sir Thomas More his witty sayings have been carefully treasured up[1] and are become familiar to most readers, his witty writings as comprised in the Epigrammata should have been entirely overlooked. Richard Pace speaks of his wit as being of no ordinary character :—like a good cook he is said to be not at all sparing in the use of acids, and to have had a way of laughing at a man in his sleeve

---

[1] The ‘Witty Apophthegms delivered at several times and on various occasions by Sir Thomas More and others.’—were published in 1658.

Latimer's
story of Ten-
terden steeple.

without allowing him the chance of finding it out.
Cresacre More says that his merry jests and witty
sayings would fill a volume. He had the gift of a
rare presence of mind and was ready on all occasions
with an appropriate anecdote. It was from 'Master
More' that Latimer derived that often-quoted story
of Tenterden steeple and the Goodwin Sands.[1] King
Henry and Queen Katharine found such a charm in
his conversation and sought it so frequently that in
self-defence he found it expedient to hide his talent
occasionally under a bushel. In order that he might
continue to enjoy that pleasant society of his wife and
children at home to which he was always accustomed,
he began, we are told, 'somewhat to dissemble his
'nature, and by little and little to disuse himself

---

[1] Upon this passage in More's Dialogue, Tyndale makes the following
remark :—

"This I have declared unto you that ye might see and feel every thing
"sensibly. For I intend not to lead you in darkness. Neither though
"twice two cranes make not four wild bees, would I therefore that ye
"should believe that twice two make not four. Neither intend I to prove
"unto you that Paul's steeple is the cause why Thames is broken in
"about Erith, or that Tenterden steeple is the cause of the decay of
"Sandwich haven, as Mr. More jesteth. Nevertheless, this I would were
"persuaded unto you—as it is true—that the building of them and such
"like is the decay of all the havens in England, and of all the cities, towns,
"bye-ways, and shortly of the whole commonwealth." He goes on to say
that "since these teachers of Romish doctrine crept up into our con-
"sciences and robbed us of the knowledge of our Saviour Christ, making
"us believe in such Pope-holy works, and to think that there was none
"other way unto heaven, we have not ceased to build them Abbeys,
"Cloisters, Colleges, Chantries, and Cathedral Churches, with high
"steeples, striving and envying one another who should do most. And as
"for the deeds that pertain unto our neighbours and unto the common-
"wealth, we have not regarded them at all, as things which seemed
"not to be holy works, and such as God would not once look upon."—
p. 279.

'from his accustomed mirth, so that he was not from 'thenceforth so ordinarily sent for.' This is stated by his admiring son-in-law, William Roper. There must have been in his conversation a characteristic raciness, and a record by some contemporary Boswell of all that passed on these occasions would have been invaluable.

He took much delight in the pleasantry of others also. Skelton, the satirist of Wolsey, and John Heywood, the prolific author of several 'centuries' of epigrams,[1] both claim the distinction of numbering Sir Thomas More among their patrons.

Erasmus said:—' Thomæ Mori ingenio quid unquam 'finxit natura vel mollius vel dulcius vel felicius?' In one of his letters Erasmus mentions a jocular remark made by More, of which he was himself the subject. A short time before this Erasmus had published a treatise, entitled, "De duplici Copiâ verborum ac rerum;" and on his complaining, as he too frequently did, of poverty, More said that after sending out his "Duplex Copia," he could scarcely expect to have anything left behind but "summa inopia." Many men have indulged their jocular propensities in the House of Commons,—as More did, and some also on the judicial bench,—as More did; some few have given utterance to witticisms in the pulpit,—as South did. Even Lord Chancellors may have made a jest of their retirement from the dignity of the woolsack,—as More

---

[1] Heywood boasts of the singular renown accruing to the Parish of North Mimms, in Hertfordshire, in which Sir Thomas More at one time had a residence :—

"There famous More did his Utopia write,
" And there came Heywood's epigrams to light."

did; who went up to his wife's pew in Chelsea Church, with his cap in his hand, before the fact of his resignation was made known to his family, and said, as one of his gentlemen in attendance had been accustomed to say, with the usual ceremonious bow,— 'May it please your ladyship, my lord is gone.' This, it will be seen, was quite in character, and we are told that the lady took it as one of his accustomed jests.

But when he proceeded to tell her gravely that he had given up the Great Seal, she lost her temper and assailed him with reproaches. Upon this he asked his daughters, who were present, whether they could 'spy any fault about their mother's dressing.' And after they had searched and found none, he replied, 'Do not you perceive that your mother's nose stands 'somewhat awry?' Lord Herbert proceeds to state that 'the provoked lady was so sensible of this jeer, 'that she went from him in a rage.'

He then told his wife and his daughters that he was now comparatively a poor man, and that their style of living must be brought down to suit their means; and that if matters should come to the worst, 'for our last refuge we will go a-begging, and at 'every man's door sing together a ' *Salve Regina* ' to 'get alms.'

Lord Herbert thinks that all this was carrying the jest too far— that it amounted to sarcasm, very inopportune and uncalled for. He says that Sir Thomas More might have betaken himself to a retired and quiet life without thus making his family or himself contemptible.' And Edward Hall, the chronicler,

---

[1] Life of Henry VIII., p. 372.

remarks that More's great wit was so mingled with taunting and mocking that he never was satisfied with himself in regard to anything which he had to communicate, unless he had 'ministered some mock ' in the communication.'

But Sir Thomas More jested even when on the scaffold. It is said of the Earl of Oxford by his friend Alexander Pope that he was accustomed to amuse himself by the composition of trifling verses, sending them round to the circle of wits with whom he loved to associate, and this at a crisis when his all was at stake. And Pope says also that he possessed at the same time such firmness of soul, that if he had been sentenced to death he would have died unconcern- edly, or perhaps even with a jest in his mouth, like Sir Thomas More.

Southey remarks that it is one thing to jest and another to be mirthful. And he thinks that in cases of a violent death, and especially under an unjust sentence, this jesting is not surprising, inasmuch as the sufferer is not wasted by long mental excitement and exertion. Edward Hall says that such jesting as More's at the time of his execution and on the scaffold cannot come from a sound mind. For as ' no one ' knows what scenes will follow the death of this ' world, and as it is a mysterious and awful change ' of being, it was as absurd for More to go to his ' grave an idle jester, as for a hardened ruffian to ' force out a horse-laugh, or to kick about his ' shoes.'

Most people, however, will agree with Addison in his more charitable and kindly observation that the innocent mirth which had been so conspicuous in

Sir Thomas More's life did not 'forsake him to the
' last. He died in a fixed and settled hope of immor-
' tality, and he thought any unusual degree of
' sorrow improper.' A similar idea has been clothed
in poetical garb by Wordsworth :—

Wordsworth's
lines.

"His gay genius play'd
" With the inoffensive sword of native wit,
" Than the bare axe more luminous and keen."

More's repu-
tation as a
Poet.

More's poetry, both Latin and English, had its
admirers among his contemporaries, and instances
are found in which he is spoken of as a Cicero in
eloquence, and in poetry something more than a
Cicero. The most popular writers of Latin verse at
the time were Pontanus an Italian and Marullus a
Greek; and in his preface to this volume, Rhenanus
places More above them both. In the reign of
James I. More is classed among the poets of former
days who continue to live in their writings :—

" In paper many a poet still survives,
" Or else their lines had perish'd with their lives,
" Old Chaucer, Gower, and Sir Thomas More,
" Sir Philip Sidney who the laurel wore,
" Spenser and Shakespeare."

In the lapse of two centuries this dictum of Taylor,
the Water Poet, has been directly reversed. In Sir
Thomas More's case the life remains, and the lines
have perished.

More's English
poetry.

The English poetry which Sir Thomas More has
left is comprised in a few pieces written, as it is stated,
'in his youth for his pastime,' among which there are
certain descriptions of childhood, youth, and age,

Shakespeare's
Seven Ages.

which it is not improbable that Shakespeare had in

his thoughts when he wrote the well-known passage descriptive of the Seven Ages.

More's schoolboy, who is bent upon his play, and whose devout wish it is that—

> " These hateful bookes all
> " Were in a fire burned to powder small,"

is a not unlikely prototype of—

> " The whining schoolboy, with his satchel
> " And shining morning face, creeping like snail
> " Unwillingly to school."

And again, the ' goodly young man,' whom ' Venus ' and her little son Cupid ' have reduced to thraldom—

> " By me subdued for all thy great pride,
> " My fiery dart pierceth thy tender side,"

is the same individual whom Shakespeare describes as—

> " Sighing like furnace, with a woeful ballad
> " Made to his mistress' eyebrow."

And More's ' old sage father,' seated in his chair—

> " Wise and discreet:—the public weal therefore
> " I help to rule,"

is identical with—

> " The Justice,
> " With eyes severe, and beard of formal cut,
> " Full of wise saws and modern instances."

In another of these early productions of Sir Thomas More, we find an anticipation of a stanza in one of Gray's celebrated odes. Fortune is described as at first showing herself to mankind, ' lovely, fair, and ' bright,' with becks and smiles for every one :—

CHAP. I.

"But this cheer feigned may not long abide,
"There comes a cloud, and farewell all our pride."

"Fast by her side doth weary Labour stand,
"Pale Fear also, and Sorrow all bewept.
"Disdain and Hatred on that other hand
"Eke restless watch, from sleep with travail kept,
"His eyes drowsy, and looking as he slept.
"Before her standeth Danger and Envy,
"Flattery, Deceit, Mischief and Tyranny."

A similar stanza in Gray's Ode.

In the more melodious, but perhaps less racy stanza of Gray, the 'fury passions' are delineated thus:—

"Disdainful Anger, pallid Fear,
"And Shame that skulks behind.
"Or pining Love shall waste their youth,
"Or Jealousy with rankling tooth
"That inly gnaws the secret heart:
"And Envy wan, and faded Care,
"Grim-visaged comfortless Despair,
"And Sorrow's piercing dart."

With one exception, the few pieces of Sir Thomas More's English poetry which are included in the volume of his works, are of a grave character, and even melancholy. In that one exception, which is styled a 'Merry Jest,' he gives a tedious history of the misfortune befalling a serjeant-at-law, who was foolish enough on a certain occasion to personate a friar. Mackintosh discovers a sort of 'dancing mirth' in the metre; Warton pronounces the piece to be long and dull.[1] The rough handling of the pretended friar which forms the catastrophe is sufficiently ludicrous; but in vain do we search throughout the

[1] Warton seems to think it possible that certain pieces of a lighter character which issued from the press of John Rastall anonymously, may have been the production of his brother-in-law More.

piece for that festive wit which marked the character
and conversation of the writer in after life. The idea
that it suggested to Cowper the original design of his
John Gilpin is scarcely admissible. It is remarkable
that among these the early compositions of one whose
reputation stood so high for wit and pleasantry afterwards, the graver pieces should be higher in point of
excellence than this lighter one.

Among other pieces of a graver cast besides those
which have been already mentioned, there is one
entitled " A Rueful Lamentation," on the death of
Elizabeth of York the wife of Henry VII., which
contains some very pathetic stanzas. The dying
queen is represented as taking a last farewell of her
several relatives ; and in the address which she makes
to her children there is a touch of the same affec-
tionate feeling with which, as we shall see presently,
Sir Thomas More himself addressed a Latin epistle
to his own children, when he was absent from them
on an embassy to Flanders.

Elegy on the
death of the
Queen.

Erasmus thought that he recognized the poet in
More's ordinary style of prose, and this he attributed
to More's fondness for writing poetry in his youth.
Tyndale, in one of his theological controversies with
More, accused him of being prone to make assertions
solely on the prompting of his imagination ; and he
ascribes this to his well-known turn for poetry.[1]
Stapleton says of him, ' Festivus fuit et poeta
' suavis.' Jortin says, with characteristic bluntness

Erasmus on
More as a
Poet.

Tyndale.

Stapleton and
Jortin.

---

[1] " Howbeit Mr. More hath so long used his figures of poetry, that I
" suppose, when he erreth most, he now by the reason of a long custom,
" believeth himself that he sayeth most true."—*Answer to Sir Thomas
More's Dialogue.* p. 247.

and brevity, that he was no bad poet, and might have been better if he had paid more assiduous court to the Muses. Mackintosh argues that the mere fact of his having taken pleasure in the composition of poems which manifest some sense of harmony, at a period when our language and literature were as yet unformed, indicates in itself a certain amount of poetical sensibility. The most poetical of his poems, however, according to Mackintosh is found in this volume of Latin Epigrammata, being addressed at the age of thirty-six to a lady who had been the object of his boyish admiration twenty years before.

On the whole it must be acknowledged that the Epigrammata contain no great amount of poetry. One of More's biographers says that they are 'witty, 'and not biting nor contumelious;' and, in respect to some of those which are strictly epigrams this may be true. It was a fashion among the scholars

of the day who had acquired the art of versifying in Latin, to dignify all such compositions with the title of Poemata. And it must be allowed that if many of the pieces in this volume had been the productions of a less distinguished person, they would long ago have been forgotten. They are the fly embedded in the amber of More's great name.

Sir Thomas More however stands pre-eminent among the historical names of our country as having been himself the subject of poetry. The affecting vicissitudes of his life, and the tragical circumstances of his death, have been a favourite theme with the poet and the dramatist, not only in our own country but among foreigners, down from his own times to the present. The tidings of his execution

produced a shock which was felt over the whole of
Europe; and we are told by Erasmus that many
persons wept over him who had never known him.
When Shakespeare put a prayer into the mouth of
Wolsey on his hearing that More was to succeed him
in the Chancellorship, that—

> —" his bones,
> " When he has run his course, and sleeps in blessings,
> " May have a tomb of orphans' tears wept on him,"—

—we cannot doubt that Shakespeare's thoughts were
recurring to that universal lamentation which some
persons then living would probably remember, and
which had already become a matter of history.   A
tragedy bearing the title of "Sir Thomas More" was
licensed for the stage by the Master of the Revels
about the year 1590.   Another which was acted in
Paris some time after this is said to have brought
tears from the eyes of Cardinal Richelieu.   Hurdis
the Professor of Poetry at Oxford published a tragedy
bearing the title of "Sir Thomas More" in 1792; and
in 1833 a tragedy with the title " Tommaso Moro "
was published at Turin by Silvio Pellico.

More the sub-
ject of trage-
dies.

The pathetic description given by Rogers of More's
parting with his daughter Margaret after his trial
and condemnation is well known :—

> " That blushing maid,
> " Who through the streets as through a desert strayed :
> " And when her dear dear father passed along
> " Would not be held.   But bursting through the throng,
> " Halberd and battle-axe, kissed him o'er and o'er,
> " Then turned and went.   Then sought him as before,
> " Believing she should see his face no more."

To some readers, however, the simple and unstudied

narrative of Cresacre More will probably have a greater charm than the rather stiff and formal condensation of it by Rogers.

It is possible that the melancholy association of Sir Thomas More's name with great historical events and much individual suffering may have absorbed all other considerations in the minds of many persons, and caused them to be indifferent with regard to his writings. His English controversial works, on which he expended very much labour and thought, are comprised in a large volume of black letter which ordinary readers seldom care to open. His Latin epistles, and the few English pieces which he wrote in early

More's Epi- life, are seldom read. His Latin poems or Epigram-
grammata
much over- mata have been almost ignored. Sir James Mackin-
looked.
tosh dismisses them with the casual and careless remark that for the most part they are merely translations from the Greek Anthology; whereas those translated from the Greek constitute barely one-fourth of the whole number. It would appear that Mackintosh had read very little further in the volume than the title-page of the first edition, where they are erroneously described as ' pleraque è Græcis versa.' And even Hallam labours under a like singular mistake when he says that More was known as a scholar by his having written Greek epigrams of some merit; —there being not a single Greek epigram of More's own composition in the whole volume.

But while Sir Thomas More's literary works in general have been suffered to drop into the category of things overlooked and forgotten, there will stand out a splendid and memorable exception in the " Utopia;" and in this work we have evidence that he

possessed much of the imagination of a poet.   It may
be styled, indeed, a political romance.   And it is by
no means an insipid romance, as Michelet termed it.
In few other books are found so many original ideas
and striking passages.   And if we estimate it according to the thought-stirring influence which it acquired
over the civilized world, perhaps it will rank as high
in the annals of literature as any poem that was ever
written.

CHAPTER II.

OLLOWING the fashion which prevailed among the literati of the period, Sir Thomas More wrote his "Utopia" and the larger portions of his poetical effusions in Latin. After the revival of literature in the fifteenth century, the study of the Latin language was cultivated with much assiduity and vigour by educated persons all over Europe; and they made use of it in their stated compositions, in their epistolary correspondence, and in their conversation. To be able to write and to converse in Latin was regarded as an almost indispensable qualification for men in public life, as well as for authors who intended that their works should be appreciated beyond the limited circle of readers in their own country.

In strength and beauty the Latin so far surpassed the vernacular languages of the different nations in Europe, that Erasmus determined to use no other.
His own language he despised, and it was his devout wish that all languages excepting the Greek and Latin might be utterly extirpated. Although he had passed several years of his life in England and in familiar association with Englishmen, he disdained to

learn the language. And having been in 1511 presented by Archbishop Warham to the living of
Aldington in Kent, he resigned it within the year,
saying that he could not pretend to feed a flock of
whose language he was ignorant.

In those cases where a writer's object was merely
to amuse himself and his friends and to air his
scholarship, he would write in Latin verse; and when
his aim was to teach, to inform, and to convince, he
wrote in prose. Hence the ponderous volumes which
Erasmus left behind him are almost entirely in
prose.

At the same time an abundant crop of Latin verse
was springing up all over Europe; and in some
countries the vernacular tongue was almost entirely
neglected. A great part of what was set forth as
Latin poetry will be pronounced to fall short of the
poetical standard, nevertheless it is possible that
some tolerable poets may have been lost to their own
country and language by this fashion of writing in
Latin. The writers had before them the best models
of style and composition in the lately recovered literature of the ancients, and they vied with each other in
imitating them. Originating at an early period in
Italy, the fashion spread over France, Germany,
Spain, and Holland; until by Sir Thomas More and
his friends under the auspices of Henry VIII. it was
introduced into England. The writers of Latin verse
in the various nations of Europe were bound together
by a sort of freemasonry of scholarship. They were
the joint proprietors of a common store of thoughts
and images and forms of expression, which each
writer strove to adapt, with more or less success, to

To write Latin
verse became
the fashion.

his own purpose. Latin verses were poured out in copious streams and in every form of composition— elegy, ode, epistle, and even epic poem. They were written upon every conceivable subject, whether sacred or secular. In the intellectual banquet thus provided the solid and substantial dishes were followed by the more piquant Epigramma. Many of the writers were ecclesiastics, and some of them were high dignitaries of the Church. Men who were supposed to be wrapped up in graver pursuits and studies were fond of trying their skill in the composition of pastoral eclogues, and sentimental or sportive odes.[1]

They formed a sort of aristocratic clique in the world of letters, comprising professors, bishops, cardinals, and even popes. By some emperors the popular Latin versifier was dignified with the office and title of Poet Laureate. The celebrated Ulric von Hutten, poet, soldier, and satirist, was crowned as Laureate by the Emperor Maximilian; and a countryman of our own who published at Rome under his Latinized name of Ghibbesius a volume of ' Carmina ad exemplum Q. Horatii Flacci quam ' proximè concinnata,' was created Poet Laureate, and presented at the same time with a medal and chain of gold by the Emperor Leopold. Some idea

may be formed of the vast amount of Latin verses thrown out by the literati of the age when we find that the number of verses in a voluminous collection of Poemata published at Frankfort in 1612, amounts on a moderate computation to something near a quarter of a million. And these, it must be observed, are the production of German writers alone.

[1] See Appendix, No. ii.

. The nearest approach to the elegance and ease of the classical poetry of the ancients was made by the scholars of Italy, many of them being dignitaries of the Church and courtiers of Leo X.: and we have also Latin verses written by scholars who were Lutherans; several pieces indeed bearing the name of Martin Luther himself are still extant. We have also an interesting volume of Epigrammata by Philip Melancthon,[1] and much Latin poetry not at all inferior to that of the Italian scholars by George Buchanan. It is unnecessary to proceed further in the history of the rise and fall of modern Latin versification; at the same time we may remark that in our own country there are still a few elegant and ingenious scholars who indulge in it as a pleasing pastime, and imitate very successfully the accredited models. A classical quotation from one of the old poets may occasionally be heard in our Houses of Parliament; and such quotations have not ceased to be, as Dr. Johnson styled them, ' the parole of literary men all over the world.'

We have a specimen of Henry VIII.'s Latin composition in his notable work against Luther, in which however it is probable that his secretary Richard Pace, who was an accomplished scholar, may have assisted him. In a dispatch sent from London by the Venetian ambassador to the Doge we have a specimen of Henry's colloquial Latin which is intelligible enough, and in some measure characteristic of the speaker. It appears that in an interview between the ambassador Giustiniani and the king—there being also present a Venetian priest who was in high favour on account of his skill in music—the king holding in

Margin notes:
Both Romish clergy and Lutherans.

Latin quotations in our own Parliament.

Latin composition of Henry VIII.

---

[1] See Appendix. No. iii.

his arms at the time the Princess Mary, who child as she was had been captivated by the priest's music, addressed the ambassador according to his own re-

port in the following words:—'Per Deum iste'— pointing to the priest—'est honestissimus vir et unus ' carissimus: nullus unquam servivit mihi fidelius et ' melius eo. Scribatis Domino vestro quod habeat ' istum commendatum.'

At the same time in regard to Latin scholarship Henry VIII. held a very creditable position among the royal and dignified personages of the day. After the death of the Emperor Maximilian, when Charles of Spain, Francis of France, and Henry of England were all competitors for the throne which he had vacated, the secretary Pace was sent into Germany to further Henry's pretensions, and he was charged with a Latin epistle, doubtless composed by himself, to the Archbishop of Cologne who was one of the electors. When this Latin letter was delivered to the

archbishop he handed it over to his brother and certain other persons who were present, confessing,— as Pace expresses it in the account of the interview which he sent to Wolsey,—'that he had not greatly ' exercised the Latin tongue.'

Charles himself who succeeded to the Empire might have made the same confession. Although he had been educated under the especial care of Adrian VI., whom he was the means of elevating to the Pope-

dom, Charles was not scholar enough to translate an ordinary letter in simple Latin. Adrian indeed himself was a sorry tutor; and by natural taste and inclination Charles would pay more attention to those who were to initiate him in martial exercises and

State policy than to the teacher of Latin composition.
When Adrian became Pope he formed a lamentable
contrast to his accomplished predecessor, Leo X. He
had no taste at all for the noble specimens of painting and sculpture which surrounded him, and very
little for the refinements of literature. He spoke of Also in Pope
the celebrated group of Laocoon and his sons as 'idola Adrian VI.
' antiquorum.' And after reading certain letters written in elegant Latin he exclaimed with contempt,—
' sunt literæ unius poetæ.'

Charles's younger brother Ferdinand was the
better scholar of the two. At the time when Charles
was preparing for his coronation at Aix-la-Chapelle,
Cuthbert Tunstall who had been sent over from
England as the ambassador to Charles, writes to report that when Don Ferdinand was informed that
King Henry was ready to do anything that Charles
might desire within the realm of England, Ferdinand
expressed his acknowledgments in Latin, regretting
also that he had not seen the King of England on
this side the sea. Tunstall adds:—' Surely he is a Don Ferdi-
' proper and wise Prince, and ready of answer to any tinity.
' thing that a man can devise with him. And he
' speaketh Latin very well.'

The appearance in the literary world of a volume Appearance
of Latin verses written by a young English lawyer Epigrammata
holding an important judicial office in the city of in the literary
London, a friend and disciple of Erasmus, as well as world.
of Linacre and Grocyn, and other English scholars
of high repute, would doubtless be regarded by the
courtly and accomplished verse-writers of Italy with
interest; and inasmuch as in a literary point of view
the Epigrammata are quite open to criticism, there

Erasmus on
More's Latin
prose.

can be no doubt that they were criticised freely. The
revival of letters had scarcely yet produced its effect
in England, and few Englishmen had as yet written
in Latin verse at all. Erasmus says of More's compositions in Latin prose that we find in them more of
the dialectic subtlety of Isocrates, than of the dif-
fuse flow of Cicero: at the same time he thinks that
in some respects More is scarcely inferior to Cicero.

In fact More wrote in a Latin style of composition
which Erasmus himself had invented, and which has

Erasmian
Latin.

been termed Erasmian, or according to Gibbon, Belgic
Latin[1]—a style created to meet the exigencies of the
times. Erasmus found that it would be impossible to
express in pure Latinity all those allusions to new
institutions and opinions and discoveries which render his familiar letters so agreeable, and which in
his theological compositions were indispensable. He
therefore endeavoured so to mould and modify his
language as to accommodate it to modern taste and

More's criti-
cism upon it.

usages. More seems to have thought that in certain instances he carried this accommodation too far,
as for instance in his usage of the word 'sabbatum'
and other expressions not strictly classical, in his
version of the New Testament.

Erasmus succeeded in this attempt to loosen the
fetters of a dead speech, as Mackintosh expresses it,
and to give it something of the liveliness of a spoken
tongue. His style was formed upon a wide acquaintance with the principal Latin authors, whether
earlier or later, in accordance with that eclectic

---

[1] Stapleton, however, who will not allow in what relates to More anything like a flaw or defect, says of his Latin writings—" quibus nihil
est Latinius."

principle which he had laid down in his "Ciceroni-
"anus:"—'scriptorem nullum fastidiemus; sed ex
' omnibus aliquid delibabimus quod nostram condiat
' orationem.'

This Erasmian style of Latin answered its tempo-
rary purpose and enjoyed a brief day of popularity.
But the time came when it was no longer required.
Most readers preferred to read books in the language
of their own country, and the writing in Latin was
left to dilettanti versifiers and professed scholars.

Although Sir Thomas More was an ardent admirer
of the languages and literature of ancient Greece and
Rome, he did not choose that his own vernacular
tongue should be disparaged. In one of his " Dia-
" logues " [1] he says that to call the English language
barbarous ' is but a fantasy.' And as to its being
barren of words, it is 'plenteous enough to express
' our minds in anything whereof one man hath need
' to speak with another.' And in writing for his
countrymen upon popular subjects, such as the points
in dispute between the Church of Rome and the Lutherans, he wrote in good vernacular English, over
which he had gained a thorough mastery.

Among the contemporaries of Erasmus there was
a clique of purists in style who excluded from their
compositions every word which is not to be found in
the writings of Cicero, and in ridicule of these Ciceronians Erasmus wrote one of the wittiest and at the
same time most learned of his works. He was also
strongly opposed to the practice which prevailed
among his contemporaries, of largely drawing for their
materials upon the ancient mythology. There are

It falls into
disuse.

More's opinion
of the English
language.

Erasmus ridi-
cules the Cice-
ronians.

---

[1] 'Touching the pestilent sect of Luther and Tyndale.' 1530.

some, he says, who pride themselves upon a modulation so perfect that the nine Muses might seem to be singing in concert, and the Graces to be moving in the dance. This was by no means to the taste of Erasmus. He had no liking for the poetry that was crowded with gods and goddesses. The poetry that he preferred must be more like prose. The aim of the writer ought to be not so much the showing off his own learning and ingenuity as the doing justice to his subject. Those far-fetched and fanciful conceits might suit the taste of certain critics, but for his own part he would rather see things represented as they are found to exist in real life.

And this is what we find in More's Epigrammata. They present us with a series of memoranda jotted down from time to time of his casual thoughts upon persons and things around him. We have a versified expression of his feelings, and of the humorous fancies that sprang up in his brain. They form indeed, so far as they go, the elements of an autobio-

graphy. We are admitted into social and familiar intercourse with him, and we seem almost to catch the words dropping from his lips, the outcome of an active, observant, and sensitive mind. He makes us acquainted with the circumstances of his first love affair, and describes his feelings on meeting with the object of that boyish passion after the interval of twenty years. He admits us into the nursery and schoolroom of his children, and. describes an interview with distinguished visitors who inspect his coins and partake of his viands at his 'poor house at 'Chelsea.'[1]   As literary productions the bulk of the

[1] So designated in the dating of some of his letters.   In this piece it is " humilis casa."

Epigrammata may be deemed almost worthless, and
the subjects are in some instances low and trivial,
at the same time we observe indications of that
strong and solid character in which he appeared
during the trials of later life, and traces also of that
tenderness of disposition which had not yet been
touched by the acrimony of polemics. His inborn and
household simplicity, his independence of thought,
and his home-spun humour, invested these unvar-
nished productions with a charm which would have
disappeared under any attempt at polish. All the
other incidents and anecdotes of More's domestic life,
and many of the wise and quaint sayings which he
uttered, come down to us by tradition, whereas all
that we find in the Epigrammata come directly from
More himself. Some of them may savour of indeli-
cacy, but many of the like effusions of that early
period are more or less indelicate. We find gross
instances in the contemporary writings of John Bale
the Bishop of Ossory. Shakespeare, who lived a century later, is by no means free from it. And even
Milton has left behind him a Latin epigram quite as
indelicate as anything of More's. At the same time
the credit must be assigned to More of never having
employed the charms of poetry in adding attractive-
ness to vice, as we find to be too often the case in
the writings of some of his contemporaries of the
Ovidian school.

The subjects of More's Epigrammata are multi-
farious. Having acquired a sufficient acquaintance
with Greek literature to lay open to his inquiring
mind the almost inexhaustible stores of wit and wisdom left by poets and moralists in the 'Anthologia,'
and finding that the brevity of the epigram suited

well for the employment of those snatches of leisure which were stolen from his more serious occupations, he amused himself by translating them into Latin; and in doing this he seems to have entered the lists

in a sort of sportive competition with his friend William Lily the grammarian, who was one of the few Greek scholars at that time in England. Their respective translations of the same epigram are printed in juxtaposition and entitled, ' Progymnas- ' tica Thomæ Mori et Gulielmi Lilii Sodalium.' By setting himself this task More was enabled to test his own proficiency in a manner both easy and agree- able, and critics doubtless would amuse themselves by comparing the two. These translations would pro- bably be made about the year 1505, at a time when More found himself obliged to withdraw from public avocations in consequence of having incurred the dis- pleasure of King Henry VII. It happened also that Lily had at this time recently returned from the island of Rhodes, having resided there for several years in order to acquire a more perfect knowledge of Greek than it would have been possible for him to acquire at home.

Where there is a moderate amount of scholarship this practice of translating from the Greek Antho-

logy affords a ready and never-failing amusement. It may be carried on during a rural walk; and Dr. Johnson in the decline of life found the use of it in beguiling the tedium of his sleepless nights. The soldier too in India, escaping from the sultry sun and obliged to spend weary hours in the seclusion and solitude of his tent, has found it a wise and a seasonable employment to revert to the studies of his youth. Such was the case with Major Macgregor, CHAP. II. who set himself to translate epigrams from the ' An- 'thologia' into English verse, and at last published a volume containing more than three thousand of them.[1]

The practice dates from a very early period. We *Early translators of Greek epigrams.* have one or more translations by Cicero, by Propertius, by Tibullus, by Ovid, and a considerable number by Ausonius. After the revival of literature the practice became almost universal. Commencing with the early part of the sixteenth century, we have translations of Greek epigrams by Erasmus, Melancthon, Scaliger, Politian, Tasso, Ariosto, Shakespeare, Ben Jonson, and Lord Bacon; also by Dryden, Prior, Hobbes, Swift, Voltaire, and Rousseau; also by Jortin, Dr. *Modern translators.* Johnson, Gray, Cowper, Rogers, Moore, Shelley, Porson, Lords Grenville, Lansdowne, and Wellesley; besides a considerable number by living scholars of very high repute.[2]

Among Sir Thomas More's translations of the Greek epigrams we find a remarkable one which has often *One remarkable Epigramma.* been quoted. It is the bidding farewell to the blandishments of hope and the freaks of fortune by one who is seeking rest; and the Greek lines are translated both by More and Lily in almost the same words. In fact the translation seems to suggest itself, and Pannonius had already given it in nearly the same words :—

> " Inveni portum.—Spes et Fortuna valete !
> " Nil mihi vobiscum.—Ludite nunc alios."

---

[1] "Greek Anthology, with Notes Critical and Explanatory."

[2] See "Anthologia Polyglotta : Versions in various Languages, chiefly from the Greek Anthology." By Henry Wellesley, D.D.

Chap. II.

The impression made upon the mind of Sir Thomas More by this epigram lasted to the end of life. While he was lying in the Tower, full thirty years after this translation had been written, Mr. Secretary Cromwell came to him with an assurance from the King that he continued to be his good and gracious lord as heretofore, and a promise also that he should not henceforward be troubled in regard to matters upon which he had scruples of conscience. Distrusting both the King and the secretary, Sir Thomas wrote with charcoal the following lines immediately after Cromwell had left him :—

Made the subject of a stanza.

> Eye-flattering Fortune, look thou never so fair,
>   Or never so pleasantly begin to smile,
> As though thou would'st my ruin all repair,—
>   During my life thou shalt not me beguile.
> Trust shall I, God, to enter, in a while,
> Thy haven of Heaven, sure and uniform.
> For ever, after calm, thus look I for a storm.

It appears that More's translation of the epigram had fallen into the hands of Sir Walter Raleigh, who in a letter written to Sir Robert Cecil at a time when he was in disgrace, gives himself over to despair with the words—

Adopted by Sir Walter Raleigh.

> Spes et Fortuna valete.

Le Sage represents these lines as placed over the gate of Gil Blas. And Lord Brougham placed them over the gate of his own château in the South of France, altering the 'nil mihi vobiscum' to 'sat me 'lusistis;' which alteration in the case of one who had been the sport of Fortune may be deemed an improvement; but it will scarcely be deemed applicable to the case of Lord Brougham.

Also by Lord Brougham.

This early practice of translating from the Anthologia led to More's taking the more independent line
of writing Epigrammata for himself; studying the
ways and characters of mankind in the busy world
around him, and exercising that power of satire of
which he had an example in his friend Erasmus.
Several of the earlier pieces were written under
the influence of a strong feeling excited by the arbitrary rule and the avarice of Henry VII.: and in
one of them he enunciates principles respecting the
dependence of government upon the consent of the
people, to which he professed his adherence in that
last examination before the Commissioners at a moment when life and death were trembling in the
balance.

After the accession of Henry VIII. he addresses
the youthful monarch in an epistle of congratulation,
and sketches out for him the outline of a glorious
reign over a happy and united people. He describes
at some length the festivities at the coronation. After
this he touches upon events connected with the wars
in which Henry engaged: the death of the King of
Scotland at Flodden Field, and the fruitless campaigns
in France. The "Novum Instrumentum" of Erasmus, probably the most important work of the period,
is the subject of several pieces, one of which is addressed to Archbishop Warham and another to Wolsey. Thus we are brought into contact as it were
with some of the historical personages of the age,
the chief actors in the drama of the reign of Henry
VIII.

One of the remarkable traits in Sir Thomas More's
character was the vigour of his mind and the faculty

Chap. II.

More begins
to write
original epi-
grams.

Covert satire
on Henry VII.

Carmen gratu-
latorium to
Henry VIII.

Coronation.

Wars.

Novum In-
strumentum
of Erasmus.

Activity of
mind in Sir
Thomas More.

D

which he possessed of exercising it upon a very wide range of subjects. He could lecture in the Church of St. Lawrence upon the treatise " De civitate Dei " of Augustine; administer law to the citizens of London in the capacity of Under-sheriff; write smart epigrams upon the follies and absurdities which he saw around him; turn a debate in the House of Commons; arrange questions of international law with the Flemish merchants of Bruges; write dispatches to Wolsey and others when acting as the King's Secretary; charm with his ready wit the supper table of the King and Queen Katharine; write theological treatises against Tyndale and Luther; and discharge the duties of his office as Chancellor with so much assiduity and skill, that—

> " When More some time had Chancellor been,
> " No more suits did remain.
> " The like shall never *more* be seen,
> " Till More be there again."

And with all this he presided over his family like some patriarch of old; surrounded by friends and familiar servants, by his wife and children and children's children; loved by them all and loving them all; causing such a charm to rest upon his ' poor house at Chelsea,' as he designates it in dating his letters—the ' humilis casa ' as it is styled in one of these Epigrammata—that in the words of Erasmus who had himself lived among them, every stranger who entered it went away happier than he was before.

And the same variety characterizes this collection of Sir Thomas More's Epigrammata. He continues to pour out, as in those English stanzas which he wrote at a still earlier period of his career, many

solemn reflections upon the uncertainty of life and the
vanity of all earthly things. And almost in juxtaposition with these solemn reflections we come upon
some sudden outbreak of his accustomed humour and
pleasantry. It is in keeping with the jests that fell
from his mouth upon the judicial bench, and were not
withheld even when he was upon the scaffold. We
see the strong lights and shadows of his character
reflected before us as in a mirror; the whole being
tinged with his predominant turn for satire. With
an unsparing hand he lays open the pretensions of
sciolists, the tricks of astrologers, the foibles of the
female sex, the misadventures of conjugal life, the
ignorance of the priesthood, and the various follies
and the vices of the world around him.

It appears from a letter which was written by Sir
Thomas More some time after the publication of the
Epigrammata, that he had come to the conviction
that it would be better policy to use caution in the
expression of his opinion upon certain subjects. This
was in consequence of an intimation given by Budaeus
that he contemplated the publication of certain letters
of Sir Thomas More in conjunction with letters of his
own. This More objects to, and he asks for time
to take the matter into further consideration; not
only because he feels some doubts as to the correctness of his Latinity, but also because through lack of
caution and circumspection in expressing his opinions
upon certain points as for instance upon questions
of peace and war, upon the prevailing manners of the
age, on husbands and wives, on the people at large,
and on the priesthood —it is probable that he may
have said things which will be laid hold of by his

calumniators and turned to his disadvantage. These remarks would seem to apply primarily to his letters, yet they are equally applicable to his Epigrammata.

It has already been stated that these Epigrammata were the production of youth and early manhood. 'The towardly youth,' as Cresacre More informs us, ' at the age of eighteen began to show to ' the world the ripeness of his wit, for he wrote many ' witty and goodly epigrams.' During the intermediate portion of his busy and eventful career his thoughts were occupied with the realities of life. But as life drew near to its close the workings of thought again took the form of poetry, and that which had been among the early occupations of his life was also among the latest. He beguiled the solitary hours of his long imprisonment in the Tower by writing verses—as the noble and gallant Earl of Surrey did some years afterwards. In an English sonnet written ' for his pastime ' he thanks his ' Ladye Lucke ' for her indulgence towards him in—

Lending me now some leisure to make rhymes.

And if his life had been prolonged it is not improbable that his name might have been added to the list of distinguished men, who having acquired in early life a taste for the elegances of Latin composition, have reverted to those studies with fresh delight in their old age.

CHAPTER III.

N Sir Thomas More's early life the study
of Latin and Greek was pursued in Eng-
land under much difficulty. The time,
indeed, had scarcely gone by when learn-
ing was little cared for excepting by those persons to
whom learning was to be the means of gaining a livelihood. Twenty years after this a certain anxious
father who consulted More with regard to the education of his son, 'non obscurè significabat cum se
' nummatum malle quam literatum:'—and Erasmus
made the remark that such was the case with most
fathers. In Shakespeare's time the Englishman was
notorious among foreigners for his lack of acquaintance with languages. Falconbridge the young
baron of England, who makes his appearance among
Portia's suitors in the "Merchant of Venice," is represented as being 'a proper man's picture' but
unable to converse except 'in dumb show.' He
understands not the lady, and the lady understands
not him. 'He hath neither Latin, French, nor Ita-
'lian; and you may come into the Court and swear
' that I have a poor pennyworth in the English.'[1]

CHAP. III.

More studied
under diffi-
culties.

Literature not
appreciated.

[1] " Merchant of Venice." Act i. Sc. 2.

CHAP. III.

In Scotland gentlemen ordered to send their sons to school.

An Eton boy's verses, temp. Edward IV.

More a diligent student.

At the time when More was at the age most suitable for learning languages, a teacher of Greek would have been as difficult to meet with in England as a teacher of Sanscrit would have been a century ago. In Scotland a statute was enacted by James IV. that all gentlemen's sons should be sent to school in order that they might learn Latin: it may be questioned, however, whether the same compulsion was exercised upon the gentry in those days which is exercised upon the commonalty by the Elementary Education Act in our own times. Latin being the language of the ordinary services of the Church, it might be expected that some at least among the higher clergy should acquire a tolerable knowledge of what we may term ecclesiastical Latin; and in regard to versification there would be a like acquaintance with the rhyming stanzas of mediæval and monkish Latin verse. But no scholars in England had advanced further than this. The youth in the noble foundation of Henry VI. at Eton had not yet been drilled in the art and mystery of verse-making; and that accuracy of metre and poetical phraseology for which they have since become famous was utterly unknown among them. If we may judge from a specimen sent rather complacently to his friends by a boy of the Paston family a few years before this, it would appear that the standard of what are conventionally termed nonsense verses had hardly yet been passed. ' Vix tenuis odor ' literaturæ melioris demigravit in Angliam'—was the remark of Erasmus. The youthful More, however, was intent upon making the most of his opportunities. He studied at Oxford under Demetrius Chalcondyles a learned Greek, and also under Grocyn who is de-

scribed by Erasmus as being in himself an absolute encyclopædia of erudition. Sir John More the
father, although an admirer of learning in the abstract
was not an advocate for what was termed the 'new
'learning,' and he did not encourage the study of
Greek. Nevertheless the young lawyer persevered.
All the time that could be spared from his other occupations was devoted to Greek; and we are told that
after his day's work was ended he might generally be
found with a book in his hand. As he advanced in
his profession there would be fewer opportunities for
classical study; for we are told that there were seldom
cases of importance before the Courts in which he was
not engaged. When the displeasure of Henry VII.
had obliged him to retire from public life, he resumed
his favourite studies and prosecuted them with vigour,
being assisted by the learned William Lily, and having also assistance and encouragement from Erasmus who was then living in his house. With many
of those great scholars of Italy the critical study of
the Latin language was the main employment of a
life, and they succeeded in obtaining something of
its accuracy of idiom and elegance of expression:
whereas with Sir Thomas More this study was merely
a pleasant and desultory recreation during intervals
of leisure. Erasmus thought that under more favour-
able circumstances Sir Thomas More might have rivalled those accomplished scholars of Italy. 'What
'might not so admirable a wit have produced if for-
'tune had allowed the chance of a fostering care and
'training; if it had been confined to the pursuits of
'classical literature; and if it had been spared to ripen
'to maturity!'

CHAP. III.

Whether More
might have
rivalled the
Italian scho-
lars.

It is quite possible that if the youthful More had
been thrown into the companionship of those accomplished scholars who were the favoured courtiers of
Leo X., he might have taken his place in the world
of letters as a Politian, a Bembo, or a Sannazarius;
and that he might have written Epigrammata with a
purity of diction and a classical polish not inferior to
theirs. But on the other hand we should probably
have lost much of that vigour and reality which constitute their peculiar charm. For it must be acknowledged that although we may derive a sort of languid
pleasure from the effeminate graces which characterize
the productions of those finished Italian scholars, we
miss the raciness and force of language which invi-

More's
writings as
we have them
are of more
value.

gorate and enliven the less correct style of Erasmus
and Sir Thomas More. In the one the eye glides
onward from verse to verse in the smooth and fluent
composition without lighting upon an idea that strikes
or arrests the attention. The appetite palls with
excess of sweetness. Whereas in the other the idea
stands out boldly, and rivets the attention at once.
We may say of More's effusions as John Skelton said
of his own :—

> " This barbarous language rude
> " Perhaps ye may mislike :
> " But blame not them that rudely play,
> " If they the ball do strike."

In More's writings whether Latin or English there
is the same point and vigour and shrewd sense that
we find in the writings of such men as Bishop Lati-

mer. The style may be often rugged and uncouth,
but it is always plain, unaffected, and intelligible.

And at times it is touching and full of tenderness.
The epistle addressed to his children in their happy
home of Chelsea is couched in numbers scarcely less
mellifluous, and in language scarcely less classically
correct than that in which the Latin versifiers of Italy
composed their odes to Neæra or Galatæa; and it is
inspired by a genuine domestic feeling to which those
dilettanti were entirely strangers.

Sir Thomas More was himself assiduous in the
cultivation of scholarship, and he was also a patron
of learning in others. He came forward on all occasions as an advocate for the 'new learning'—that is
for the study of the ancient languages and literature,
and more particularly the Greek. And doubtless
to his friend Pace and the other Englishmen who
were striving to raise the literary reputation of their
country, the countenance and support of a man in Sir
Thomas More's position would give much encouragement. He delivered a public address to the University of Oxford in which he reproached that learned
body for their remissness in this matter, and at the
same time held up the sister University as an example. And on another occasion being commissioned
by the King to undertake the defence of the 'new
'learning' in reply to a certain scholastic divine who
in his sermon at Court had been denouncing it as
heretical, he conducted his defence so successfully that
the unfortunate preacher was put to silence, and the
King gave order that he should be prohibited from
appearing again to preach before the Court.

Although Sir Thomas More was far behind Erasmus
in the prompt and ready command of Latin composition, it is not unlikely that some of these Epigram-

mata were composed extempore, like many of the
short and similar poetical pieces of Erasmus. We
are informed by Froben who collected and edited
and also printed the Epigrammata of Erasmus, that
at the time when he was labouring with incredible
industry upon his great work, the " Novum Instru-
"mentum," he was frequently interrupted by the
dropping in of friends to ask for some scrap of
verse, some ' epigrammation or epistolium,' which he
was too goodnatured to refuse.   And that he would
throw off in the space of ten minutes, as it were
' stans pede in uno,' a string of verses so clever that
his critics and detractors would not be able to produce in ten mouths a single line worthy to be compared with them.[1]

Erasmus himself says of his Epigrammata that they
were by no means studied performances, some of
them being written during his walks, or while sitting
at wine with his friends.   He says also that certain
of his too partial friends had caused a few of them
to be printed at Basle in the same volume with the
Epigrammata of Sir Thomas More.   With a show of
modesty he professes to deem this an advantage to
himself, inasmuch as the facetious Epigrammata of a
writer like More who is well known to excel in such

---

[1] Politian complains in a letter to his friend Donatus that in attending to impertinent requests of this nature much of his time is thrown
away.   One person comes to ask for a motto for the hilt of his sword—
another the posy of a ring—another an appropriate verse for his bed or
his bedchamber—another an inscription for his silver plate :—others ask
for set pieces, grave and merry, sacred and profane ; odes, songs, and
ballads.   And if he chances to leave the house he is at once beset by
petitioners of a lower grade, who lead him about through the street as
an ox is led by the nose.

compositions, may be expected to attract readers to the rest of the volume.

Both More and Erasmus, and doubtless many other men with active minds and studious habits, were accustomed to turn to good account the slow and solitary hours which they had to spend in their journeys on horseback. By those sixteenth century travellers our present luxurious speed of locomotion would have been classed with the incredible stories of Palæphatus. Erasmus composed a Latin poem of two hundred and fifty lines upon the ills and grievances of old age, while, as he expresses it in those lines, he was creeping over the snowy Alps:—and being without any means of writing them on paper he brought them away in his memory. The celebrated " Encomium Moriæ " was devised during a journey from Italy to England, while he was brooding over the conclusion at which he had arrived, that a land of ceremonies and a land of inquisition was no proper place of abode for a man of temper like his own. He tells his friend that he gave his mind a subject to work upon—' ne totum hoc tempus quo equo fuit ' insidendum ἀμούσοις et illiteratis fabulis tereretur.' The embryonic sketch was put into form and completed by him after his arrival at the house of his friend More at Chelsea. And if, as is probable enough, the successive portions of it were submitted to More's perusal, we may well imagine that his kindred spirit would appreciate all the strange wit and reckless satire which it flings about.

Sir Thomas More himself composed that charming and characteristic epistle to his children at home, while he was journeying on a sorry and stumbling nag over miry roads in Flanders,[1] such being even for ambassadors and statesmen the usual and only mode of transit. More was at that time no less a personage than Master of the Requests, a Member of the King's Privy Council, and his special commissioner for the settling of certain questions of commercial policy with the ministers of the Emperor Charles V.

In consequence of the frequent and long journeys which Erasmus had to undertake on horseback he found the horse an indispensable part of his ordinary contingent; and his letters abound with allusions to the weary distances he had to travel, the horses which he had to ride, and the adventures which befell them both. He writes to Wolsey on one occasion that when he was on his way from England to Basle, he found the Rhine so swollen by the melting of the snow that all the country about Strasburg was under water, and the journey was performed by swimming rather than by riding. He is constantly reminding his wealthy friends and patrons that nothing would be more acceptable to him than the present of a horse. To Bishop Fisher he particularizes the kind of animal that would suit him:—pleasant to ride, easy to manage, and able to endure a good amount of work. A man accustomed to indulge when riding, as Erasmus indulged, in occasional fits of dreamy abstraction, would have found a mettlesome steed at

---

[1] The Latin verses of Sir Henry Halford, which were published with the title of "Nugæ," were composed as he traversed the streets of London in his carriage. And Dr. Lettsom, another eminent physician, was accustomed to place at the heading of some of his letters—"super "strata viarum."

times rather inconvenient. Archbishop Warham gave
him a horse which he describes as being devoid of all
mortal sin excepting laziness and gluttony, and at
the same time endowed with a combination of virtues
such as might adorn the character of a father confessor, being humble, modest, sober, chaste, gentle,
and prudent. The generous Bishop of Basle had
given him a horse which he could easily sell for fifty
golden florins. While he was staying with Bishop
Fisher at Rochester in the autumn of the year 1513,
Sir Thomas More being also the Bishop's guest at
the time, a horse was sent down to him from London
by his friend Ammonius, who had just before been
appointed to the office of Latin Secretary to the
King. The horse was a white one, and Erasmus
received it with the graceful acknowledgment—'per-
'placet equus candore insignis ac magis animi tui
'candore commendatus.' Urswick the Recorder of
London gave him a horse which as he states ought by
this time to be at least as wise as Ulysses. Ulysses
had visited many cities—' mores hominum multo-
' rum vidit et urbes '—but Urswick's horse had visited
quite as many universities.

During his residence in England Erasmus had
reason to be well satisfied with the supply of horses,
but in his studies he was much troubled at times by
the difficulty he had in meeting with an amanuensis.
Such he said was the laziness of the people in England that a scribe to copy out his writings for him
was not to be met with at any price. It is probable
however that the fault lay with the writer himself.
If the handwriting of Erasmus had been as bold
and legible as that of his English friends More and

Tunstall, the English transcribers would have escaped this imputation of laziness.

We are told by Roger Ascham in his "Toxophilus" that when Erasmus was resident at Cambridge as Lady Margaret Professor of Divinity and also Professor of Greek, he was accustomed for his health's sake to ride about the Market-hill. 'When he had

'been sore at his book, as Garret our bookbinder has 'very often told me, for lack of better exercise he 'would take his horse and ride about the Market-'hill.' A rather limited sphere of action this would be, and especially so when compared with the constitutional circuit taken by professors in our own times.[1]

It has been already stated that More's Epigrammata were collected by Erasmus and printed by

Froben. This was done without any express sanction from More himself, who says in a letter to Erasmus, 'I never was much pleased with them, as you 'are well aware; and if you and some others had not 'thought better of them than I do, the volume never 'would have appeared.' He acknowledges to a 'cacoëthes scribendi,' and he thinks indifferently of the result. His own poetry he makes little account of, and he complains that it has damaged his reputa-

---

[1] It is said that the following rather flippant lines upon a grave subject were addressed to Sir Thomas More by Erasmus, who had borrowed a palfrey and forgotten to return it: but whether there is evidence for this story it is not easy to ascertain :—

Quod mihi dixisti
De corpore Christi
Crede quòd edas—et edis.
Id tibi rescribo
De tuo palfrido—
Crede quòd habeas—et habes.

tion as a writer of prose. His opponents twit him
with having indulged his imagination so far as to
deaden his apprehension of the truth.

In remarking upon the treatment which writers
often meet with after having done their best for the
instruction and amusement of their readers, Sir
Thomas More states the result of his own experience. He says that some readers care for nothing
but what is old. Others care for little excepting what
they write themselves. Others are fickle and versa-
tile, professing one thing while they remain seated and
another thing after they have risen up. Others like
to sit over their wine in taverns and great houses,
passing judgment upon books as it were 'ex cathe-
'drâ,' and plucking at the sentences in a man's writings as they would pluck at the hairs of his head :—
being themselves secure all the while, inasmuch as
they write nothing of their own. These worthy persons are so smooth and clean shaven that there is
not left upon their heads a single hair to pluck at.
And there are found others so ungrateful that although they may be pleased with the work itself,
they choose to take a dislike to the author. They
resemble those churlish guests who, after they have
partaken to the full of an entertainment, will coolly
depart without giving a word of civil acknowledgment
to their host, perhaps even reviling him among themselves.

While Sir Thomas More was living these Epigrammata appear to have been rated as much above their
merits as they have been underrated since. In his
prefatory epistle Beatus Rhenanus expatiates upon
their excellence, and places More upon a par with the

favourite writers of Latin poetry of the age. Leland says that Pontanus is a second Ovid, Vida is divine, Marullus sweeter than honey;—but More is an unrivalled and universal genius, at once a poet and an orator. In his Epigrammata all that he aimed at was to show what he could do off-hand as it were and without effort; and with the same materials and opportunities he would have rivalled Martial. As we come lower down in point of time, Huet commends More's Epigrammata on the whole, but rather singularly giving the preference to his translations. Thomas Peake, who translated some of the Epigrammata into English, styles him ' that upright Lord Chancellor and ' facetious poet.' The author of the life of " Tommaso " Moro," printed at Venice in 1753, says of the Epigrammata that they are not the less witty though abounding in sound and practical sense. Dr. Johnson gave his opinion in a Greek epigram, apparently an original one, which appears in his diary of a journey into Derbyshire in 1774.[1] In this epigram the first crown of merit is assigned by the Muses to More, the second to Erasmus, and the third to Micyllus. Micyllus, or Moltzer, was a Professor at Heidelberg, and a friend of Philip Melancthon, to whom he addressed a long and interesting epistle in Latin verse. His writings were much commended at the time, and by the fact of giving to More's Epigrammata the preference Dr. Johnson showed that he held them in considerable estimation. Walter Savage Landor thought that the early writers of Latin verse in England, among whom he specially mentions Sir Thomas More, are not entitled to any particular commendation as

[1] Croker's " Boswell," ii. 195.

Latin poets; and it is probable that critics in general will be of the same opinion. In the Epigrammata we must not expect to find much classical poetry; but we may pick up notes and records which will assist us to follow the footsteps of one of the most remarkable men of his age, during a life full of interest in its progress and pre-eminently tragical at its close.

Among the writers of Latin verse in our own country about that period were William Lily, More's friend and fellow-student; Leland the laborious antiquary; and George Buchanan the historian of Scotland. Leland wrote encomiastic verses upon the great men of the day in an easy and pleasant style: and to Buchanan was assigned by Julius Cæsar Scaliger the distinction of being numbered in the highest rank of modern Latin poets, styling himself a mere barbarian in comparison. Both Leland and Buchanan were writers of Epigrammata. In the next century we have the notable little volume of " Joannes Owen, " Cambro-Britannus," who is said to have been disinherited by a rich relative for writing satirical epigrams upon the Church of Rome. Owen's reputation as an epigrammatist extended over Europe. We meet with his epigrams translated by various writers into English, and also into French by Le Brun, and by Francisco de la Torre into Spanish. In times nearer to our own the name of Landor stands pre-eminent. The facility acquired by Landor in imitating the models of classical antiquity in their own style of composition, whether epigrammatic or otherwise, places him almost without a rival.

The volume of More's Epigrammata has become rather scarce; and when met with it will be found to

CHAP. III. labour under the serious defect of being without arrangement and also without index. For a reader to refer to the several pieces in the original would be tedious and irksome and in some cases almost impossible. And the interest unquestionably lies in the matter rather than in the diction. It has therefore

Certain translations given. been deemed convenient to give the substance in certain cases by a translation. One of these, apparently

Sir Nicholas Bacon. never before published,[1] is by Sir Nicholas Bacon, who received the Great Seal from Queen Elizabeth within about twenty-five years after it had been delivered up by Sir Thomas More into the hands of her father. Several of the translations are taken from a work entitled, "Flowers of Epigrams, out of sundry "the most singular authors selected, as well ancient "as late writers, pleasant and profitable to the ex-

Kendall. "pert readers of quick capacity:—by Timothe Ken- "dall, late of the University of Oxford, now student "of Staple Inn; 1557." Others are from "Emblems

Thynne. "and Epigrams by Francis Thynne;" dedicated to Lord Chancellor Egerton in 1600: these translations however are coolly passed off by the writer as original epigrams. For a few we are indebted to the "Parnassi

Pecke. "Puerperium" of Thomas Pecke, published in 1659. One or two of the longer translations were written

Wrangham. by Archdeacon Wrangham: and for the rest the author of this work must himself be held responsible.

More's age at the time of publication. At the time of the original publication of the Epigrammata Sir Thomas More was about forty years of age. Within the two previous years two editions of the "Utopia" had been published, the one at Louvain and the other at Basle. His reputation was now fully

---

[1] See Appendix, No. iv.

established as an able lawyer and an eloquent speaker.
The next ten years of his life were a career of unin-
terrupted success. He became in succession Treasurer of the Exchequer, Speaker of the House of
Commons, Chancellor of the Duchy of Lancaster,
and in 1529 Chancellor of England.

CHAPTER IV.

 HE earliest incident in More's life which is alluded to in these Epigrammata took place about the year 1494. His fondness for female society and the susceptibility of his temperament in early life have been alluded to by his friend Erasmus; and the reminiscences of a A boyish attachment. boyish attachment are here placed upon record by himself. At the mature age of thirty-six, being now the husband of a second wife, and the father of four children, he chanced to meet with a lady who had captivated his affections at the early age of sixteen. From that time down to the present they had never met: and the tender remembrance of the past came so powerfully over his mind, that although surrounded by many and stirring avocations, he found time to pen an epistle which is pronounced by Jortin to be the most poetical, and by Mackintosh to be the most pathetic and elegant of his compositions. After restoring to the lady all those youthful charms of which she had been spoiled by the lapse of twenty years, he proceeds to tell how their companions were amused with his artless attempt to dissemble what he felt, hinting at the same time that there were reasons for

believing that the feeling was mutual. He ...
however, even before Shakespeare, that

"The course of true love never did run smooth."

for the maiden was placed by her friends und
strict surveillance, and the boyish lover was for-
den to enter the house. His earliest affection ...
blighted in the bud; and although he was married
twice it is doubtful whether there was much genuine
love in either case. He concludes with a prayer that
after the lapse of another twenty years they may again
meet, each as now in the enjoyment of health and
happiness.

The following is Archdeacon Wrangham's transs-
lation:—

"To ELIZA, WHOM HE HAD LOVED IN HIS YOUTH.

"Thou liv'st, Eliza, to these eyes restored,
O more than life, in life's gay bloom, adored.
Many a long year, since first we met, has rolled,
I then was boyish, and I now am old.
Scarce had I bid my sixteenth summer hail,
And two in thine were wanting to the tale,
When thy soft mien — ah, mien for ever fled!
On my tranced heart its guiltless influence shed.
When on my mind thy much-loved image steals,
And thy sweet long-lost former self reveals,
Time's envious gripe appears but half unkind,
Torn from thyself, to me thou'rt left behind.
The grace that held my doting glance, though those,
Has flown thy cheek — to make my breast its throne
And as by gentle blast the flame is fed,
And mid cold ashes rears its languid head,
So thou, though changed — ah, changed indeed — to view
Kindlest the love that once was thine, anew.

Now on my memory breaks that happy day,
When first I saw thee with thy mates at play.
On thy white neck the flaxen ringlet lies,
With snow thy cheek, thy lip with roses vies.

Thine eyes, twin stars, with arrowy radiance shine,
And pierce and sink into my heart through mine.
Struck as with heaven's own bolt, I stand, I gaze,
I hang upon thy look in fixed amaze.
And as I writhe beneath the now-felt spear,
My artless pangs our young companions jeer.
So charmed me thy fair form; at least to me
Fairest of all the forms it seemed to be.
Whether the glow that thrills our early frame
Lit in my breast the undecaying flame :
Or some kind planet at our natal hour
Deigned on our hearts its common beam to pour :
For one who knew with what chaste warmth you burned
Had blabbed the secret of my love returned.
—Then the duenna and the guarded door
Baffled the stars, and bade us meet no more.

Severed, our different fates we then pursued,
Till this late day my raptures has renewed.
This day, whose rare felicity I prize,
Has given thee safe to my delighted eyes.
Crimeless, my heart you stole in life's soft prime,
And still possess that heart without a crime.
Pure was the love which in my youth prevailed,
And age would keep it pure, if honour failed.
O may the gods, who five long lustres past,
Have brought us to each other well at last,
Grant, that when number'd five long lustres more,
Healthful, I still may hail thee healthful as before ! "

It was precisely at the end of those 'five long lustres more' that More's chequered and eventful life was brought to an end on the scaffold.

A passage very similar to one in these lines occurs in Milton's "Elegia septima," which was written under circumstances in some degree similar. Milton was then at the age of eighteen, and he tells us that hitherto he had bade defiance to the god of Love and laughed at his archery. However the Cyprian boy appeared at his bedside very early one

morning in May, and warned him that the time was
at length arrived for him to feel the smart of those
arrows which he had been so daring as to ridicule.
In the course of the day he went to a promenade and
place of public resort, where he saw a bevy of nymphs,
beautiful as goddesses, pacing to and fro. One of
them appeared to him to be Juno and Venus in the
same person, and upon this one he rashly fixed his
admiring gaze. The god of Love placed himself upon
vantage ground and at once commenced the attack.
The result is thus given in Cowper's translation.

> " Now to her lips he clung her eyelids now
> Then settled on her cheeks and on her brow :
> And with a thousand wounds from every part
> Pierced and trans-pierced my undefended heart :
> A fever, new to me, of fierce desire
> Now seized my soul, and I was all on fire."

While the youthful poet lay in this unhappy plight,
the lady departed, all unconscious of the mischief she
had done.

> " But she, the while, whom only I adore,
> Was gone, and vanished to appear no more."

Upon this he goes on in the true classical vein to
compare his feelings at the moment to those of Vul-
can when he was cast down from Olympus, and to
the feelings of Amphiaraus when his horses plunged
into the abyss and he looked up at the sun for the
last time.

Sir Thomas More breaks off his tender reminiscences by blandly and courteously breathing good
wishes to the lady for her future health and happiness. Milton cools down to the serious reflection that
the little god has made a fool of him, and he returns

a wiser man to his studies in the shady bowers of
Academe.

That this early disappointment may have produced
an effect upon More is by no means improbable. In
his first marriage he gave his hand to the elder of two
sisters, although in his heart he is said to have pre-

More's two
marriages.
ferred the younger. And in his second marriage the
choice of his wife, as it is reported, reminds us of
those bygone days when busy lawyers were said to
employ their clerks to choose their wives for them.

Character of
his second
wife.
Madame Alicia was neither 'bella' nor 'puella,' and
moreover she was a shrew. At the same time she
was a notable housewife, successful in the manage-
ment of her household: and in that singular epitaph
which More wrote for himself and his two wives he
places it upon record that she was to his children a
good stepmother. There is no doubt that the temper
of Xantippe was displayed too prominently in her
character, at the same time it must be allowed that
her Socrates was at times a provoking husband.

Erasmus a
stale guest.
The manner in which she treated her guest Erasmus
was neither hospitable nor courteous. He complained
to Ammonius that she was keen and penurious, and
that she plainly gave him to understand that she
thought his stay with them had been long enough.
The starveling and sickly scholar from Holland had
already begun 'to stink in the nostril,' as he puts it in
plain terms. On the other hand she made herself so
agreeable to Ammonius himself, who was the King's
secretary and a great man at Court, that he found her
as he stated to Erasmus most gentle and courteous and
easy to please. And he adds that she never mentions
the name of Erasmus without expressing a kind wish

towards him. Although the over-long visit of Erasmus had been a trial to her equanimity as a prudent housewife, she seems to have deemed it only prudent to speak civilly after he was gone of the great scholar who was the common friend of both Ammonius and her husband. And Erasmus on one occasion gives his friend's wife a good word in return. On another occasion however he tells a story which will be looked upon as rather question-able. He says that More had confided to him his resolution that he would not a second time marry a widow: and that if his present wife should be taken away from him he intended to marry a lady of rank and fortune. It will be allowed that this looks very like a sly and rather impertinent suggestion thrown out in a merry mood, 'more suo,' by Erasmus himself.

Anthony Wood speaks of Dame Alicia More in terms which will be pronounced undeservedly harsh. He says that in a letter addressed to Secretary Crom-well at the time when Sir Thomas More was a prisoner in the Tower, which letter he had seen, she implores him to 'be kind to her poor old husband,' and states that she is reduced almost to poverty, having been driven to sell 'certain implements and old stuff' in order to satisfy the wants of her household. In the breast of most men this natural expression of distress would have excited pity, but Wood summarily dis-poses of it as the idle intrusiveness of a 'whining ' woman.'

During the lifetime of his first wife, to whom in the epitaph which he wrote for her he applies the endearing term of ' uxorcula,' there is reason to believe that Sir Thomas More enjoyed a full share of domestic happiness. It appears from the epitaph that it was his intention that his own remains and also those of the second wife should be deposited in the same tomb with his former wife; and he ventures upon the licence of a poet so far as to declare that if the two ladies could have been his wives at the same time, the happiness of the trio would have been complete. The epitaph is thus translated by Wrangham :—

Translated by
Wrangham.

" Within this tomb Jane, wife of More, reclines :
This for himself and Alice More designs.
The first—dear object of my youthful vow,
Gave me three daughters and a son to know.
The next—ah, virtue in a step-dame rare—
Nursed my sweet infants with a mother's care.
With both my years so happily have passed,
Which the more dear, I know not—first or last.
O ! had religion, destiny, allowed,
How smoothly, mixed, had our three fortunes flowed !
But be we in the tomb—in heaven—allied ;
So kinder death shall grant what life denied."

Epigrammata
on kings and
tyrants.
A.D.circa 1508.

We come now to certain Epigrammata upon kings and tyrants which were very probably written before the death of Henry VII., who being provoked by More's opposition in the Commons to a vote of money which he expected to be given on the marriage of his daughter, had committed his unoffending father Sir John More to the Tower, upon a charge, as Mackintosh supposes, of having infringed some obsolete statute; and it was only by paying a heavy fine that he regained his liberty. The son found it expedient to withdraw from public life; and we are told that at one time he contemplated a journey into foreign parts. At this crisis he seems to have occupied himself by giving expression in Latin verse to the moody thoughts which were uppermost in his mind, making them the subjects of his Epigrammata. The drift of these is plainly signified by their headings. 'De 'Principe bono et malo.' 'Quid inter Tyrannum et 'Principem.' 'Bonum Principem esse Patrem non 'Dominum.' 'Dives avarus pauper est sibi.' In one of these the tyrant is boldly admonished that, if he allows himself to assume airs because the multitude bow their knee before him and uncover their head in his presence, and because he holds in his hand the disposal of life and death—if on this account he exalts his crest and lords it over the people—in what is he better than a lunatic? For where is all his glory in the time of sleep? He is then no better than a senseless trunk, a corpse newly dead. And if the chamber where he lies were not by bolts and bars well secured, his life would be at the mercy of any vagabond who might choose to take it.

Kendall has translated the Epigramma thus:—

> " A tyrant in sleep differeth not from a common person.
>
>   " Dost therefore swell and pout with pride
>   And rear thy snout on high,
>   Because the crowd doth crowd and couch
>   Whereso thou comest by:
>   Because the people bonnet-less
>   Before thee still do stand;
>   Because the life and death doth lie
>   Of divers in thy hand?
>   But when that drowsy sleep of thee
>   Hath every part possessed,
>   Tell then where is thy pomp and pride,
>   Thy porte and all the rest?
>   Then, snorting lozzel as thou art,
>   Thou liest like a block:
>   Or as a carrion corpse late dead,
>   As senseless as a stock.

Kendall's translation

> And if it were not that thou wert
> Closed up in walls of stone,
> And fenced round—thy life would be
> In hands of every one."

The Epigramma which bears the reading, 'Sola mors tyrannicida est,' must have been written either at the time of Henry VII.'s death or in the immediate prospect of it. All victims of kingly oppression are exhorted to take courage and hope for better times; for if no other change should occur to befriend them death the tyrannicide, the avenger of the persecuted, will sooner or later hurl down the oppressor from his throne and lay him prostrate, an object of scorn and derision, at their feet,

> "— miser, abjectus, solus, inermis, inops."

This train of reflections would be suggested to one in More's circumstances by the death of his persecutor; and we recognize the spirit at least of those models of classical antiquity which had been of late the subject of his studies.

The next incidents in point of date which are commemorated in the Epigrammata are the accession and the coronation of Henry VIII. in 1509.

Address on the accession of Henry VIII.

Upon this there are several pieces, the first being a gratulatory address to King Henry himself. It is prefaced by an epistle in prose, which exhibits characteristic touches of More's natural vivacity and humour. Some delay having occurred in the presentation of this poem he deems it expedient to state the cause; and proceeds accordingly to explain that the artist who had undertaken to embellish it with an appropriate device was incapacitated by a fit of the gout. He expresses a fear lest in waiting for these adventitious attractions, which he compares to the artificial bloom in a lady's complexion, he had deprived his verses of their chief recommendation, the charm of novelty. He doubts after all, whether the advantage accruing from the adroitness of the artist's *hand*, is sufficient to make amends for the damage sustained through the incapacity of his *feet*. He alludes to the well-known story that when the people of Ilium came after a long time had elapsed to offer their condolence to the Emperor Tiberius on the death of his son Drusus, he offered to them in return his own condolence upon the death of their brave fellow-citizen Hector. At the same time he intimates that his own tardiness cannot be deemed quite so ridiculous as theirs, inasmuch as the subject of his congratulations is an event of such universal joy, as to be impressed upon men's minds with a vividness which it would take ages to efface.

No prince could have succeeded to a throne under brighter auspices than Henry VIII., and in the national enthusiasm with which he was received by the people no one had greater reason to participate than More. To him it was the entering upon a new life. Emerging from his hiding-place and entering once more into the arena of public affairs he fearlessly gives utterance to the indignant feelings of his heart. And in those feelings the mass of the people would more or less participate. They were overjoyed by the exchange of an aged recluse whose selfishness went on increasing with his years, for a king in the vigour of his youth, prince-like and of commanding presence, fond of regal state, free, generous and openhanded. The allusion made in this piece to 'tot 'turum tot uncas manus,' and to 'leges nocere coactæ,' would be quite intelligible to most of his subjects. It will be allowed, however, that when we find in this piece on the one hand very biting satire upon the sordid and rapacious character of the late monarch, and on the other hand very lavish encomiums upon the present, we are inclined to think that if Henry had felt any filial respect for his father's memory, these lines so far from recommending their writer to his good graces would have produced an impression altogether the reverse. The reign of Henry VII. had been a beneficial reign to the

country, and like his son he was for some time after his accession a popular king. He had been eulogized by Erasmus quite as unreservedly as his son is here eulogized by More :—

> " Hoc regnum ille putat, patriæ carissimus esse,
>   Blandus bonis, solis timendus impiis."

But More remarks in his " Life of Richard III.," that 'the gathering of money is the only thing that 'withdraweth the hearts of Englishmen from the 'prince.' And even Bishop Fisher in his funeral sermon of the Lady Margaret, Henry VII.'s mother,

says that ' avarice and covetyse she most hated, and ' sorrowed it full much in all persons, but specially ' in any belonging to her,'—which is quite as intelligible as the passages in More's address.

The single good quality which More allows to the father is prudence. And this appears to have been introduced for the purpose of making good an assertion that from each of his progenitors the young king had inherited a characteristic good quality. The noble

heart of his grandsire Edward IV., the piety of the *[Edw. IV.]*
Lady Margaret his father's mother, the kindly disposition of Elizabeth of York his own mother these
rare qualities combined with the prudence of his father
will make up the character, as More states, of such a
monarch as had never reigned over England before.

The personal advantages which Henry possessed, *[More's]*
his stature and gait, his manly vigour, the fire of his *[young ...]*
eye and the beauty of his complexion, are described
minutely, and at the same time due stress is laid upon
his skill in martial exercises and his love of literature.
At a time when scholars and courtiers were vying
with each other in the extravagance of their eulogies,
and when a foreign ambassador was likening him to
the deities of Greece and Rome ; when Erasmus was
extolling his discreetness and his piety ; when Ammonius declared that his genius was developing itself
into something almost divine ; it can scarcely be said
that More's panegyric is much overdrawn. It is be- *[A deserved ...]*
yond doubt that Henry was every inch a king. In *[of reason.]*
form and bearing and in features he was said to resemble his grandfather Edward IV. who was pronounced to be the handsomest man in Europe. In
the tournament few could enter the lists with Henry.
He was a good linguist, a fair scholar, and a practised
theologian. His State papers and his letters evince a
power of expression as well as a vigour of purpose ;
and in the judgment of Mr. Froude they are in no
degree inferior to those of his distinguished ministers
Cromwell and Wolsey.

It was a happy thing however for More that he could
not look into the future. That high-flown laudation of
Henry's modesty, his ingenuous humility, and above

all the tenderness and clemency of his heart, proceeding as it does from one of the future victims of his tyranny, must give birth to sad reflections. The worst crimes of the father, selfish and unfeeling as he was, and the cruel wrongs which he inflicted upon the family of More, are mild and gentle when compared with the cruelties perpetrated by the ' princeps ama-'tissimus' upon him who is now writing the panegyric.

Softened by no recollection of familiar intercourse, that communion of counsels and studies and social pleasures which usually forms an indissoluble bond of friendship—he trampled under foot all the obligations of humanity; and after putting his faithful friend and servant to the lingering torture of a twelvemonth's imprisonment in the Tower, caused him at last to be beheaded as a traitor.

The result of Sir Thomas More's long experience in the ways and tempers of royalty may be taken as embodied in his advice to Secretary Cromwell. ' Tell

' the King what he *ought* to do, but never tell him ' what he *can* do. So shall you be a right worthy ' counsellor and a true and faithful servant. For if a ' lion knew his own strength, hard were it for any man ' to rule him.'

Allusion is made in this gratulatory address to Henry's marriage, which is rendered the more interesting by the fact of More's adherence to that marriage having proved eventually the cause of his disgrace and downfall. It is clear that he could not have acquiesced in Catharine's divorce without abandoning the sentiments expressed in these lines. In ordinary cases when the muse is invoked to sing the praises and celebrate the virtues of a youthful queen, it is allowable to put into requisition all the flowers and figures of poetry, but in this instance even the bounds of poetic licence seem to have been overpassed. The young queen is exalted to a pre-eminence over all the heroines of antiquity. She is described as excelling Cornelia in eloquence, Tanaquil in wisdom, and Alcestis in devotedness to her husband. Penelope's constancy is as nothing in comparison with that of Catharine, who, resisting the calls of her sister, her parents, and her country,

" Sola tui longâ mansit amore morâ."

Her female infant is represented as the anchor of the succession, firm and secure, in the event of there being no further progeny. But the poet boldly promises a son; and proclaims that Henry's descendants in the male line shall succeed to their father's sceptre for countless generations. No foreign wars shall molest him, even if France and Scotland should league together; nor shall his peace be disturbed by intestine commotion, all contending interests being united in his own person. The nobility, kept so long at a cold and cautious distance,—' nomen inane diu.'—now begin to lift up their heads: the merchants are relieved from their oppressive imposts: and the race of informers is extinct. These lines in short as illustrative of the general state of affairs at Henry's accession to the throne, and the universal joy with which the nation received him, possess considerable historical interest: and they are referred to by Hume among his authorities for the events of the period.[1]

Chap. IV.

The reign begins auspiciously.

[1] An elegant Latin Epithalamium was written on the marriage of Henry's father with Elizabeth of York, which More probably took for his model.

F

Besides the 'Carmen Gratulatorium,' there are several shorter pieces relating to the accession of Henry VIII. and the festivities connected with it. The ceremony of the coronation was performed at an immense cost, and with much splendour. The royal pair, arrayed in vestments of the richest material and glittering with precious stones, went along streets hung with tapestry from the Tower to Westminster, attended by nine youths on stately coursers, representing the nine kingdoms and provinces which Henry governed. While this goodly procession was advancing a shower of rain began to fall; the sun however continuing to shine as before. Hence the poet takes occasion to remind us that both 'Phœbus' and 'Jovis uxor' conspire to bestow their auspices upon the event. After the coronation came the jousts and tournaments, which were on a scale of unusual magnificence; and More commemorates the fact of their having been concluded without a single misfortune. No transfixed knight had bedewed the arena with his blood, no unlucky plebeian had been struck by a mis-directed lance, or trampled upon by a rampant steed, or crushed by the fall of a scaffold: they had been distinguished by an 'innocentia'—an absence of all mischief—which 'innocentia' was at that time believed to be, as the writer intimates, characteristic of the natural disposition of King Henry himself.

At the last coronation several lives were lost. While the multitude were pressing forward to cut off and secure for themselves pieces of the striped cloth upon which Queen Katharine had walked from Westminster Hall to the Abbey, some persons were trampled to death. And if the King had not interposed between

Chap. IV.

the Knights of Diana and the Knights of Minerva in the tournament when they were proceeding to fight *à outrance*, the entertainment would not have been so bloodless as it is here represented to have been.

A.D. 15..

Another coronation which took place in More's lifetime was regarded by him with very different feelings from those which are expressed in this address. A pageant perhaps even more splendid than the present passed along the streets of London at the coronation of Queen Anne Boleyn in the year 1533, which was at the closing period of More's public life. He had resigned the Chancellorship, and had been for some time at variance with the King on the subject of his divorce from Queen Katharine. Cresacre More informs us that he received an invitation from 'three great Bishops,' Gardiner of Winchester, Clark of Bath, and Tunstall of Durham, to bear them company in the ceremonial, and also to accept a sum of money wherewith to provide 'a gown,' and defray other necessary expenses. Sir Thomas More was now a poor man, and he did not refuse the money: at the same time believing as he did that Katharine was still the King's wife, he declined to be present at the coronation of her whom he did not recognize as the Queen. At their next meeting he addressed the three prelates in a merry mood, and told them according to his wont an amusing anecdote. At the same time he warned them of troubles and dangers a-head. 'As for my-'self,' he said, 'it lieth not in my power but that they 'may devour me; but God being my good Lord, I 'will provide so that they shall never deflower me.'

Coronation of Queen Anne Boleyn.

More refuses to attend.

This piece is followed by two others which are also connected with the accession of Henry VIII. In the

Others on the accession of Henry VIII.

Chap. IV.

A.D. 1509.

Union of the
Two Roses.

Battle of
Flodden Field.

one it is intimated that according to Plato's theory of a succession and revolution of seasons, the Iron age—that is the reign of Henry VII.,—is now ended, and we are entering upon a Golden age. The other piece is descriptive of the union of the White and Red Roses, from which union there springs a rose combining all the beauties of the other two. Whatever there was to admire and love in each of the two other roses, the same may be found to exist in this single rose.[1] After this comes the sting of the epigram. Should any person be found so base and churlish as to withhold his admiration from this single rose, that man needs to look well to himself:—

" Nempe etiam spinas flos habet iste suas : "

—a veritable fact which the writer himself lived long enough to realize.

The next of these pieces in point of date refer to the attempted invasion of England by the Scotch, and the battle of Flodden Field in 1513. In one of them it is stated that at the time when the pious King Henry was engaged in asserting the Pope's rightful authority over France—' the father of all Christians ' as he styled himself—Henry's brother-in-law, the impious King of Scotland, was marching his hostile armies into England. Regardless of all oaths and treaties he allied himself with the enemies of England, and set his mind upon sinking the ship of St. Peter.

---

[1] Upon the binding of certain books which may probably have belonged to the library of Henry VIII. there is a device containing the royal arms in an upper compartment, and below them a full-blown rose encircled with the following lines :—

" Hac rosa virtutis de cœlo missa sereno
" Æternum florens regia sceptra feret."

This act of impiety however cannot be wondered at, for when he was little more than a child he imbrued his hands in the blood of his own father. It is by the will of God that he and his army have perished. Their crime is followed by retribution.[1]

Immediately after his flight from Bannockburn, where his son a youth of seventeen had appeared in arms against him, the late king was assassinated in a miller's cottage under circumstances of peculiar atrocity.[2] The son is said to have worn ever after by way of penance an iron girdle, the weight of which was added to in every successive year.

The siege of the castle of Norham in Northumberland is the subject of another piece written at the same time. This fortress which is situated on the Tweed, was repeatedly taken and retaken, and had a principal share in all the border warfare of the period. It is intimated in these lines that James professed to lay siege to it, although at the time it had been already betrayed into his power; and that the traitor was afterwards put to death by his command. After the battle of Flodden Field in which James was slain, Norham of course fell once more into the hands of the English. This succession of events affords to More the opportunity of investing the place with a mysterious kind of fatality. The miscreant who betrayed it and the king to whom it was betrayed are both dead; while the 'arx invicta' itself is again in the

---

[1] This epigramma is found in the edition of 1518, but not in the subsequent editions.

[2] The mysterious death of the late king is alluded to by Skelton :

"Though ye untruly your father have slain."

"Against the Scots," v. 119.

possession of its rightful owners. It is curious to find a tradition still lingering on the spot that the castle was won by treachery, and that the traitor was afterwards hung for his pains. It seems to be hinted at by Scott in his poem of Marmion:

> " And first they heard King James had won
> " Etall and Wark and Ford;—and then
> " That Norham castle strong was ta'en :—
> " At that sore marvell'd Marmion."
>
> Canto v. 34.

More's epitaph upon the King of Scotland. This is followed by a few lines upon James's untimely end, being an epitaph of that unusual kind which contains much invective and but little eulogy. With all due admiration for his valour and sympathy with his misfortunes, the poet denounces in round terms the duplicity of his dealing with England, and represents him as calling upon all his brother monarchs to take warning by him, and to stand firm to their plighted faith.

His body said to be conveyed to London. It was reported at the time that a body found on the field of battle and supposed to be that of the King was enclosed in a leaden coffin and conveyed to London, where under the pretence that he had been excommunicated by the Pope, it was kept ignominiously without the rites of sepulture in a lumber room at the monastery of Sheen. Possibly the lines may have been suggested by that rumour. In Scotland however the belief was that James had escaped, and that the corpse taken to London was that of some His sword. other person. His sword fell into the hands of the victorious Lord Surrey, and after being for a long period in the possession of the Howard family, it was deposited in the Heralds' College, where it probably still remains.

Among the Latin poems of Buchanan is an epitaph, which may be set in contrast with that of More, as indicative of the national feeling in the two countries. 'Cease' the monarch exclaims 'to enquire the 'place where my remains are deposited: if the fates 'would grant me a burial-place correspondent with 'the greatness of my soul, the whole compass of ' Britain would be too narrow for my sepulchre.'

By James's side in this battle fell his natural son, a young man of great personal comeliness and a peculiarly amiable disposition. A few years before this, being already the Archbishop of St. Andrews, he had been a diligent and promising student at Padua under the direction of Erasmus.

While the Earl of Surrey was conducting the English arms with so much success on the borders of Scotland, King Henry himself was occupied with his warlike operations against France both by sea and by land. A century had now elapsed since the days of [1] Agincourt, but the jealous feeling of the French had lost none of its bitterness: and the wits amused themselves by attacking our countrymen in epigrams and lampoons. At that time the Emperor Maximilian, Louis XII. of France, and Pope Julius II., three ambitious potentates, were bent upon war and conquest.

---

[1] The battle of Flodden Field caused great rejoicing all over England. In his peculiar strain Skelton wrote

> " At Flodden hills our bows and bills
> " Slew all the flower of their honour."

He composed also a few indifferent Latin verses on the same subject.

CHAP. IV.

A.D. 1512.

Our own Henry VIII. joined the league against France, and being young and inexperienced he sent out an army in 1512 under the command of the Marquis of Dorset into the southern provinces of France. This army was long detained in a state of inactivity through the manœuvres of the King of Spain, and at A disastrous last being reduced to extremities through sickness expedition. and famine the men returned home crestfallen, mutinous and in disorder. Upon this a derisive poem Lampoons by issued from the French press with the title "De the French. "Anglorum è Galliis fugâ;" and in one of his letters More complains of other productions of a similar character. Erasmus, who had no great liking for the French and happened to be staying at that time in England, retaliated upon the wits of France and gratified also his English friends by addressing to Henry Answered by VIII. a Latin epigramma upon the flight of the French Erasmus. cavalry before the mounted English archers at Guinegate in Artois in the month of August 1513, which escapade was by the French themselves designated the Battle of Spurs. Erasmus takes up the idea suggested by Martial's well-known epigram upon the solemn entrance of Cato the Censor into the theatre during the exhibition of the immodest games of the Floralia. As Cato was asked whether he walked in with his austere countenance for the sole purpose of walking out again, so the Frenchman may be asked whether he had set himself forward to encounter the prowess of the English archers at Guinegate merely that he might have the opportunity of showing them his back in flight: whether the trial was in the fleetness of foot rather than in the strength of arm. Cato of old could not face women; the modern Gaul can-

not face men.   Cato could not change the severity of
his countenance; the Frenchman cannot change the
cowardliness of his heart.

During the war with France several events occurred to call forth the exercise of More's poetical
ingenuity; and one of these, a disastrous catastrophe
at sea, was eventually the means of involving him
in a strange dispute upon the merit of his own epigrams. By land Henry made several acquisitions
which in some degree compensated for his losses by
sea; and tended as he thought to impress foreign
princes with an idea of his prowess and resources.
After a tedious resistance of nearly two months,
Terouenne, an inconsiderable town on the fron-   Terouenne
tiers of Picardy, surrendered to his arms; and on   taken.
September 20, 1513, he took the rich and important
city of Tournay, after a siege of only two or three   Also Tournay.
days.[1]   The latter acquisition supplied More with a

---

[1] According to an old ballad, some of the London apprentices who
had been concerned in the outbreak on " Evil May Day," were par-
doned on condition of their serving in the French war.

> " And when King Henry stood in need
>   " Of trusty soldiers at command,
> " These prentices proved men indeed,
>   " And feared no force of warlike band.
>
> " For at the siege of Tours in France
>   " They showed themselves brave Englishmen :
> " At Bullen too they did advance
>   " St. George's lusty standard then.
>
> " Let Tourine, Tournay, and those towns
>   " That good King Henry nobly won
> " Tell London prentices' renowns,
>   " And of their deeds by them there done."

In this ballad, apparently written some time after the event, there is a

subject for some complimentary verses. When Julius Cæsar invaded Gaul, a desperate opposition was made to his victorious legions by the Nervii, the ancient inhabitants of this district, and the slaughter that ensued was immense: it follows, therefore, according to the poet's logic, that Henry, who had become master of Tournay without any bloodshed at all, is a commander at the same time mightier and more merciful than Cæsar. Henry reaps laurels while Tournay reaps the advantages of his protection. How much Henry was delighted with such victories appears from the reply which More made to Roper when congratulated by him on his familiar footing at Court:—
' Howbeit, son Roper, I have no cause to be proud
' thereof; for if my head would win him a castle in
' France, it should not fail to go.'

At length More himself was provoked into an open conflict with the wits of France. One of the French king's courtiers by name Germain de Brie, wrote a Latin piece which he called " Chordigera," arising from the circumstances of a naval fight which had taken place near the French coast. The two commanders Sir Edward Howard and Admiral Primauget fell in with each other near the harbour of Brest, and at the very commencement of the engagement the French ship ' La Cordelière '—' Chordigera'—was set on fire. Her captain finding the destruction of his vessel inevitable, bore down upon the ' Regent' an English first-rate and grappled with her; thus involving in one common fate two of the finest ships in the world and nearly two thousand men. This act of

confusion of dates: at the same time its eulogy of the apprentices may have been founded on fact.

desperation was much applauded by the Frenchman,
who seems indeed to have been carried by the warmth
of his national prejudices far beyond the limits not
only of courtesy but of truth; deliberately charging
the English with the violation of treaties, and perjury.
More proceeded to ridicule the poem in a series of
epigrams for its falsehood, plagiarism, and bombast.
The author, a young man ambitious of the reputation
of scholarship, and living in familiar intercourse with
some of the first scholars of the age, felt his pride
mortified by More's satire; but conscious of the
weakness of his cause, he subdued his indignation
and remained silent. At length however, after a
lapse of five or six years, the volume of More's Latin
poems came out, including all the offensive epigrams,
although he himself with much prudence and good
feeling had expressly desired that they should be
omitted. This seemed to de Brie a fair opportunity
of gratifying his revenge. Having scrutinized all the
real and imaginary faults which could be discovered
in More's Epigrammata, he summed up his animad-
versions in an elegiac poem bearing the portentous
title of "Antimorus," and thus the 'bellum interne-
cinum' between the two ships kindled a spirit of warfare no less furious and determined between the two
scholars. A rumour of de Brie's intention soon
reached the ears of Erasmus, who felt himself bound
not only by a regard for the parties concerned, but more
especially by a consciousness of having been the cause
of the publication of these epigrams, to use every possible effort and argument to soothe the angry feelings
of the combatants. He wrote immediately to de Brie,
urging him most strenuously to abstain from pub-

lishing the satire not only on More's account, but also
on his own : reminding him that the offensive epigrams
were written during the war, that their sarcasms were
rather national than personal, and that if he were
better acquainted with More he would acknowledge
that the world did not contain a man more worthy
of his esteem and affection. He urges too the danger
lest the cause of literature should be disgraced and
its progress impeded by the squabbles of its professors.

This well-intentioned epistle was not received by
de Brie, according to his own statement, until the
"Antimorus" was already in the press, and this fact
he assigns to Erasmus as the cause of his not having
complied with the request. At all events the "Anti-
"morus" made its appearance, and if the author's wit
had been equal to his virulence, the chastisement inflicted upon More would have been tolerably severe.
In reply to the charge of having borrowed too largely
from the ancients, he retorts that More himself has
no occasion to be afraid of such a charge, inasmuch as
he is indebted to no one unless it be to the poets of
his own Utopia. He censures him for having published his poems too hastily, and makes him responsible for all the errors of the press. 'The mistakes,'
he says, 'are as numerous as the waves on the sea,
' the blades of grass in the spring, the leaves in
' autumn. He ought to have licked his cubs into
' better shape.' He condemns the implied censure
passed upon Henry VII. in the gratulatory verses
addressed to his son : and severely animadverts upon
the want of classical taste displayed in a rhyming
epitaph upon Henry Abyngdon, omitting to notice

More's statement of the circumstances under which it was written. The want of candour in these criticisms is so evident, that perhaps More's reputation even as a scholar would have been very little the worse if he had suffered the affair to drop. This view of the case was urged upon him by Erasmus, who cautions him at the same time against that acrimonious and quarrelsome spirit of which he complained in his antagonist. In writing to de Brie he tells him plainly that the " Antimorus " meets with few readers, and still fewer admirers, and that More's abilities and learning and loftiness of character are such as to place him far out of the reach of attacks like this. To More he says, ' If you are determined to prosecute the affair, I ' conjure you to pursue the course you have already ' adopted, and to set down your adversary by reason ' and erudition rather than by hard words.'

Although More had already got his rejoinder not only written but printed, he complied so far with this appeal as to delay the publication of it until Erasmus's further pleasure should be known. The language, however, which he used must have militated strongly against any project of a reconciliation, and in fact he soon gave his angry epistle to the world, stimulated as it would appear by some further irritating remarks made by de Brie in the preface to another work. Erasmus, who had previously seen it in manuscript, observes to Budaeus, that although his own satire is thought by some to be rather biting, it is altogether toothless when compared with this epistle. ' I have no reason,' More says at the commencement of it, ' to complain that my own lot is ' harder than that of mankind in general: for I am

Gives advice to More.

More's reply to Antimorus.

' aware that no one, however inoffensive his demea-
' nour, can pass through life without an enemy.
' Since this is the case, how much reason have I to
' rejoice that the friends whom fortune has given me
' are of the noblest stamp, and that the only enemy I
' have is a person whom no one would wish for as a
' friend, or care for as a foe; a man who when kindly
' disposed has it not in his power to do me a service,
' nor when malignant to do an injury. And yet I
' should have been angry with myself, if even such a
' person had become my enemy from any fault of my
' own.'

If it were advisable we might proceed with the detail of More's defence of himself and his poems; the
pains which he took to show that de Brie was the ag-
gressor; his allusion to a wrestler who springs up
from the ground after a fall, and spits in the face of
his antagonist; and his professed intention of publish-
ing the "Antimorus" himself. He prays that the gods
may be propitious to both and correct what is wrong
in each of them: that in him they may chastise all
solecisms of speech, and in his opponent all solecisms
of temper; that they may eliminate from his own
compositions all barbarous words, and from his opponent's breast all barbarous manners; that in their
benignity they will grant that he may himself have
sound feet in his verses, and that his opponent may
have a sound head upon his body.

But the most curious inquirer will scarcely be inclined to investigate the matter any further. To
bring out the details of such a quarrel from the
oblivion into which they have descended, and to expose the irritability and jealousies of these patriarchal

scholars, comes not within the scope or spirit of our
present inquiry.

The fact of a man of high position in the Court of
France thus placing himself in the arena of literary
polemics against an English Chancellor of the Exchequer, and sending forth a long Latin poem in order to
expose the defects in his adversary's hexameters, is a
remarkable evidence of the high estimation in which
classical knowledge was held by the community at
large. And nearly three centuries afterwards a rather
singular scene occurred in our own House of Commons. The Chancellor of the Exchequer, when
making use of a Latin quotation, gave a certain word
with a false quantity. This was at once pounced
down upon by the noble leader of the Opposition.
The Chancellor of the Exchequer disputed the point,
and held that he was right. The Speaker was referred
to as the legitimate adjudicator. The Speaker sent
for a Gradus, and after having solemnly consulted it
he pronounced an authoritative judgment upon the
question. A false quantity perpetrated in public is
still a very serious matter; and it has been already
remarked that classical quotations have not yet ceased
to be, as Dr. Johnson styled them, the parole of
literary men all over the world.

CHAPTER V.

ETWEEN the years 1514 and 1523, More was engaged in several embassies to Flanders, chiefly for the purpose of settling disputes upon questions of commercial reciprocity: an employment which involved much loss of time and was in other respects irksome to him. The Flemish merchants were perverse and impracticable, and many difficulties were thrown in the way by the intrigues of diplomacy on the part of France. There was constant travelling to and fro across the country, and State emissaries sometimes found it necessary to transmit important messages by word of mouth. On one occasion, Pace, the King's Secretary, at the moment of his leaving Calais for Antwerp, picked up accidentally from the post certain facts bearing upon the movements of the French army, and happening to meet with More on the road, he desired him to make Wolsey acquainted with these facts without delay, which of course would be done; at the same time Pace wrote to Wolsey a special despatch on his arrival at Antwerp, which document is now extant bearing date October 25, 1515.

During these unsatisfactory visits to the Low

Countries More appears to have lost not only his temper but his health. Being of a constitution rather delicate, with his mind harassed and over-anxious, and always longing after the company of his 'very sweet 'children Margaret, Elizabeth, Cecilia, and John,' at home, moreover breathing the air of an insalubrious climate, he fell into an illness which Erasmus represents as in some degree dangerous.' At the same time it is to this foreign mission that we owe an epistle in Latin verse addressed to his children which is one of the most interesting and valuable pieces in the volume.

The most amiable and perhaps the distinguishing feature in More's private character was the affection which he bore for his children; and if there were no other proof of the sweetness of temper so often extolled by his associates, we should not hesitate after reading these lines to sanction the frequent use of the superlatives 'suavissime,' 'mellitissime,' applied to him by his friends Ammonius and Erasmus.

It is stated by his biographers to have been his constant practice when absent from home, to maintain an intercourse by letter with his children; receiving from them an account of every step in their progress, and giving them in return whatever counsel and instruction he deemed requisite. Of such epistles the one before us is an elegant and valuable specimen. It gives us at once an insight into the detail of his paternal superintendence; we are presented with the pleasing spectacle of this great man in his nursery, depicted without reserve or affectation by himself. We see him folding the younger ones in his bosom; opening to them his store of sweetmeats, the mellow

apple and the comely pear; and gratifying a father's
pride by procuring for them rare and costly garments
of silk. He could not bear to see them weep: and
the account which he gives of his gentle mode of
chastisement, winding up with the words,—

Ah ferus est, dicique pater non ille meretur,
    Qui lacrymas nati non fleat ipse sui,—

could not have been written by any but the ten-
derest of parents. The outspoken minuteness with
which he describes the process forms an agreeable
contrast to the picture given by Erasmus of a flagel-
lation which he had himself seen inflicted upon an
unoffending boy of tender years by one of the
'magistri strenuè plagosi' of the day. And yet—
More goes on to observe—this is nothing more than
the love with which every parent is endowed by
nature, independently of any desert on the part of
his offspring. He then proceeds to tell how their
engaging manners, their early accomplishments, their
graceful mode of speech, and the correctness of their
language have so won upon his affections, that all his
former love appears as nothing when compared with
that which animates him now; and he exhorts them
to persevere in the same course of improvement until
all his present love shall appear as nothing when
compared with that which he shall feel for them
hereafter.

No one after reading More's simple and touching
lines can be surprised to find so many pleasing allusions made by Erasmus and others to the affection
and harmony that prevailed throughout the household. And we turn from them to take a still deeper

interest in the record of those acts of filial duty and
tenderness with which, in the last dark period of his
life, these children evinced the strength of their affection and gratitude to the kindest and best of parents.

In the Life of Cresacre More will be found several
letters to his children in English prose, which like
the Latin epistle afford evidence at the same time of the
warmth of his affection and the pains which he took
to encourage them in their studies. In one of these
letters he refers to the progress which they had made
in astronomy, and admonishes them to 'let that ex-
'cellent and pious song of Boethius sound in your
'ears, whereby you are taught to penetrate heaven
'with your minds also; lest when the body is lifted
'up on high, the soul be driven down to the earth
'with the brute beasts.'

The passage to which he alludes is probably the
following :—

Sunt enim pennæ volucres mihi,
Quæ celsa conscendant poli ;
Quas sibi cum velox mens induit
Terras perosa despicit.
Aeris immensi superat globum,
Nubesque post tergum videt.

Lib. iv. 1.

The celebrated work of Boethius " De Consolatione
" Philosophiæ " was much read at this time, and it
seems to have been held in especial estimation by Sir
Thomas More. The volume is introduced into one
of the paintings of the More family by Holbein.

In his fondness for children More much resembled
his friend Colet, of whom it is recorded in one of
the epistles of Erasmus that he took pleasure in
watching their ways, and that from the pulpit he

used to remind his hearers that Christ himself charged his disciples to imitate their guilelessness and innocence, comparing them to angels. Doubtless More was among those who had heard this from Colet's own lips, and it would touch a chord that vibrated responsively. In More's expression of love for his children there is a feeling congenial with that which is embodied in Colet's address to the children in his newly-founded school. 'I pray you all little 'babes, all little children, learn gladly this little 'treatise, and commend it diligently to your memories, 'trusting that of this beginning ye shall proceed and 'grow to perfect literature and come at the last to be 'great clerks. And lift up your little white hands 'for me which prayeth for you to God :—to whom be 'all honour and imperial majesty and glory. Amen.'

His address to them.

Sir Thomas More's love of his children is thus referred to by Hurdis in his tragedy,

Hurdis quoted.

'I love to listen to the simple chat
'Of prattling infants. From the lip of youth
'I draw a sweeter pleasure to remark
'How reason dawns unto her perfect day:
'How passion kindles and impels the soul
'To all the useful purposes of life.'

He repeatedly tells his friends that any amount of honour which may accrue to him from the success of his Flemish embassies is altogether insufficient to compensate for the anxiety caused by the long separation from his children. And in a letter to Erasmus referring to the duties of an ambassador, he states his opinion that for the undertaking of such duties a priest is better suited than a layman. He says that the clergy, wherever they may be sent, can easily

Priests rather than laymen should be ambassadors.

procure all the comforts to which they have been accustomed at home; whereas a layman is perpetually
drawn away by the desire to be with his wife and
children. The clergy can take about with them their
servants, and all are maintained at the King's expense: whereas in his own case there are two house-
holds to be provided for, one with him abroad and
the other at home. And he adds with a touch of
characteristic humour that although a man may be
a kind husband and an indulgent father and a good
master, he cannot expect his family to have so much
consideration for his purse as to live upon air until
he comes back.

Yet after all his complaints of the annoyances and
loss of time in these embassies, Sir Thomas More
allows that they were in some degree counterbalanced
by the acquisition of several valuable friendships. At
Mechlin he made the acquaintance of Jerome Buski-
den, an opulent and learned ecclesiastic, in whose
house he found a progress made in the accommoda-
tions and ornaments of domestic life which excited
his admiration as expressed in several of these Epigrammata. He was also associated in the embassy
with Cuthbert Tunstall, afterwards Master of the
Rolls, and eventually Bishop of Durham; whom he
much esteemed for his high character and his learning, and with whom he enjoyed much agreeable companionship. And he became acquainted also with
Peter Ægidius of Antwerp, to whom he afterwards
addressed his "Utopia." Erasmus writing from
London to his friend Ægidius informs him that two
of the most learned of Englishmen are at that time
staying at Brussels, namely Tunstall, the Chancellor

CHAP. V.

Friendships formed when in Flanders.

Busleiden.

Tunstall.

Ægidius.

of the Archbishop of Canterbury, and Thomas More, 'to whom I addressed my Moria.' He adds that they are both very much his friends, and that if anything should occur to give Ægidius an opportunity of being of service to them it would be acknowledged by him as a favour.

Busleiden's library.

Of Jerome Busleiden it was said by Erasmus that although he possessed a noble library his mind was better furnished than his own or any other library. In presenting one of his own works to Busleiden Erasmus wrote :—

> Non ego Buslidicæ decus adfero bibliothecæ,
> Sed decus apponit bibliotheca mihi.

His collection of coins.

Several of More's Epigrammata are addressed to him. In one of them he is remonstrated with for not consenting to give to the world the poetry which he had written; keeping his Muse in durance under lock and key. In another More launches out into a strain of admiration of the Roman medals which Busleiden possessed. He says that as the city of Rome was saved from the incursions of her foreign enemies by the Imperators, so Busleiden saves the Imperators themselves from the incursions of Time. And he proceeds :—

> Those medals—gathered in the love thou bear'st
> To bygone ages—form thy choicest wealth.
> The arch of triumph moulders in the dust,
> Not so the laurelled chief who won the triumph.
> E'en the proud pyramid that holds the dust
> Of mighty kings, will prove a monument
> Not so enduring as thy Cabinet.

In another of these pieces he dwells with rapture on the recollection of Busleiden's mansion, so well arranged in all its compartments that it must have been the contrivance of Daedalus. You appear, he says, to have prevailed upon the fates to restore to life all the great artists of antiquity. Your sculptures, paintings, casts, and carvings seem to be the work of Praxiteles, Apelles, Lysippus, and Myron; while the distich to each appended is such as might have excited the jealousy of Maro himself. Every thing about you savours of classical antiquity excepting your organ; and that it would have been beyond the power of antiquity to produce. He concludes with a wish that old age may be slow in its advances both upon the house and upon its possessor. Busleiden died however before this volume was published; leaving by his will an endowment for three Professorships in the University of Louvain.

In regard to the remuneration which More received for his services in the foreign embassies we have evidence that he was especially careful to preserve his independence of character. In one instance on his return after an absence of six months he had an annual pension assigned to him by the King as an extra reward for his services. He reports this to Erasmus, and acknowledges at the same time that such an addition to his income would on more accounts than one be very acceptable. Nevertheless he declined to receive it. He tells Erasmus that upon that point his mind is fully made up. He says that it he were to accept the pension it would become necessary for him either to relinquish his present position in the city, or to retain it against the wishes of his fellow-citizens. For as he goes on to explain if any question of privilege should arise between the citizens and

Chap. V.

the King, they would look upon their own officer as holding a retaining fee for the Crown;—and to this imputation he did not choose to expose himself.

In the early part of his life, whatever may have been the case afterwards, there can be no doubt that More's political sympathies were rather with the people than with the Crown. There was nothing of the courtier in his composition. He strenuously opposed a financial measure in the House of Commons which Henry VII. was bent upon carrying, and it was reported to the King that his wishes had been thwarted by a beardless boy. The office of Under-sheriff which he held was an elective office, to which he had been appointed by the suffrages of his fellow-citizens. In the tragedy of "Sir Thomas More" which was brought on the stage about the year 1590, the Earl of Surrey is represented as speaking of 'Master 'More' as—

Keeps aloof from the Court.

> ' One of the Sheriffs, a wise and learned man,
> 'And in especial favour with the people.'

And More in his letters repeatedly expresses his satisfaction in feeling himself altogether independent of the Crown.

Such was the case down to the time of the publication of these Epigrammata in the year 1518. More's resignation of the popular office which he held would in some measure separate him from his fellow-citizens, and his appointment to the office of Treasurer of the Exchequer two years afterwards would place him among the chief officers of State and bring him nearer to the Court. What had been his sentiments with regard to kings and courtiers in his earlier days is

Drawn nearer to the Court.

clearly shown in some of the Epigrammata. And although he was eventually admitted to terms of social familiarity with the King himself it is evident that he was drawn into it reluctantly, and that among courtiers he felt altogether out of his element. It was said of him that he tried as hard to keep away from the Court as many men try to get into it. Simple in his attire, primitive in his manners, and in spirit independent, he had no mind to accommodate himself to the splendid constraints of a Court. ' Herein do I ' hang as awkwardly as one who never rode sitteth in ' a saddle.' Such was the confession which he made to his friend Bishop Fisher.

He well knew that the tenure of a Prince's favour is extremely precarious, and in one of the Epigrammata he administers wholesome advice on the subject, giving evidence at the same time of the existence of that almost prophetic sagacity which has been attributed to him by his biographers.

> Thou boastest access free to kingly ears,
>   Jesting with royalty in sportive mood :
>   Just so men sport with the tamed lion's brood,
> Withouten harm, though not withouten fears.
>
> From cause unknown grim fury 'gins to chafe,
>   And in thy sporting sudden death ensues.
>   Pleasure like thine, though great, I would refuse ;
> Less pleasure choosing, an' I find it safe.

In another of the Epigrammata a simple rustic who has joined a crowd of people waiting to see the King pass, is represented as taken by surprise on finding that the King appears to be nothing more than a man wearing a fine dress and mounted upon a great horse.

The following is Kendall's translation :—

' A clown in forest fostered up
　The city came to see,
Than forest Faun or Satyr wood
　More homely rude was he.

Much people all the streets about
　Together thick did throng :
And nothing but—' The King doth come '—
　They cried the street along.

The seely rustic half amazed
　To hear so strange a cry,
Much mused, and tarried there to see
　What should be meant thereby.

At last upon a sudden comes
　The King with sumptuous train ;
All brave, bedecked with glittering gold
　He gorgeous did remain.

On comely courser hoisted high :—
　Now everywhere the crowd
With strained throats—' God save the King '—
　They cry, and cry aloud.

' The King—the King—O where is he ? '—
　The clown began to cry :
Quoth one, with finger pointed out,—
　' Lo where he sits on high ! '

' Tush, that is not the King,' quoth he—
　' Thou art deceived quite.
' That seemeth but a man to me,
　' In painted vesture dight.'

In another Epigramma written as it would appear during one of the embassies in Flanders, he describes a clown as coming to a bridge on which the Prince is seated with a retinue of attendants standing around him. At a reasonable and respectful distance the man seats himself also upon the bridge. The by-

A clown seated on a bridge beside the King.

standers tell him that thus to sit upon the same
bridge with the Prince is an act of monstrous presumption. He replies by asking what would be the
amount of presumption if the bridge should happen
to be ten miles in length.

In another of the Epigrammata it is held that a
good and pious King can never lack children, inasmuch as whatever may be the number of his subjects
he is a father to them all.[1] In another piece the King
is represented as being the head of a body politic,
each citizen being a member. To lose one of his subjects is like the losing a limb, and it gives him pain.
And the members in return are ready to brave all
dangers in defence of the King, their head. In another
piece the good King is compared to the watch-dog
who chases away the wolf from the sheepfold, the
wolf being the bad King. This comparison may
perhaps have been suggested to More by passages in
the annals of his own country.

Some of the Epigrammata touch with much free-
dom upon the advantages and the disadvantages of the
different forms of government. It is shown in what
respects a popular form of government is to be preferred to a monarchy, and vice versâ: and although
the summing up is a little vague there is not much
difficulty in discerning on which side the bias lies.
In another place we are told that the security of a
King does not rest upon hoarded wealth, nor upon
mercenary satellites, nor upon princely palaces, but
upon a belief on the part of his subjects that a King
is of more service to them than any other ruling

---

[1] It seems probable that Melancthon who wrote an epigramma upon
the same subject may have seen those of Sir Thomas More's.

power could be. And if a Prince who thus holds his power at the will of others should exhibit towards his subjects a proud and disdainful bearing, it is absurd and childish. In another piece it is maintained that in the case of many men being ruled over by one man, that one man has no right to continue his rule any longer than the many may think proper to submit to it. When Langland among other personages introduces a King, he says that 'might of the Com-

Populus Regem creat.

'mons made him to reign.'[1] 'Populus regem creat' was a dictum of Cardinal Pole. Nevertheless when More in the course of his examination in the Tower said to the Solicitor-general Rich that the King could be made by Parliament and deprived by Parliament, but the Parliament could not make the King chief head of the Church, this was pronounced by the Court of Commission to amount to treason.

We find that the same line of thought was followed out and the same comparisons introduced by Sir

Speech in the opening of Parliament.

Thomas More when he made his opening speech in Parliament as Lord Chancellor in the year 1529. The King being seated upon his throne and the Commons attending at the bar, the new Chancellor stated the reasons for the present summoning of the High Court of Parliament. And in doing this he spoke of the King as a good shepherd who foresees things that may be hurtful or noisome and makes provision accordingly. He also said that it is not riches nor grandeur nor dignity that make a man a Prince, but the multitude of his people. And proceeding with the comparison of a King and his subjects to the shepherd and his flock he delivered a studied eulogy

---

[1] Prologus to the Vision concerning Piers the Plowman, l. 113.

of the King and an invective against Wolsey his pre- CHAP. V.
decessor who was now in disgrace, to which reference
will be made in a future page.

The satirist who had handled Kings so harshly
and freely was not likely to spare the courtier.

> Dismounting with a lordly air,
> " Hold me this horse, you fellow there."
> A courtier cried.   As if afraid
> T'advance a step, the peasant said,
> " Good sir, an' I be not too bold,
> That rampant steed can one man hold?"
> " Aye, one can do't."   " If so it be,
> Hold him thyself, no need of me!"

It is pretty clear that More did not much disapprove
of this unmannerly wit at the expense of the fine
gentlemen of the Court, and that he felt some pleasure in recording it.   Erasmus intimates that by
nature he had been always averse to the companionship of courtiers, and that he preferred to be familiar
with persons nearer to his own position in life, provided that he found them of a kindred and congenial
spirit.   This would be More's feeling down to the
end of the reign of Henry VII.

After the commencement of the reign of Henry Character of
VIII. as he became better acquainted with the Court the Court of
Henry VIII.
he found in it men of a very different stamp from
those whom he had made the objects of his satire.
We have the testimony of Erasmus and others that
in the early part of this reign the Court had attained
a very creditable character in the estimation of
foreigners.   The King himself, Erasmus says, is by no
means an indifferent scholar, and he possesses great
natural abilities.   He has succeeded in bringing about
him a greater number of scholarly and distinguished

men than are to be found in any of the Universities.
Pace was at this time his chief secretary—Linacre his
physician—Colet and Grocyn favourite preachers,
and Tunstall Master of the Rolls. Erasmus himself had been invited and pressed to join them by
his friend Lord Mountjoy [1] who stood high in the
King's favour, and by Wolsey, and also repeatedly
by the King himself. He excused himself to the
King on the ground of his delicacy of health ; stating
also to one of his friends that although he had heretofore never felt a liking for Courts he would have
joined them gladly if he had been a younger man.
Erasmus writes also about the same time to Sir
Henry Guildford the King's Master of the Horse that

the Prince of Bergen, a man of great learning and
sagacity, is desirous to send his son to the English
Court as a school in which he will be well trained for
an important position, and at the same time suffer no
harm from the contagion of those vices which are too
often prevalent in Courts. Margaret of Savoy wrote
also in behalf of the same youth to Henry himself.
This occurred in the year 1519. Hence it would
appear that there must have been a lamentable de-
generacy if all be true which is stated with regard to
the open immoralities practised in Henry's Court ten
years after this.

For a long period after the commencement of this

[1] William Blount, Lord Mountjoy, had studied under Erasmus in
Paris, and he continued to be to him through life a generous friend and
patron. He was a good scholar as well as an accomplished courtier,
and many letters of his written in neat Latin are still extant. He
married a daughter of Sir William Say of Lawford in Essex ; and in
1526 Sir Thomas More presented to the Rectory of Lawford by con-
cession from Sir William Say the patron.

reign the influence and example of Queen Katharine
would have its effect, and the Queen's character would
in some measure form the character of the Court.
Henry himself at that period took especial pains to
keep about him wise and able councillors. Pace
writes to Wolsey in 1521 that 'as old men decay
' greatly the King wishes that young men be made
' acquainted with his affairs,' and he desires Wolsey
to make Sir Thomas More and Sir William Sandys
' privy to certain negotiations at Calais.' And in the
following year Henry expresses his wish to have
about him besides Sir Thomas More others of a like
character:—'as well to receive strangers that shall
' chance to come, as also that the same strangers shall
' not find him so bare as to be without some noble
' and safe and wise persons about him.'

In the early part of Sir Thomas More's life he had
an aversion not only to the Court and to courtiers,
but to a town life in itself. At the age of about
twenty-six, being then in London, he wrote a Latin
epistle to his friend Dean Colet in the country, which
will remind the reader of certain passages in Johnson's
celebrated " Imitation of the third Satire of Juvenal."
He asks what there is in a city like London to induce
a man to lead a life of virtue. At the moment when
he is striving to tread the narrow and arduous path,
how many thousand devices there are to prevent him,
—how many thousand allurements to draw him into
the vortex of sin. On the one hand he hears the voice
of counterfeited love and poisonous flattery—on the
other hand he hears the babble of slander, jealousy,
and hatred, and the clamour of the Courts of Law.
Around him he sees nothing but tradesmen's shops

with all manner of tempting dainties—fish, flesh, and fowl—catering to the appetite and ministering to the world and to the devil the prince of the world. The clear and cheerful light of day is hidden from you by the overhanging tops of houses. In the country there is the smiling face of nature to feast your eyes upon, and the grateful temperature of wholesome air to refresh you, and the free aspect of the sky overhead to enliven you. Your friends can scarcely wonder if you prefer to remain for a while longer where you are, in the country, in the quiet enjoyment of the benign gifts of nature.

Thus Johnson to his friend who preferred the country to the town.

The same ideas in Johnson's London.

> Though grief and fondness in my breast rebel,
> When injured Thales bids the town farewell.
> Yet still my calmer thoughts thy choice commend,
> I praise the hermit, but regret the friend;
> Who now resolves, from vice and London far
> To breathe in distant lands a purer air.
>
> *   *   *   *
>
> There, stretch thy prospect o'er the smiling land
> For less than rent the dungeons of the Strand;
> There every bush with Nature's music rings,
> And every breeze bears health upon its wings.
> On all thy hours security shall smile,
> And bless thy evening walk and morning toil.

The Utopia also written in early life.

Both the Epigrammata and the "Utopia," which is beyond question the most important of his works, were written by Sir Thomas More in early life, at a time when he had not yet been tempted to mix with courtiers and to bask in the smiles of royalty. In regard to principles of philosophy More was at that time an eclectic. There was no sect of

philosophers in which he did not find something to
approve; and the more he found of this, the more he
admired the sect. This was said of him by his friend
Richard Pace in his treatise, 'De fructu qui ex doc-
'trinâ percipitur.' He seems to have sat down to
write the Utopia at a time when his thoughts were
running upon Plato's Republic and the True His-
tories of his favourite Lucian. There can be little
doubt that in that ingenious fiction a satire was intended upon the demoralized state of society around
him. Erasmus in a letter recommended his friend
Cope a learned physician at Basle to send for the
book at once. 'If you wish to trace the fountain
'head from which spring most of the evils that vex
'our commonwealth, read the Utopia.' Its grave
irony and its repressed humour are skilfully employed as a veil to keep out of the sight of the
uninitiated political sentiments which it would have
been dangerous to broach at a time when the
sovereign's will was paramount. In this book Sir
Thomas More figures before modern eyes as the
most daring innovator of his age, and thirty years
passed over before it could be printed at an English
press. It was probably in reference to the Utopia
and the Epigrammata that More himself said:—'I
'would not now translate even some works that I
'myself have written ere this, into English:' and to
this he was bold enough to add, 'albeit there be no
'harm therein.' [1]

No one in
England dared
to print it.

[1] The Utopia was published at Louvain in 1516, and in the course
of another year or two it was reprinted at Antwerp, Paris, Basle, and
Vienna. It did not issue from an English press, either in the original
or in a translation, until the reign of Queen Mary : nor did any English

An attempt has recently been made to enumerate all the works in various languages which may be supposed to have emanated from the Utopia as a prototype, but at present the list is far from complete.

translation appear until it had already been translated both into Italian and French.

CHAPTER VI.

E find Sir Thomas More acting occasion-
ally in the capacity of secretary to the
King, although he may not have received
the formal appointment of Secretary of
State, which appears to have been the case with his
friends Pace and Ammonius.

A letter is extant addressed by Pace to Cardinal
Wolsey in the year 1519, from which it appears that
a certain nobleman whom he styles 'my Lord Mar-
'quis'[1] was 'making suit unto the King's Grace' with
a view to obtain for his brother the vacant Archdeaconry of Colchester; and that when the King was
informed that the annual value of the preferment
was a hundred marks, he said that it would be 'more
'meet' for his Secretary Pace; and that 'he immedi-
'ately commanded Mr. More' to write to the Bishop
of London to that effect. All this was reported by
More himself to Pace, the writer of this letter, who
adds that the appointment was made 'without any
'intercession or knowledge' on his own part. Within
the space of two days he was installed as Arch-

Chap. VI.

A.D. 1519.

More acting
as secretary
to the King.

Pace appointed
Archdeacon of
Colchester.

---

[1] Probably the Marquis of Dorset, whose son, created Duke of
Suffolk in 1551, was the father of Lady Jane Grey.

deacon in the cathedral church of St. Paul; and before the end of the year he succeeded Colet in the Deanery.

Among other documents connected with More's secretaryship we find the record of an interview

which one Arthur Poole had with the King in reference to a matter in dispute between himself and the Earl of Arundel. In this transaction the prudent forbearance of Sir Thomas More appears to advantage. Poole states that when he described the manner in which he had been treated the King was 'greatly

'miscontent,' and gave directions that 'Mr. More 'should devise a sharp letter' to the Earl of Arundel. Mr. More however—as Poole goes on to state— 'thought it better to send the Earl a loving letter 'first.'

On another occasion More informs Wolsey that the King had expressed to him his entire satisfaction with the draft of a letter which had been written by

Wolsey in the King's name to the Queen of Scotland his sister. And More subjoins rather emphatically a like assurance from himself. 'I never saw him like 'anything better, and, as help me God, in my poor 'fantasy not causeless. For it is for the quantity one

'of the best made letters for words, matter, sen- 'tence and couching that I ever read in my life.' We learn in another place that after a while More began to show himself more frequently at Court, and that he paid marked attention to the Cardinal. It appears therefore that Wolsey's strong and determined character had already acquired some amount of ascendancy over a man who was by nature so little of a courtier as Sir Thomas More.

In a letter written by More to Wolsey in November 1524 he gives the detail of a conversation between himself and the King on matters connected with a certain Genoese who had come over as an ambassador from Francis I. to negotiate a peace. When More came into the King's presence he 'made ' the Cardinal's recommendations,' and the King expressed himself well pleased to hear of the Cardinal's health. More was holding in his hand at the time certain letters which had been sent to the King by Wolsey, and when he was about to deliver his message respecting the letters the King 'prevented' him by exclaiming, 'Ah, ye have letters by John Joachim,'— and he intimated that he knew the purport of the letters. The King however was wrong in his surmise. More rejoined, 'Nay verily Sir;' and he proceeded to explain that no letters at all had been received from John Joachim, neither did he believe that John Joachim had received any letters from his master the King of France. On hearing this the King 'very ' much marvelled,' for he knew that John Joachim had received dispatches two days before. More respectfully stated that this fact was not known to Wolsey, assigning his reasons for making this statement. The King then delivered into More's hand certain letters and 'advertisements' which he had received from Pace, and these documents were transmitted to Wolsey along with this letter of More's; the King desiring that Wolsey will return them without delay in order that they may be laid before others of the Council and also before the ambassador,—for the contents, he adds, 'will do him little ' pleasure.'

CHAP. VI.

A.D. 1524.

An ambassador from Francis I.

More's conversation with the King.

After this the King 'fell merrily' to the reading of the letters from Pace, and also the abstracts and other writings which More had brought, with which he was 'highly contented.' He thanked the Cardinal most heartily for his 'good and speedy advertise-'ment,' and then he communicated the news to 'the 'Queen's Grace and the other about him, well 'noting upon every material point;' 'and they were 'all marvellous glad to hear it.'

It appears from some of the letters that in most cases Henry was careful to keep the reins in his own hands; he being himself the deviser of plans, and Wolsey the instrument to carry them out. In the following instances however it was not so. At a time when the Duke of Suffolk had entered upon a campaign in France with a large army, the question

arose whether he should march forward to the frontiers of Germany, or remain where he was and proceed with the siege of Boulogne. Wolsey recommended the latter, and it was approved by the King, who said that Wolsey had 'hit the right nail on the 'head,' and was 'determinately resolved that the 'siege should be experimented.' Wolsey however re-

considered the matter and changed his mind. When the King was informed by Wolsey of this he directed More to write a letter in reply which is justly pronounced by Mr. Brewer to be equally honourable to the writer

and to his royal master. In this letter Wolsey is assured that 'his Highness thinketh that Councillor 'to be very commendable who, although there be no 'change in the matter, yet forbeareth not to declare 'the change of his own opinion, if he perceive, or think 'that he perceiveth, the contrary of his former coun-'sel to be the more profitable.'

In another instance when Wolsey had deemed it advisable in a very delicate negotiation to depart in some measure from his instructions, he gave his reasons for this change to Sir Thomas More and Sir William Fitzwilliam: and in writing to apprize the King of it he 'begs credence' for More and Fitzwilliam, venturing also to advise the King to confer with them upon the matter.

In conjunction with Ruthal Bishop of Durham, Tunstall Master of the Rolls, and Pace the King's chief Secretary, Sir Thomas More, Councillor, signed and solemnly swore to the Treaty of Intercourse between the King of England and the Emperor Charles V. in the presence of Cardinal Wolsey, the Earl of Surrey Admiral of England and certain others. By this treaty it was arranged that Charles should land on a certain day at Sandwich, and that he should proceed with Henry who would meet him there to visit the relics of St. Thomas at Canterbury: a special remission being granted to all such visitors in the present year which was the year of jubilee. It appears however that Charles landed at Hythe and that he was met there by Wolsey. He spent several days in conference with the King and Wolsey at Canterbury, and on the day of his departure Henry crossed the Channel and proceeded to meet his great rival Francis in the field of the Cloth of Gold.

At length More's frequent and continued absence upon other duties rendered it necessary for him to resign his favourite and popular office of Under-sheriff, and in 1521 he was appointed Treasurer of the Exchequer, an office of considerable profit as well as dignity, being in some respects identical with that of the modern Chancellor of the Exchequer. When we find it noted among the official memoranda of the year 1523 that Sir Thomas More could not 'be 'spared from the Exchequer in consequence of the 'great matters at the knitting up of this term,' we are reminded of the opening the Budget in our own days. And by the duties of the office he was brought into closer communication with the Court. When the Emperor came to England as the affianced husband of the Princess Mary it was arranged that he should be met at Canterbury by a splendid cortége of Lords spiritual and temporal followed by a considerable number of knights, among whom was Sir Thomas More. As they approached London they were met by the Lord Mayor and the City Companies; and by special appointment from the King More delivered

More's Latin address to Charles V.

an oration in Latin, congratulating the two mighty monarchs on the love and amity subsisting between them; to the 'great content' of all those who heard it.

A.D. 1521-25.

The period between the years 1521 and 1525 was probably the happiest portion of More's life. During

More's rapid advancement.

that brief space the important offices of Treasurer of the Exchequer, Speaker of the House of Commons, and Chancellor of the Duchy of Lancaster fell to him in quick succession. He stood high in favour both with the Court and with the community at large. In his inauguration as Speaker the Chancellor by the King's command described him as a man distinguished by the possessing three qualifications rarely found to exist in the same person—wit, learning, and discretion. And to this eulogistic speech of the Chancellor the Commons gave their very cordial assent.

Office of Treasurer of the Exchequer.

In reference to the first of these appointments Erasmus writes to his friend Budæus that the office itself is very honourable and the emolument very considerable. Also that there had been no solicitation whatever on More's part, and that another person was desirous to take it without receiving that additional salary which had been assigned to More. And he adds that knighthood, the prelude to future honours, had been conferred upon him by the King.

It appears that More in the unreservedness of their close friendship avowed to Erasmus about this time that there were many circumstances which tended to make his life a happy one, and that for all these he was indebted primarily to his love of learning. It was by his literary attainments that he had gained the favour of the King. They had tended to make his companionship the more acceptable both to his own countrymen and to foreigners:—his conversation is the better suited to please his friends, and he is the happier himself. He has been raised to a position which affords him the means of being useful to his own kindred and rendering service to his country. He is the better qualified to hold his own among the nobles of the land and the great men at Court. He is supplied with the means of keeping up a better style of living, and he is recruited in health. And last of all he becomes the more and more sensible of the thankfulness due to a kind Providence which has showered down upon him so many blessings.

The office of Speaker of the House of Commons to which More was appointed in 1523 although elective was virtually disposed of at the pleasure of the King. In the discharge of its duties Sir Thomas More acted with his usual spirit of straightforwardness and independence, making a noble stand for the privileges of the House, as Lord Campbell has fully stated in his Lives of the Chancellors. And although the House on one occasion by their demur and long debate in the matter of a subsidy [1] incurred the marked displeasure both of Wolsey and the King, Sir Thomas More lost nothing in the King's favour. Cromwell in speaking of him before the House styled him their ' right worshipful, best assured, right wise and discreet ' Speaker '—epithets which would not have been used by an aspiring courtier like Cromwell if the King had not been quite disposed to assent to them. He added also the words ' excellently lettered ' which would be duly appreciated both by the King and by Sir Thomas More himself.

Extra allowances.

As More became more closely connected with the Court it became necessary that he should meet the increased expenditure in his household by availing himself of certain pensions and extra grants which were among the usual modes of remunerating the officers of State; at the same time it appears that he became a recipient reluctantly. Wolsey in a letter to the King asks for permission to grant to Sir Thomas More a sum of one hundred pounds usually given to the Speaker ' for the better maintenance of his house- ' hold and other charges:' adding that he writes thus in More's behalf, ' well knowing that he is not himself

---

[1] On the subsidy question a Convocation of the Clergy was summoned by the Archbishop to meet at St. Paul's, and on their meeting at St. Paul's they were summarily ordered by Wolsey in virtue of his authority as the Pope's legate to meet at Westminster Abbey. Hence Skelton's bold and very popular epigram :—

Gentle Paul lay down thy sweard,
For Peter of Westminster hath shaven thy beard.

'the most ready to speak and solicit his own cause.'
This is coldly put by the lofty and patronizing
Cardinal who was by no means a good friend to
More. In the stronger language of Erasmus he was
'a sordido lucro alienissimus.'

The King complied with Wolsey's request and gave
his permission; nevertheless More had occasion to
refresh the Cardinal's memory by a very respectful
letter which is extant. Alluding to the fact that the
King had been 'graciously content' that beside the
hundred pounds to be taken at the 'receipt of the
'Exchequer' there should be paid him another hundred pounds out of 'the King's coffers by the hand of
'the Treasurer of the Chamber,' More prays 'in most
'humble wise' that Wolsey who had obtained for
him this allowance will direct Mr. Wyatt to deliver
it—'to such as I shall send for it.'

From a letter addressed to Cromwell by More's
learned friend Sir Thomas Elyot, who was himself a
courtier and had been employed in several embassies.
it appears that a courtier's life was by no means free
from pecuniary embarrassment. The pay for official
services was both scanty and precarious. He assures
the Secretary that although he possesses a considerable landed estate it is altogether impossible for him
to maintain the state and appearance expected from
one who serves the King. A lawsuit had cost him
more than a hundred pounds, and nearly four times
that sum had been claimed from him as an executor.
Having served the King 'without fee or reward more
'than the ordinary,' he had got nothing for all his
'long unthankful travail,' but the 'colic and the
'stone, together with an almost constant distillation

' of rheums which ministers to abbreviate my life.'
And he makes the melancholy remark that although
his life may be in other respects ' of no great impor-
' tance,' nevertheless ' some ways it might be neces-
' sary.' His estate being impoverished and his public
services thus scantily remunerated he had been
obliged to dismiss ' five honest and tall personages '
of his attendants, until he shall be able to ' recover '
himself ' out of debt.' And thus it has come to pass
that he is altogether ' out of power to serve his Grace
' —according to my expectation, and as my poor heart
' desireth.' [1]

It appears from official documents that in 1522
a grant was made to Sir Thomas More of a manor
and advowson in Kent which had fallen into the
King's hands by the attainder of the Duke of Buck-
ingham; and in 1523 the wardship of the son and
heir of Sir John Heron was granted to him.[2] He
received also from the King a " corrody " or annual
rent-charge, payable out of the revenues of the monastery of Glastonbury to a person nominated by the
King.[3]

---

[1] Sir Thomas Elyot was one of those men of literary reputation in
whose society Henry VIII. took pleasure and whom he liked to have
about him at Court. He was the author of the " Governor " and many
other works popular at the time.

[2] Cecilia the youngest of Sir Thomas More's three daughters, at
this time in her fifteenth year, became eventually the wife of Giles
Heron.

[3] The corrody—from the Italian corrodare to furnish—was originally
a right of sustenance or provision in the Abbey for one of the King's
retainers. In this case it amounted to £5 per annum. A letter is
extant from the Abbot of Glastonbury to Secretary Cromwell respecting the arrears accruing from the corrody after Sir Thomas More's
death; concluding with the emphatic asseveration that ' it hath been

In 1525 Sir Thomas More was raised to the office of Chancellor of the Duchy of Lancaster, and thereby his connection with the Court became still closer, insomuch that Erasmus in a letter intimates some fear lest the prosperous gale of fortune should bear him away from his old and familiar friends. Erasmus states also that nothing would have broken through his reserve and brought him out of his seclusion but the courteous and engaging manners of the King himself, who—as we learn from Roper—would come 'unlooked for' to dine with him at his house at Chelsea, and after dinner would 'walk with him by 'the space of an hour, holding his arm about his 'neck.' It has been remarked that Kings are entitled to commiseration on the ground that their isolated rank deprives them of those ordinary pleasures of friendship which are among the purest in life. Henry VIII. however was not so shut out from the pleasures of friendship. He sought them and he seems to have found them. There was doubtless in the familiar condescension of such a man an almost irresistible fascination, and although More by this time must have been sharp-sighted enough to discern something of his real character, he could not stand aloof. Having begun to taste the sweetness of royal favour he was drawn over to court it. King Henry entered the lists as a theological polemic by sending out his 'Assertio' against Luther, for which exploit he was rewarded by Pope Leo X. with the title of Defender of the Faith. Luther was ready with his reply, treating his royal opponent with little ceremony.

'herebefore always used to be paid at Michaelmas, as knoweth our 'Lord.'

CHAP. VI.

More as Ros-
sæus attacks
Luther.
Presently came forward a mysterious champion who fought under the name of Gulielmus Rossæus, attacking Luther with even less ceremony than Luther had attacked the King. This unknown writer is supposed to have been More.[1] In 1529 he entered the field without disguise as the avowed author of a "Dialogue "against Luther and Tyndale." And in the same year he was appointed by the King to succeed Cardinal Wolsey as Chancellor.

More succeeds
Wolsey as
Chancellor.
The appointment was doubtless a popular one. In the address which is said to have been delivered on the occasion by the Duke of Norfolk he spoke of Sir Thomas More's 'admirable virtues and matchless 'gifts' as well qualifying him to fill the office, although it had heretofore been held by none but very learned prelates or noblemen of high degree. And we are told that the people received this address 'with great 'applause and joy.'

More's speech
on the occa-
sion.
The speech which is represented as having been made by Sir Thomas More, 'with his usual modesty' in reply, is considered by Lord Campbell to rest upon

---

[1] Bishop Atterbury in his remarks upon this work says that Sir Thomas More—'much a Christian, much a gentleman, naturally of great mildness and candour, so far forgot himself in this answer to Luther that he has there given himself no other reputation than that of having the best knack of any man in Europe of calling bad names in good Latin.' One of Sir Thomas More's admiring biographers quotes from the book of Proverbs—'Answer a fool according to his folly, lest he be wise in his own conceit.' And he says that Sir Thomas More 'so dressed Luther with his own scolding and jesting rhetoric that 'he burst his very heart.' He adds that More suppressed his own name 'inasmuch as it seemed not agreeable to his gravity;' setting it forth in the name of one William Rosse, 'a mad companion that then wandered 'in Italy, and for the manner of his behaviour was well known of most 'men.'

questionable authority. It is not in More's style, and
he points out in it a singular anachronism. It contains however a classical allusion which to some of
his audience would be new, and to others would not
yet have lost the charm of novelty.—' Were it not for
' the King's most singular favour and all your good
' wishes towards which your joyful countenance doth
' testify, this seat would be no more pleasing to me
' than the sword was to Damocles which hung over
' his head tied only by a horse's tail, when he had store
' of delicate fare before him, seated in the chair of
' state of Dennis the tyrant of Sicily.'

Certain details of Sir Thomas More's Chancellorship
as they have been gathered from traditionary anecdotes preserved by Roper and others are well known,
but very little is known of that part of it which is
strictly judicial; there being no record of cases
decided by him nor any allusion in the law books
to his arguments or judgments. His assiduity in
clearing off the suits that were brought before him
is commemorated in a well-known epigram which has
been already quoted.

We have also the record of that memorable act of
filial reverence which in the case of many other persons would have been liable to the suspicion of a
striving after effect. Every day after entering Westminster Hall the Chancellor was accustomed before
he took his seat to kneel before his venerable father,
at that time the senior judge of the King's Bench,
and to ask for his blessing :—a scene not less touching
than that which took place between More himself and
his daughter Margaret after his condemnation, and
prompted by a like spirit.

Sundry other anecdotes connected with his Chancellorship and not less interesting have been recorded, but it would be beyond the scope of the present work to recapitulate them.

A comparison has been drawn by John Owen in one of his Latin epigrams between Sir Thomas More and Lord Ellesmere who held the same office of Chancellor in the reign of James I. Like some other writers of Latin epigrams Owen had learned the art of pouring delicate flattery into the ears of great men, and he draws the parallel so ingeniously as to convey to Lord Ellesmere a neat and well turned compliment. After pointing out the leading traits of excellence in the two Chancellors—the integrity, genius, and eloquence of More—the wisdom, gravity, and grace of countenance in Egerton; he pronounces them to be in spotless purity of character upon a par, and at that point he breaks off the comparison. Alike in most respects, in one respect they signally differ. Egerton is a second More until you come to the axe and the scaffold.

> Excipias Mori casus et flebile fatum,
> Et causam mortis :—cætera Morus eris.

A comparison has also been made between Sir Thomas More and another of his distinguished successors, Francis Lord Bacon. It may be allowed perhaps that Bacon stood the higher of the two in point of intellect, and that it would probably have been beyond More's capacity of thought to produce a philosophical work equal to the "Novum Organum." But in all other respects More stands on an unapproachable eminence. Bacon was corrupt, servile,

rapacious, and profuse; More was upright, indepen- Chap. VI.
dent, unselfish, and averse to all ostentatious expenditure. Bacon in his later days sank into degradation
and infamy. More cheerfully laid down his head upon
the block for conscience sake; deaf to the entreaty of
friends and regardless of the tears of his children.

As an instance of a distinguished man appearing at
a certain crisis of his life mean and contemptible,
Swift adduces Lord Bacon at the moment when he
was convicted of bribery: and among those who have
made a great and noble figure in some particular era
of their lives he points to Sir Thomas More in his
imprisonment and at the time of his execution. Sir
James Mackintosh allows to Lord Bacon the designation assigned to him by Pope as the 'wisest of
' mankind,' at the same time suggesting that the
distinction of having been the most illustrious of Lord Somers
Chancellors will belong of right either to a More or on a par with More.
a Somers.

CHAPTER VII.

HERE can be little doubt that More had received in early life strong religious impressions from those around him. He was brought up in the household of the most eminent ecclesiastical dignitary of his day, John Morton, Archbishop of Canterbury, Cardinal and Chancellor: a man to whom he looked up with reverence as being no less venerable for his wisdom and virtue than for the high reputation which he bore. Such is the character of Morton given by More himself in the introduction to his Utopia. And there can be no doubt that More's general character was in some degree formed by this early association: for he tells us that the Archbishop was accustomed to test the mental qualities of those about him by speaking with them sharply and at the same time without giving offence, thus discovering their spirit and their self-command.

In the house-
hold of Car-
dinal Morton.

More's fondness for theological study is evinced by the fact of his having delivered lectures on the ' De ' civitate Dei ' of St. Augustine while he was yet only a youth. At one time indeed he entertained thoughts

of entering the monastic life, and had begun to practise certain austerities by way of preparation. After
this his inclination was turned to the priesthood; but
he feared that the restraints of a priestly life might
prove too strict for him. At length by the direction
of his 'ghostly father' he abandoned the idea of
celibacy and settled down to the profession of the
law; retaining perhaps much of his predilection for
the Church, though as it appears from his Epigrammata with rather less respect for some of the clergy.

He placed himself under the spiritual guidance,
both publicly and in private, of that able and exem-
plary divine John Colet the Dean of St. Paul's.
Cresacre More states that he 'chose that worthy
'Dean for his ghostly father, and was obedient to
'him in all spiritual affairs as he was to his own
'father in all dutiful obligation.' In the year 1504,
being then about twenty-six years of age, he writes
to Colet who was at that time absent from London,
a Latin epistle couched in terms of very strong affection and reverence; telling him how much he values
his society and his wise counsel and his weighty
sermons, and how much he strives to follow in daily
life the excellent pattern which he sees always before him. He says that by following this example
he had escaped as it were from the very jaws of hell.
According to his wont he continues to attend the
sermons at St. Paul's, but he complains that the
preachers there in Colet's absence are very sorry
physicians:— in fact none are so sick as the physicians
themselves. And inasmuch as there can be but little
hope of a patient's recovery without confidence in
the skill of the physician, not only More himself but

CHAP. VII.

the whole city of London are very anxiously longing for their Dean's speedy return.

The young lawyer continued to be regular in his attendance at the Dean's sermons, and those sermons were eminently calculated both in regard to doctrine and delivery to leave an impression upon the minds of his hearers. Erasmus said of Colet himself that there was not in England a man of greater piety or a truer knowledge of Christ; and that his sermons were expositions of Evangelical truth;—there was something inexpressibly grand in his delivery of them and he preached like one inspired. Colet's teaching was that religion does not consist in the superstitious observance of rites and ceremonies such as were practised around him, but in a full self-sacrificing loyalty to Christ. Colet was one of that pious and devout body of men who saw the necessity of a thorough reform in the Church and who ardently desired it: but like some others he hesitated to identify himself with the avowed partisans of Luther.

Colet's sermons.

In that very important work entitled "The Oxford "Reformers," it is ingeniously argued that both Dean Colet and Sir Thomas More may be taken as admirers and to a certain extent followers of the Dominican monk of Florence, Jerome Savonarola.[1] Colet was in Italy at the time when Savonarola was electrifying the Florentines by announcing the advent of regeneration in a corrupt Church; and he came home strongly impressed with a sense of the need of that regeneration. In More's translation of the Life of John Picus of Mirandula, Savonarola is spoken of as 'a man of God' and 'most famous as a

Colet and More admirers of Savonarola.

[1] Oxford Reformers:—Second edition, p. 159.

'preacher.' Colet would confirm this from his own knowledge. And More's knowledge of the character of the clergy around would be quite enough to satisfy him that the regeneration spoken of by Savonarola was needed quite as much in England as it was needed in Italy.

Although the name of Erasmus is not usually included in the list of Reformers, and although it may not have been strictly true that more Protestants were made by his Colloquies than by all the ten tomes of Calvin, those Colloquies must have furthered materially the progress of the great religious revolution then commencing, by laying open the emptiness of the superstitious forms which had been made to take the place of true Christian piety. The book was eagerly sought for and universally read. It having been bruited about that the University of Paris were about to condemn the work, twenty-four thousand copies were at once issued by one bookseller.

Between Erasmus and the youthful More—the latter being scarcely twenty years of age and Erasmus being by ten years his senior an intimacy sprang up which soon ripened into a close and life-long friendship. In the month of October, 1499, Erasmus writes to More in terms of warm affection, and it appears from allusions made to certain letters eagerly looked for but not yet come to hand, that a tolerably brisk correspondence had already commenced. It was almost certain that two such men if thrown together would fraternize. More's genial playfulness caused him to be a favourite companion to all grades of men from the palace to the cottage, and it could not fail to tell upon Erasmus. Each had a keen eye for the foibles and faults of those around him,—a lively sense of the ridiculous,—and an aptitude to 'shoot folly as it flies.' Each wrote satire under the form of allegory. It was while staying as an inmate in More's house at Chelsea that Erasmus put into form the witty conceptions which had been springing up in his mind as he journeyed across the Alps, producing therefrom that memorable satire the "Encomium Moriæ." And it was immediately after leaving the company of Erasmus that More being then at Bruges wrote his celebrated Utopia. Each of them was a devoted lover of literature. Each of them took pleasure in ridiculing the monks for their ignorance and self-sufficiency. Each held the same opinions with regard to the superstitions and corruptions of the secular clergy. The terms of admiration which these two men used in writing and speaking of each other can scarcely be surpassed: in fact the character of More as depicted in one of the letters of Erasmus is little short of a model of the Christian scholar and gentleman.

It may fairly be assumed that in this closeness of intimacy the elder of the two, whose reputation as a scholar and a wit was already spreading itself over Europe, would gain a certain ascendancy over the younger: or at all events that there would be no great divergence of opinion between them. It was quite natural that in the event of the elder of the two being assailed with impertinent and unfounded charges the younger should stand forward in his defence. Erasmus was incessantly worried by the petty malice of the fraternities of monks and friars, and by one of them in particular—'monachus qui-

'dam'—he was openly denounced as a sciolist, a
pseudo-theologian, a vagabond, a sycophant, a schis-
matic, a heretic, and the forerunner of Antichrist.
These foul-mouthed names were contained in a sort
of cautionary letter which the monk addressed to
More, warning him of the danger to which he exposed himself by associating so much with the learned
and speculative foreigner: to which letter More wrote
a long and elaborate defence of Erasmus in reply. In
reference to the charge that Erasmus had maligned
the Fathers by intimating that certain of them were
occasionally liable to fall into error, More quotes
several instances in which Augustine alleges that
Jerome has mistranslated a passage and Jerome per-
sists in asserting that his translation is the correct
one; and he then asks whether the one or the other
is not in error. He touches also upon the doctrine
of the immaculate conception, intimating that although the Christian world of the present day for
the most part denies it, the belief of the saints of old
was that the blessed Virgin was conceived in original
sin. In reference to the system of Mariolatry which
was then prevalent he says that a certain Franciscan
monk had been preaching to the people at Coventry
that whoever daily goes through the Psalter of the
blessed Virgin can never be damned; and that he
was asked to give his own belief upon that point.
He says that at first he laughed at the question as
absurd. In the course of a discussion upon the subject afterwards he said that in the case of an earthly
prince you might easily find one who would grant a
pardon if his mother were to intercede for it: but
that no prince would be found so foolish as to create

Chap. VII.

More's defence of Erasmus.

He defends Erasmus.

He argues against Mariolatry.

among his subjects a spirit of insubordination and
insolence by granting a remission of punishment to
all criminals, provided only that they conciliate the
favour of his mother by paying her a certain amount
of obsequious reverence.

He proceeds to denounce the fraternities of the
monks themselves in terms very similar to those in
He denounces
the monks.
which Christ denounced the Pharisees of old: he
said that while they were strict observers of the
rules of this Order they lived in open neglect of the
commonplace virtues of faith, hope, charity, and low-
liness of heart, making the word of God of none
A remarkable
story.
effect by their traditions. He tells a strange story
which might indeed have been deemed almost incredible if he had not himself declared it to be a
fact. A certain man of the most approved religious
character, the head of a convent and a most punctilious observer of the rules of his Order, meditated
the commission of an atrocious crime—a combination,
as he states, of murder, parricide, and sacrilege;
and he engaged certain men of desperate character
to be his accomplices. Having brought these men
together, before he proceeded to explain to them the
deed which they were to commit he conducted them
to a private chapel, and there they propitiated the
Virgin by offering to her the accustomed salutation
upon their bended knees. More had been told this
by the men themselves, probably in the course of
some judicial investigation.

The Enchiri-
dion of Eras-
mus.
Erasmus was the author of a book with strong
Protestant tendencies which he entitled 'Enchiridion
' Militis Christiani.' In writing to Colet he states
that his object in writing this book was to counter-

act the prevailing error of those persons who think
that religion consists in the observance of certain
ceremonies almost Jewish, in which the body only is
concerned, while the inward and spiritual essence of
religion is almost forgotten.[1] This letter was written
by Erasmus when he was about to join his friends
More and Colet in England. Some time before this
More himself had written and printed a translation of
a similar treatise bearing the approximate title of
' Twelve weapons of spiritual battle which every man
' should have in hand,' by John Picus of Mirandula.
In the course of conversation by the three friends
the Enchiridion and Twelve weapons of spiritual
battle would be brought up as subjects of discussion, and the Protestant tendencies of the Enchiridion would be explained and enforced. More as the

[1] The epigramma which Erasmus placed ' in fronte Enchiridii' is to
be commended rather for its pious sentiment than for elegant Latinity.

> Nil moror aut laudes levis aut convicia vulgi,
>   Pulchrum est vel doctis, vel placuisse piis :
> Spe quoque majus erat mihi si contingat utrumque :
>   Cui Christus sapit,-- huic si placeo, bene habet.
> Unicus ille mihi venae largitor Apollo,
>   Sunt Helicon hujus mystica verba meus.

In one of his epistles Erasmus states that he had given a copy of
this ' Pocket-dagger' to a certain maker of guns at Cambridge, whom
he calls ' Joannes bombardarum artifex.'

> John Gun-maker with me agreed
> As Glaucus once with Diomede
> Arms to exchange, as pledge and token
> Of amity and faith unbroken,
> John gave to me a little sword,
> I gave to John my Enchiridion,
> That sword of John's I never use,
> Nor does John use my Enchiridion.

youngest of the three would at all events be an attentive listener and more or less a convert: Colet being his spiritual adviser and Erasmus a scholar and a theologian whose services to the cause of religion he acknowledges in these Epigrammata with unbounded admiration.

In reference to the fact of More's leaning in early life to the party whose aim it was to effect a reformation in the priesthood, it may be noted that More's son-in-law Roper, who married his eldest and favourite daughter Margaret, lived as an inmate in More's household for some years before the marriage took place; continuing also to be an inmate and member of the family until More's death. What may have been Roper's religious opinions in the first instance

Roper a Lutheran at the time of his marriage.

does not clearly appear; but at the time of his marriage he was unquestionably a zealous and active Lutheran. And if the father's attachment to the Church of Rome had been at that time, namely in the year 1505, as strong and his opposition to Lutheranism as determined as it became afterwards, it is difficult to suppose that this long and intimate association with the family could have taken place, terminating as it did in a marriage with the favourite daughter. Nor can we believe that Margaret More would have consented to become the wife of the zealous Lutheran Roper if she had been firm at the time in her attachment to the Church of Rome.

Scandals among the clergy.

Not the least powerful among the causes which brought on a reformation of the Church was the demoralized character of the clergy. The ostentatious routine of an imposing ritual, and the presumed exercise of an awful and supernatural power in the sacrifice of the Mass and in the rite of sacerdotal absolution, never fail to produce their natural effect in generating priestly pride : while the social position of the clergy, kept apart from the companionship of domestic life, gave rise to scandals innumerable and by no means unfounded. One of the first Acts of Parliament passed in the late reign was an attempt to check the public scandals caused by the immoralities of 'priests, clerks and religious men.'

The Church was dishonoured and religion itself was thought lightly of in consequence of the evil conduct of the accredited ministers of religion. More saw this: his friend and adviser Colet saw it: and all thoughtful men were grieved thereby. More saw instances not a few in which those sacerdotal restrictions by which he had himself been deterred from entering the priesthood were openly disregarded. And as Colet gave public utterance to his thoughts in the solemn prose of his famous Convocation sermon at St. Paul's, so did More scatter abroad his satire upon the ignorance and shortcomings of bishops, monks, and parish priests in these Epigrammata. Without losing his respect for the office, the individuals themselves he held in undisguised contempt. Like Erasmus and like many other scholars of the day who were not priests themselves, he looked upon ignorant and unworthy ecclesiastics as a fair subject for the exercise of his powers of ridicule; and he did not spare them.

More however was by no means indisposed to give honour where honour was due. Among his Epigrammata we find one in which he treats Archbishop Warham with marked respect and reverence. And

Erasmus has left more than one in which he takes the part of the clergy against a certain courtier who showed a bitter and unfounded animosity against them. This man is pronounced by Erasmus to be more foolish than Midas and more violent than Malchus. And he expresses a wish that either Apollo would decorate his head with the ears of an ass as he decorated Midas, or that Peter would cut off both the man's ears as he cut off one of the ears of Malchus.

Holy orders obtained by artifice.

There is no doubt that through lack of due supervision admittance was often obtained into the order of priesthood by a sort of artifice. This fact is stated by More in one of his Dialogues. He says that there are men who obtain a presentation to a living from the patron and take it to the bishop, 'having secretly ' discharged it;' that is, having entered into a private covenant with the patron that they will proceed to use the title no further than as a means to procure ordination. 'The bishop is blinded,' More says, ' by ' the sight of the writing, and the priest goeth a ' begging.' He complains that in consequence of this

Degraded condition of some priests.

they have in the country such 'a rabble of priests,' that for lack of proper maintenance some of them are driven to undertake the duty of menial servants, ' in ' as vile office as that of a horse-keeper.'

Priests in Utopia.

Very different from this is the condition of the priesthood as devised by More in his imaginary Utopia. The priest is there selected so carefully that they secure a man who is ' ex bonis optimus;' and we read that it rarely happens that a man so selected, solely on the ground of his suitableness for the dignity, is found to degenerate into indolence and vice.

A letter is extant written by Fitzwilliam the Treasurer of the King's household to Cromwell with instructions that a certain priest should get preferment solely on the ground of his cleverness in training the King's hawks. 'His Grace hath a priest that yearly 'maketh his hawks; and this year he hath made him 'two which fly and kill their game very well, to 'his Highness' singular pleasure and contentation.' Henry was fond of falconry, and he desired that this priest might have as a reward for his pains 'one of 'Mr. Bedell's[1] livings,' or some other when 'it shall 'fall void.'

Another letter is extant addressed to Cromwell by one Edward Baxter a merchant at Newcastle which shows that money was offered for preferment even to the great officers of State almost as a matter of course. Baxter states that he has educated one of his sons at great cost and that it is his desire to 'purvey' for this son 'some good spiritual living, 'to be God's servant and a man of the Church.' And knowing Cromwell to be 'in good favour' with Cardinal Wolsey 'who hath gift and collation of many 'good promotions,' he begs that he will procure for his son 'some substantial preferment.' And he undertakes to 'bear all charges,' and also to 'do unto my 'Lord's Grace and yourself such large pleasure as 'yourself shall devise, according to the value of the 'promotion.'

By a statute passed afterwards in the reign of Elizabeth this transaction if carried out would have

CHAP. VII.
—

Preferment for training the King's hawks.

Money offered for preferment.

---

[1] Thomas Bedell had been appointed Archdeacon of Cornwall: he was also a Commissioner to visit religious houses and a Clerk of the Council.

brought upon both the Cardinal and Cromwell the
charge of simony, rendering them liable to a penalty
'according to the value of the promotion.' So little
was Baxter himself aware of the nature of simony,
that after having made this offer he concludes by
commending his correspondent to 'the keeping of
'the Holy Ghost.'

The Epigrammata which More levelled at the priesthood are among the most severe in the volume. A
certain parish priest, whom he styles Candidus, is congratulated on his appointment to a living. His flock,
too, are congratulated upon their new pastor:—
'Unless I am blinded by partiality, it would be
'almost impossible to find another like him. With-
'out a spark of that useless learning which serves
'only to puff up its possessor with pride, he is en-
'dowed with such a combination of rare virtues as
'could scarcely be equalled even among the ancient
'fathers of the Church. He shows in his own con-
'duct, as in a glass, what his people ought to do,
'and what to leave undone; all they require being a
'simple admonition to *practise* whatever they see him
'*avoid*, and to *avoid* everything which he *practises*.'

> As a faithful mirror view it,
>   Showing what to do,—what shun.
> All he shuns, take care to do it:
>   All he does, take care to shun.

The same priest is represented in another place as
much given to sound the praises of the good men of
old, but slow to walk in their steps. If you imitate
them you envy them. But Candidus who only praises
them keeps himself thereby clear of the sin of envy.

In another place the priest of More's own parish, which would either be St. Lawrence in the Jewry where his father lived, or Bucklersbury where he lived himself after his marriage, is said to have given public notice to the following effect:—To-day is the great and memorable festival of the martyr St. Andrew, and it is well known to you that St. Andrew was right dear in the sight of God. I therefore forewarn all who are here present that according to ancient custom and by direction of the holy fathers of the Church you must keep *yesterday* as a solemn fast.[1]

An ex post facto notice of a Saint's day.

Among the Epigrammata we find one upon the subject of auricular confession which no strict adherent to the Church of Rome would have ventured to circulate among his friends, and much less to print. The story is told that during a storm at sea certain sailors confessed their sins to a monk who was among the passengers, and then threw him overboard. This story has given rise to unseemly ridicule from that time down to the present. Although probably nothing more than an idle fiction it serves to show which way the wind blew.

An auricular confession.

The following translation is by Archdeacon Wrangham :—

A squall arose; the vessel's tossed ;
The sailors fear their lives are lost.
Our sins, our sins, dismayed they cry,
Have wrought this fatal destiny.

[1] A French preacher on the same occasion is said to have told his audience that he had made known to them a year ago all that he could learn respecting St. Andrew, and that the Saint did not appear to have distinguished himself in any way whatever during the twelvemonth. 'I have therefore'—he said—'nothing more to add.'

A monk it chanced was of the crew,
And round him to confess they drew.
Yet still the restless ship is tossed,
And still they fear their lives are lost.

One sailor, keener than the rest,
Cries—with our sins she's still oppressed;
Heave out that monk, who bears them all,
And then full well she'll ride the squall.

So said, so done:—with one accord
They throw the caitiff over-board.
And now the bark before the gale
Scuds with light hull and easy sail.

Learn hence the weight of sin to know,
With which a ship could hardly go.

Another translation by Sir Nicholas Bacon will be found in the Appendix.

Although the Utopia cannot be referred to as containing the writer's settled opinion upon the subjects which are introduced, there is nevertheless some significance in the fact that while representing the practice of Confession as generally adopted by the Utopians, he mentions it as in a marked degree unconnected with sacerdotalism. Not to the priests but to the heads of families Confession is made.

Erasmus in one of his letters complained that the priest was sometimes bemused in the performance of sacred services by the potations in which he had indulged, and he relates a story showing what inconvenience may result therefrom to the persons confessing. A certain penitent confessed to a drowsy priest that among other delinquencies he had broken open his neighbour's escritoire. At this point the priest fell asleep. The penitent observing this ceased his confession and departed. Another penitent took

Mistake made by a drowsy priest.

his place and began to confess. But when he per-
ceived that the priest was asleep he awoke him with
a loud exclamation that he was not listening. The
priest declared that he was listening :—adding by way
of proof,—'you told me that you had broken into
'your neighbour's escritoire.'

Thus—as Erasmus goes on to remark,—the crime
of the one penitent was divulged by the priest to the
other penitent.

More took pleasure in exposing the pretensions of
the Scotists. A singular story is told by his friend
Pace, showing at once the turn of More's satirical
humour, and also his dislike to any ostentatious
attempt to display superior knowledge. It happened
that he was in the company of two popular preachers,
of the class who had attacked Dean Colet for his
famous sermon against the war. Their conversation
turned upon the fabulous King Arthur, of whom
Pace remarks that some people say he never was
born; and that others say he never died, but that he
disappeared and that it was never known how he
disappeared. One of the divines stated it as a known
fact that the cloak worn by King Arthur was woven
out of the beards of giants slain by him in battle.
This fact so alleged More ventured to question.
Upon which the elder of the two divines addressed
him with a patronizing air as little better than an
ignoramus, and told him that the fact was easily explained, inasmuch as the skin of a dead person is
capable of a vast amount of tension. To this the
other divine at once assented, deeming the explanation
to be characteristic of the well-known subtlety of a
Scotist. More then said that the alleged fact had

K

never before come to his knowledge, but that he was well assured of another fact;—which other fact was this, that his two opponents were very like two shallow-brained philosophers of old commemorated by Lucian; the one of whom milked a he-goat and the other held a sieve. Perceiving that they were altogether in the dark as to the meaning of the Greek proverb, More laughed at them in his sleeve and departed. And here Pace goes on to say that whenever in conversation with ecclesiastical dignitaries More makes a clever and learned remark upon theological matters, which he understands as well as they do, they invariably profess to regard him as a mere novice. Not that his remarks are at all like the rhapsody of a novice, but because they envy his wonderful genius and his consummate knowledge of things of which they are themselves ignorant. In fact, the novice is a much wiser man than the professor.

Favourite quotations from the Vulgate.

It was a common practice with the priests and friars to keep in readiness a few short passages from the Vulgate, and with such hackneyed quotations they often succeeded in cutting short an argument. Chaucer's Sompnour is represented as taking his quotations from the Decrees.

> ' A fewe termes had he, two or three,
> That he had learned out of some Decree.'

In the introduction to the Utopia a smart skirmish is described as taking place at the table of Cardinal Morton by the discharge of these missiles, the combatants being a jester and a friar. One of the texts most frequently quoted was ' occidit littera,'[1] which

---

[1] 2 Cor. iii. 6.

was a favourite weapon with the Scholastic divines
in their attack upon the Lutherans. Another was
'scientia inflat.'[1] Both of these are introduced by
More in the Epigrammata. A divine whom he styles
Posthumus is represented as perpetually quoting the
text, 'occidit littera;'—and yet he has no reason to
be afraid, for of 'litterae' he knows nothing. At the
same time, if he *should* chance to be killed by the
'littera,' it would be a hopeless case, for he possesses
not the Spiritus to give him life again.

Thynne has translated the Epigramma thus :-

> For lest that this dead letter should thee kill,
> Thou didst beware the letters for to learn.
> And aptly this, since of God's holy will
> The quickening spirit thou never could'st discern.

To a certain portly father who was fond of quoting
the text 'scientia inflat,' More says :—

> Much knowledge puffeth up, thou say'st,
> And what thou say'st is true.
> But looking at thy breadth of waist
> Scant knowledge doth it too.

A few severe lines in Latin verse upon the monks
are found in one of More's letters to Erasmus. In
describing a picture in which Erasmus and Ægidius
were represented by the painter Quintin Matsys in
conversation together, More resorts to his classical
authorities and compares them to Castor and Pollux.
Tunstall, who was at that time associated with More
in an embassy had gratified him by praising the lines.
But a certain monk found fault with the comparison
to Castor and Pollux. To compare the two to Pylades
and Orestes—he said,—would have been more appro-

[1] 1 Cor. viii. 1.

priate, inasmuch as they were really and truly friends, whereas Castor and Pollux were only brothers. More professes to acknowledge to Erasmus that he thinks the criticism quite fair, and that in order to relieve his mind he had written some indifferent lines on the subject. In these lines he states that he asked the paltry monk,—'fraterculus'—whether any amount of friendship can be imagined closer than brotherhood? The monk smiled at More's ignorance of the world and replied, that within the walls of his own monastery there were at least two hundred brethren, and yet among them all he did not think there could be found any two who were friends.

This letter was written at Calais; and it was finished in great haste under circumstances which serve to make us in some degree acquainted with the postal arrangements of the sixteenth century :—'Valdè ' festinante tabellario, urgente opinor illum aurigâ.'

Another Epigramma records an interview between More and a certain bishop, who little thought at the time that the young lawyer with whom he was conversing would one day be numbered among the most illustrious Chancellors of England, and that the only record of himself would be the discreditable anecdote now before us, in which he figures as,—'episcopus ' quidam sordidus et perparcus.' A bishop in the sixteenth century was as a rule ' given to hospitality' when he was at home, and a welcome was held out to all comers: so that whenever the doors of the episcopal palace were closed in consequence of the master's absence, there was a general complaining throughout the diocese. In the present case however the bishop was at home, and he received his visitor with formal courtesy. There were no signs of hospitality however until the last moment, and then in order that his departing guest might taste at least a modicum of his tawny wine, he proceeded to extricate from his pocket slowly and with an ill grace the key of the wine-cellar.

> If even to a Sybil's life
>   My own should lengthened be,
> Never shall I forget the boon
>   That bishop gave to me.
>
> A princely prelate he, I trow,
>   Lord of a wide domain:
> He never moves without five score
>   Of lacqueys in his train.[1]
>
> Though he so great, and I so small,
>   He rich, and I so poor,
> He took me in, he spoke me fair,
>   A stranger at his door.
>
> And when I left, to taste his wine
>   He deigned to make me free:
> And slowly from his grudging pouch
>   Drew forth the cellar key.

A singular and characteristic story of a visit paid by John Skelton to the Bishop of Norwich will be found in the Appendix, No. iv.

Skelton and the Bishop of Norwich.

In another of the Epigrammata More states with some humour and in a vein of bitter irony what he would represent as the ordinary qualifications for a bishop. Any priest who aims at a bishopric must possess two qualifications,—that of reading ill and

The two qualifications for a bishop.

---

[1] Skelton said of Wolsey:

> 'Then hath he servants, five or six score,
> Some go behind and some before.'

Wolsey however was by no means ' perparcus et sordidus.'

that of chanting ill. If he lacks either of these it will spoil his promotion.

> So *ill* thou chantest, one might almost deem
> Thee destined as the lord of some rich see;
> So *well* thou readest, one can never dream
> Aught better than thou art that thou wilt be.
> Chanting and reading well, in simple troth,
> If thou would'st thrive i' the Church, eschew them both.

It is probable that in the latter part of the reign of Henry VII. sundry elevations to the episcopal bench may have taken place on very questionable grounds; and upon one of these appointments More animadverts with an especial degree of severity. Professing to be delighted that so high and sacred an office is not now disposed of at random as had heretofore been the case, he says that this person, whom he designates Posthumus, has evidently been selected with extreme care, inasmuch as it would have been utterly impossible to find a worse,—

> Stultior haud possit, deteriorve legi.

And whoever this Posthumus may have been, it is evident that he was notoriously deficient both in piety and learning.

Such an appointment as this is more likely to have been made by Henry VII.—in the latter part of whose reign some of these Epigrammata were written—than at the beginning of the reign of Henry VIII. Henry VII. as he grew older became still more unscrupulous and fond of appropriation, but the young King his son and successor at the beginning of his career was much the reverse. In those congratulatory verses which have been already quoted More ascribes to him among other good qualities a just and conscientious selection of men to fill high offices : not selling them to bad men, but conferring them upon worthy and good men. And as if pointedly referring to this appointment of Posthumus to a bishopric, he says that the prizes which have been heretofore carried away by ignorant and unworthy men are now bestowed upon men of learning.

About three years before the death of Henry VII. namely in the year 1506, an individual was appointed to the rich see of Ely whose character corresponds precisely with the Posthumus of Sir Thomas More. This individual was James Stanley a younger son of the first Earl of Derby, who was the step-father of the King. Godwin the ecclesiastical historian after recording Bishop Stanley's neglect of his episcopal duties and the open scandal of his life, concludes with the following passage :—'sic voluptatibus immersus, familiâ 'à quâ natus est nobilissimâ tantoque munere indig- 'nus vitam exegit, et nullâ re præstitâ memorabili 'anno 1515 interiit.'

In an ancient metrical history of the house of Stanley the bishop occupies his place among the men of note. The admiring rhymester says all that he can find to say in the bishop's favour, allowing at the same time that although a priest, he had within him very little of the 'priest's mettle.'

> ' As many, more pity, sacred orders do take
> For promotion rather than for Christis sake.'

He was a 'goodly tall man' in stature : and he had a strong will, generally accomplishing whatever he took in hand. Withal he was of a lofty spirit :

'What proud priest hath a blow on his ear suddenly
And turneth the other likewise for humility?
He would not do so, by the cross in my purse,
Yet I trust that his soul fareth never the worse.'

Like Wolsey—and very unlike More's bishop Posthumus—he kept up princely hospitality in his
household:—

'A great viander, as any in his days,
For bishop that then was, here was no dispraise.'

Like Wolsey also he availed himself of that conventional licence to set aside the restrictions of celibacy,
which appears to have been allowed almost as a
matter of course to the higher ranks of the priesthood.   He left behind him a natural son known as
Young John Stanley, who inherited the gallant spirit
of his grandfather the Earl of Derby.   Under the
command of his uncle Edward who was created for
his services on that occasion Lord Monteagle, he led
the retainers of his father the bishop at the battle of
Flodden Field.[1]

[1] When Godwin states that Bishop Stanley died without having performed any act worthy to be commemorated he probably refers to the
Bishop's own cathedral at Ely, in which Alcock one of his more recent
predecessors and West his immediate successor erected the chapels
which are distinguished by their names.   Bishop Stanley is said to have
much improved the episcopal residence at Somersham, but his name is
not found among the special benefactors to the cathedral itself.   It
must also be acknowledged that he appears to disadvantage in the
early annals of St. John's College in the University of Cambridge,
where he is shown to have persisted in throwing impediments in the
way of Bishop Fisher the executor of the will of the foundress: that
foundress being the Lady Margaret Tudor by whose interest with her
son King Henry VII. Stanley had obtained the bishopric.   To the
church at Manchester however both he and his son were liberal benefactors, and in a chapel which he erected there the bishop lies interred.

We come now to examine the probability of Dr. Knight's belief that this James Stanley was the same individual who had some time before applied to Erasmus, at that time acting as a sort of private tutor in Paris, to assist him in the acquiring of a sufficient amount of scholarship to enable him to make a tolerable figure when placed upon the bench of bishops.[1]

In a letter written at Paris about the year 1498 Erasmus informs his friend Nicolas Werner that he has lately fallen in with several Englishmen of high rank, and that one of them a priest holding very valuable preferment had declined the offer of a bishopric made to him by the King, on the ground of his avowed insufficiency in scholarship. The offer of the bishopric however being made a second time within the year and being pressed with much urgency, the intended bishop desired to qualify himself in some measure by employing Erasmus to furnish him with the required amount of learning, promising most liberal terms of remuneration. Erasmus however, unwilling to have his thoughts and attention diverted from important study, and also feeling some pride in showing the rich Englishmen that he cared little for their money, declined the proposal of the bishop designate with something like contempt.

It is important to show that the age of this applicant who came to Erasmus for assistance in his studies in the year 1498 will correspond with the age of James Stanley at that time.

His father the first Earl of Derby died in 1504.

---

[1] Life of Erasmus. p. 19.

Marginal notes:
- Chap. VII.
- A.D. 1498.
- A bishop designate desires to be instructed.
- Erasmus declines.

Although he had led a stirring life and was advanced in years, the details of his will which was made a very few months before his death argue a full possession of mental vigour.[1] If his age be set down at seventy-five the year of his birth would be 1429; and if his first marriage took place at the age of twenty-four the date of that marriage would be 1453; in which case the birth of James his sixth son cannot be fixed much earlier than the year 1465.

And if James Stanley was born about the year 1465 he would be at the time of the interview with Erasmus at Paris about thirty-three years of age.

Stanley corresponds in point of age.

The fact of the applicant being in point of age eligible for a bishopric proves that he was over thirty, and the fact of his being styled by Erasmus 'adoles-'cens' shows that he was under forty. So far the circumstances correspond with those of James Stanley.

And of preferment also.

And the valuable preferments held by the applicant correspond also, Stanley being at that time Dean of St. Martin's-le-Grand and Warden of Manchester.

It is not at all improbable that the fact of Erasmus having refused to undertake the task of qualifying James Stanley for a bishopric may have been the cause of his for the second time declining the offer. There is reason to believe that it was the bishopric of Worcester which he declined. When the rich and important see of Ely fell vacant some years after this Stanley no longer pleaded 'nolo episcopari,' and he consented at last to assume the pastoral staff and the mitre.

[1] He bequeaths a cup of gold to the King, his stepson, praying him to be 'a good lord' to his three sons whom he mentions by name.

Cast. VII.

And at this point we find corroborative evidence that More's Posthumus was no other than James Stanley. In the year 1506 when he was appointed to the bishopric of Ely, More and Erasmus were living together on terms of the most familiar intimacy in More's house at Chelsea. The King's appointment of his mother's stepson, a notoriously unepiscopal person, as Godwin testifies—to one of the most important and most coveted sees in England, would be the subject of general animadversion. Erasmus would tell to More the story of all that had occurred some time before at Paris between himself and the English ecclesiastic who required help in his studies. And if that well-beneficed priest was indeed James Stanley, of which there is little doubt, the statement made by Erasmus would not be lost upon the listener. And More, who was amusing himself at that time by writing satirical Epigrammata upon all manner of subjects public and private, and whose feelings towards the King had been embittered by harsh treatment, would naturally take this discreditable appointment as a subject for his satire. Corroborative evidence.

The honest and out-spoken Thomas Baker in the preface to his edition of Bishop Fisher's funeral sermon on Margaret Countess of Richmond and Derby alludes to James Stanley as having been 'probably 'promoted to the see of Ely by her interest.' And at the same time he pronounces that exercise of her interest to have been ' the worst thing she ever did.' Which strong assertion of Baker coincides very remarkably with the no less strong expression of More : Baker's condemnation of the appointment.

' Stultior haud possit, deteriorve legi.'

It would appear that Baker's words as quoted above are incapable of being misunderstood or misrepresented. Yet in his Memorials of Westminster Abbey, Dean Stanley endeavours to make it appear that Baker's usage of the words,—'the worst thing 'she ever did,'—was directed, not at the misuse of her influence in procuring her stepson to be made a bishop, but at her interference with the studies of Erasmus by asking him to become Stanley's tutor. But it was not the Lady Margaret,—it was Stanley himself who attempted to entice Erasmus from his studies. Erasmus states this plainly and unmistakably. And the charge of having caused an unworthy man to be made a bishop is laid by Baker very reluctantly but most unequivocally upon the memory of the foundress of his college, whom he would have desired to represent as almost faultless.

Throughout the whole of his life,—whether as a young man writing epigrams, or as in mature age administering justice,—Sir Thomas More was accustomed never to spare an unworthy or delinquent priest. We are informed by one of his biographers that 'those who were naught of the clergy and fell 'into his hands for any manner of crime, found so 'little favour of him that there was no man living to 'whom they were more loth to come.' And yet we find him complaining in his 'Apology' that he is charged with being partial to the clergy. He adds however that he 'marvels whereon they gather it.'

CHAPTER VIII.

HE imposing accessories of ritual in the Church of Rome and the splendid luxury of its Court may be said to have reached their culminating point in the Popedom of Leo X. Two centuries before that period they were sufficiently striking to evoke the satire of Petrarch, who in an imaginary dialogue between the Pope and St. Peter under fictitious names represents the Apostle as lamenting the altered condition of the flock which he had bequeathed to the care of his successors:—once healthy and thriving, now demoralized and degraded. While the shepherds are sunk in luxury and sloth all the lambs of the original stock have been suffered to die off, and the fold is occupied by goats and unclean swine. Whither—he asks—are gone all the profits of the fold? The Pope replies that the profits have been devoted to good and legitimate purposes. Regarding with pity the rustic tastes of those who went before us, we have assumed —he says— a style more becoming to our position. We have dyed the white fleeces of the sheep with Sidonian purple. By the distribution of seasonable presents we have secured to ourselves powerful friends.

My spouse the Church now makes herself seemly with jewels. Her head-gear sparkles with gems, she wears costly ornaments of gold upon her neck, and her feet are adorned with bright colours. She abides in a state of dignified retirement and comfort. She is neither frozen by cold nor burnt up by the sun, which was the usual plight of the foul old woman your own spouse during the time that you had the supervision of the sheep and the sheepfold yourself.

As it is wittily put in one of the most biting of all satires, the shoulder-knots, the gold lace, the silver fringes and the embroidery had been attached one by one to the plain coats bequeathed to the three sons by their father; and in direct contravention of the careful instructions given by the father in his will.

The plain coats tricked out with ornaments.

There are doubtless many even among the more thoughtful members of the community who do not object to the use of ornament and grandeur in religious services, so far as it may conduce to the edification of the worshippers and the glory of Him to whom the worship is offered. At the same time all thoughtful persons strongly object to that spiritual pride and pretentious sacerdotalism which the exhibition of a gorgeous ritual tends to generate in weak minds among the officiating priesthood. By one class of the community it is witnessed with grief and indignation, by the multitude at large it is either regarded with indifference or turned into ridicule. Wolsey's pomp and processions were made the subject of derisive satire in the reign of Henry VIII., and Laud's riding in solemn state like another Wolsey caused much merriment in the reign of Charles I. The nations of Southern Europe are more addicted to this blending

The effect of religious pageantry.

of parade with religion than we are in the North: it
is in fact a main characteristic of Protestantism as
opposed to Popery.

In Sir Thomas More's time the English people
were becoming more and more convinced that mere
ceremonial is not religion. They were beginning to
regard with impatience and aversion those magic
forms and those imposing spectacles to which they
had hitherto been accustomed. They were beginning
to understand from the Word of God itself that the
true service is the service of holiness and purity and
humble obedience to His will. Hitherto they had
been living in ignorance of the plainest truths in the
Bible. And now those truths were taught not only
by Tyndale and others in secret with fear and trembling, but openly and boldly by Dean Colet in his
preaching at St. Paul's.

So long as literature was locked up in manuscripts
which were almost inaccessible, or in printed books
which were rare and costly, even the better educated
among the people were without the means of acquiring much real knowledge of Scripture. In the ordinary services of worship the prayers were muttered
over in an unknown tongue,—' sacra verba mussi-
' tant sacerdotes '—as Erasmus remarked. Sermons
were rare even in the towns, and in the villages there
were none at all. The only attempt to bring religion
in any degree into the minds of worshippers was
made through the medium of the senses. In the great
churches and the cathedrals there was an imposing
array of paintings and sculptures and gorgeous vestments and processions and pageants for the eye to
feed upon: and for the ear to drink in there were to

The eyes of
the people
were opened.

Worship had
hitherto been
sensuous.

such as were susceptible of that influence the strains
of vocal and instrumental music,—'the pealing organ
' and the full-voiced quire.' To a portion of those
who were assembled for worship all this might probably be a source of actual enjoyment: and when set
against the excitement of many of the ordinary pleasures of life there was so far something gained by it.
But there was little or no implanting in the mind of
religious truth. There was nothing to lead the people
to reflect that unless there go up together with this
an earnest aspiration and a prayer that both the heart
and the body may be directed and sanctified and
governed in the ways of the divine laws and the
works of the divine commandments, there is no real
and spiritual worship.

And these æsthetic appliances were confined for the
most part to the cathedral cities and to the great towns.
In the more remote villages recourse was had to a rude
and bold style of painting upon the internal surface
of the wall of the church. . Figures and scenes were
there depicted which could scarcely fail to make an
impression upon the mind of the illiterate worshipper.

Fresco paint-
ings. The bloody martyrdom of St. Thomas of Canterbury;
St. Michael weighing the souls of the righteous and
the wicked in a balance; and the terrors of a place of
torment. And a certain amount of religious instruction was conveyed also through the Block books or
Biblia Pauperum as they were called. In the rural
districts these were the channels through which illiterate persons derived their scanty lessons of divine
truth.

And it is easy to understand that so soon as the
vital and fundamental truths of religion began to be

proclaimed from the pulpit by ardent and eloquent preachers, there would be a rushing to and fro to hear them. The preacher being sufficiently well versed in Scripture to throw light upon the most important of all subjects, would bring to each individual a special message which had never been delivered to him before. And when they were told of man's spiritual needs and the spiritual help which is provided for him, they would test his doctrine by the written Word of God which was now circulated among them in their own language. In this state of things it is easy to see that the old system of æsthetic ritual would gradually but inevitably crumble to pieces.

The form of worship which More frequented was the simple service in his own parish church at Chelsea, at that time a small and quiet country village, where he sought rest and retirement when wearied with the noise and bustle of London. On one occasion he was found by his friend the Duke of Norfolk in the quire of this church, wearing a surplice and taking a part in the services; and the Duke took him to task for so far demeaning himself as to appear before the people as a parish clerk. In opposition to this reproof administered by his co-religionist the Duke of Norfolk, we may set the commendation given for the same act of devotion by the Protestant Bishop Aylmer in a sermon preached at St. Paul's Cross in the reign of Elizabeth, who pronounced Sir Thomas More to be a man 'who must be honoured for his zeal' although he was no Reformer.

In an imaginary conversation between Sir Thomas More and Southey written by Southey himself, More

L.

is represented as arguing that the effect of a splendid ritual upon the clergy by whom it is enacted will be to make them feel the temporal and spiritual importance of religion. He says that although the mind may not be impressed, it is at least engaged and occupied, and that there is something to feed the eye and to excite the imagination. Should the heart remain unaffected it is nevertheless entertained in a state which makes it apt to receive devout impressions and open to their influences.

This specious plea for æsthetic services is put by Southey into Sir Thomas More's mouth, but it is very much to be doubted whether such words were ever heard to come out of it. More would have said that the effect upon the actors in an ornate and quasi-theatrical ritual must necessarily be to impress them with a feeling of self-importance rather than with a sense of the importance of religion, and to produce a class of priests such as those whom he satirizes and exposes in these Epigrammata.

In an age which affected much punctilious ostentation and splendour in the ordinary costume Sir Thomas More was indifferent in such matters, and even careless. His gown he wore so loosely upon the shoulder as to give to his figure the appearance of deformity. He appointed a simple and homely servant by name Wood to have the charge of his expenditure and his apparel. A severe satire upon the love of show is introduced into his Supplication of Souls. Some of the souls in Purgatory are represented as undergoing a special punishment for their desire when on earth to be buried with a pompous funeral. They are brought back by their evil angels in order that

More himself careless as to costume.

Satire upon pompous funerals.

they may be witnesses of their own funeral, and they
stand invisible among the press being 'in great pain,'
and are made to gaze upon their own 'carrion corpse'
as it is borne out to the grave. They confess with
much sorrow that when on earth 'they studied not so
' much how they might die penitent and in good
' Christian plight, as how they might have gay and
' goodly funerals.'

Among the people of Sir Thomas More's Utopia
all the wearing of rich apparel and golden rings and
ornaments and precious pearls and diamonds and
jewels of every description was a mark of disgrace
and ignominy. Their gold and silver they put to the
vilest of all household uses, and to wear a chain of
gold was the mark of a slave. It is recorded among
the anecdotes of the More family that More's daughter-
in-law, who being the heiress of the family of Cresacre
was entitled to some amount of consideration, 'made
' petition ' to him that he would buy her a pearl necklace. From time to time he 'put her off' with many
' pretty slights,' until on one occasion when she asked
him on his returning home whether he had brought
her the necklace, he said, ' Aye marry I have not for-
' gotten thee.' And sending for a box out of his study
he solemnly placed it in her hands. She opened the
box with great joy and took therefrom the necklace :—
but it was not the pearl necklace for which she had
petitioned—it was a necklace of peas. It is said that
the poor young lady ' almost wept for very grief.'
Her prudent father-in-law however 'gave her so good
' a lesson that she never after had any great desire to
' wear any new toy.'

Another stroke of satire upon the lovers of finery

occurs in the Supplication of Souls, where wives in Purgatory who had been in the habit of wearing in their lifetime many ornaments and jewels, assail their husbands with reproaches for having gone to great cost in thus indulging their conceits; causing them thereby to be 'higher-hearted and the more stub- 'born' in their demeanour toward the husbands, and also to lose the favour of God.

We are told by Erasmus that when Colet was appointed to the Deanery of St. Paul's, instead of assuming the purple vestments usually worn by dig-

nitaries of his position he wore only a plain black robe. Colet, it will be remembered, was More's confidential friend and spiritual adviser. It is probable that when More in one of his English works speaks of the 'pompous and proud' apparel of certain of the higher clergy, 'the fashion of which had been intro- 'duced by the pride and oversight of a few,' he may have adverted to the pomp of Wolsey and the better example set by Colet. It is not without significance that he represents the clergy in his Utopia as for- bidden to wear any rich and embroidered vestments; assigning to the High Priest no other mark of distinc- tion than the carrying before him of a wax-light. A

lurking satire may here be found upon the appearance in public of the stately Cardinal with his two great crosses of silver and his two great pillars of silver ' glorious to the eye,'—his men-at-arms bearing gilded poleaxes to keep away from him the pressure of the crowd.

We are told by one of More's biographers that ' he ' so much loved the beauty and the glory of the House ' of God that if he had seen a fair and comely man of

'personage he would say that it is pity yonder man
'is not a priest, for so he would become an altar
'well.' This anecdote however is so little in accordance with More's strongly-expressed condemnation of unworthy priests as to render it impossible to
believe that the sight of mere comeliness of personage
without any apparent reference to other qualities
could have thus caused him to regret that a man had
not been made a priest. It is to be observed that the
reporter of this anecdote is a writer of strong Romish
proclivities, and that his biography was published a
full century and a half after Sir Thomas More's
death.

From the record which we have of a Pageant exhibited in Whitehall on February 13, 1511, it appears
that to the ecclesiastics of the day it was almost a
matter of indifference whether the piece in which they
were required to take a part was of a sacred or a
secular character. This Pageant was called the Golden
Arbour in the Orchard of Pleasure, and the chief per-
formers in it were the members of the choir of the
King's chapel with the Sub-dean at their head. The
orchard was set out with orange and pomegranate
trees and 'all manner of trees.' The arbour was
decorated with a profusion of flowers, and within the
arbour were twelve lords and ladies. On the sides
of it were eight minstrels richly apparelled and
playing upon strange instruments. On the steps at
the front stood 'divers persons disguised,' the chief
one being 'Master Sub-dean,' wearing a garment
'of a strange fashion' in the making of which were
used sixteen yards of blue damask. Upon his head
he wore a 'rolled cap' like that of a Baron of the

A.D. 1511.

The clergy
take a part in
the pageants.

The Sub-
dean's 'dis-
guise.'

'Exchequer.' Before him there stood a desk adorned with leaves of vine and laurel, and upon the desk a standish. By the side of the Sub-dean was 'Master 'Cornish' the choir-master,' whose gown and bonnet wherein 'to play his part' consumed fourteen yards of green satin. There were also two gentlemen of the Chapel wearing garments of russet satin 'like 'shipmen.' On the top of the arbour were the children of the Chapel, singing, being habited in cassocks of yellow sarcenet. The framework which supported this pageant was 'marvellous weighty,' there being borne upon it thirty persons; yet it was drawn from one end of the hall to the other end and back again. Most of the costly dresses worn on this occasion were probably retained by the wearers as perquisites, having been entered in the King's Book of fragments as 'spoiled.'

As Sir Thomas More fell by degrees into the routine of Court ceremonial he would occasionally be required
More's ap-
pearance in
State
pageantry.
to take an official part in pageantry and processions in which he could not be altogether at his ease. When Campeggio the Pope's legate made his public entry into
A.D. 1528.
London in the year 1528 he was accompanied by a cavalcade full two miles in length; the way on both sides being lined by friars and monks and priests singing hymns, wearing copes of cloth of gold, and bearing crosses of gold and silver and banners, throwing up clouds of incense as the legate passed and sprinkling him with holy water. And when the procession arrived at Cheapside Sir Thomas More was appointed to address him in a Latin oration. What he may

---

[1] William Cornish is mentioned by Sir John Hawkins as a composer of some repute, but not over-refined in his selection of words.

have said in this oration on the subject of Queen Katharine's divorce which was the great object of Campeggio's mission, and upon which he had been carefully reticent, it is not easy to conjecture: but in regard to the glitter and the pomp of the spectacle in which he played so prominent a part it may have crossed his mind perhaps that such things were ordered very differently in Utopia.

In order to meet the growing indifference of the people to her ritual the Church of Rome attempted to make it more attractive. The gorgeous ceremonial became more gorgeous still, and the musical services more elaborate. Henry himself was fond of pomp and pageantry, and being well skilled in music also [1] he took no small interest in these services. And all persons who were well versed in the craft, whether singing-men or singing-boys or organists, became persons of more than ordinary importance. The King, the Cardinal, and the Archbishop competed with one another for their services.

It appears from letters that are extant that the Archbishop having been given to understand that the Cardinal was desirous to take into his choir 'one 'Clement of my chapel which singeth a bass part,' conveyed at once to the Cardinal a polite assurance that not only Clement—whom he states to be a man of 'very sad, honest, and virtuous behaviour'—but any other servant that he had should be always at the Cardinal's command.[2]

[1] Erasmus states that Henry composed offices for the Church; and there is extant in the books of the royal chapel an anthem composed by him which is allowed by musicians to possess considerable merit.

[2] All the arrangements of Wolsey's chapel were on a scale of almost

It appears on another occasion that the excellence
of Wolsey's choir had given rise to a jealous feeling
on the part of the King, who complained to Cornish
his choir-master that 'if a piece had to be sung *ex*
'*improviso* it would be handled better and more surely
'in the Cardinal's chapel than in his own.' Upon
this Pace the King's secretary wrote to Wolsey that
were it not for the personal love borne for him by
the King,—'his Grace would surely have out of your
'chapel both boys and men.' The hint thus given
could not easily be misunderstood; and we find a
subsequent letter in which Pace informs the Cardinal
that a certain 'child of your chapel' who had been
transferred to the King's chapel, is much approved :—
the choir-master 'doth greatly laud and praise him,
'not only for his sure and cleanly singing, but also
'for his good and crafty descant. And he doth in
'like manner extol Mr. Pygote for the teaching of
'him.'

regal magnificence. The Dean of the Chapel 'was a great clerk and a
'divine,' and under him there were a Sub-dean, repeater of the quire,
gospeller, epistoler, and twelve singing priests. There were sixteen lay
singing-men, twelve children, and a master of the children; with a
yeoman and two grooms to attend upon the men, and a servant for the
children. Besides all these there were 'divers retainers of cunning
'singing men who came up at the principal feasts.' Of Wolsey's insolence in levying contributions for the maintenance of his own state and
splendour there are many instances. He sent to demand from the Earl
of Northumberland certain choral books which were in the Earl's chapel
—antiphoners, graduals, and others,—for the use of his own chapel, and
the Earl thought it prudent to submit. This characteristic imperious-
ness in Wolsey is ably illustrated by Shakespeare in his Henry VIII.,
where information is brought that certain valuable horses had been
seized 'by a man of my Lord Cardinal's who took them from their
'keeper by commission and main power, with this reason, that his
'master would be served before a subject if not before the King.'—
Act ii. sc. 3.

For one of these important personages by name Abyngdon, More was requested to compose a Latin epitaph.

In rather indifferent lines he commemorated the deceased Abyngdon as having been for a long time the pride of the cathedral at Wells,—then the pride of the King's chapel, and now exalted to be an additional glory in the celestial quires above.

These lines however were not at all suited to the taste of the survivors. They could not indeed desire anything higher in the way of glorification, but they would have been better pleased with something more musical in sound; after the manner of the rhyming and jingling verses of the monks which had been hitherto the only kind of Latin verse in vogue.

He then wrote another epitaph which gave entire satisfaction, running thus :—

> Hic jacet Henricus semper pietatis amicus.
> Nomen Abyngdon erat si quis sua nomina quærat.

And so on to the end of an epitaph of eight similar lines which were engraved on the tomb. In order to express his sense of the bad taste of those who had rejected the first written epitaph he set himself to write a third time, explaining the whole affair. He says that scholars might reasonably enough have found fault with the lines, but that the man who rejected them had done it in his ignorance: and that he ought for his obtuseness to be buried in the same tomb with the defunct Abyngdon and have his memory embalmed in the same epitaph.

Erasmus wrote an epitaph upon a certain musician which seems to have been intended as a burlesque upon the prevailing style of ultra-classicism. Invoking Apollo and Calliope he calls upon them both to mourn. Such was the magical power of the voice of the departed one that it moved the very stones. As it rolled along the sacred roof the ears of both mortals and celestials were soothed by it. Death the tyrant is informed that although mankind must all submit to his iron rule, music and its professors belong solely to the gods.

Music unduly exalted.
The inordinate exaltation of music in the services of religion caused some of the more intelligent and thoughtful persons to murmur, although they might be lovers of music in the abstract. Erasmus complained that 'multa canuntur ac fiunt in templis ' inepta.' He condemned the foppery of that style of singing which prevents you from catching and **Erasmus on musical services.** understanding the words. The sole object, he said, ought to be the creating a more ready entrance into the mind of the words and therewith of the ideas signified by the words. In the celestial region he apprehends that there is heard no sound whatever of voices, praise being there offered by the emotions and affections of the spirits. He would have in the church a choir, but he would make the choir subordinate to the reader and the preacher, and he would have it conducted with solemnity and devotion. The chief place in the service he would assign to the preacher, and to the silent inward prayer of the worshipper. He introduces St. Paul's comparison of the sounding brass and the tinkling cymbal. He says that in the time of Augustine some bishops did not allow any singing at all in the services, but only reading or recitation. And he complains that

he finds in England the services comprised in one continuous modulation of sounds out of which it is not possible to extract any intelligible words of sense: and that the people are required to resort to these services at all hours of the day on peril of their salvation.

In an imaginary dialogue between Cardinal Pole and Thomas Lupset, which was written by Thomas Starkey one of the King's chaplains and is supposed to give a fair statement of the opinions of Cardinal Pole, he is represented as saying in reference to church music that 'they use a fashion more con-'venient to minstrels than to devout ministers of 'the divine service,' inasmuch as 'the words be so 'strange and so diversely descanted that it is more 'to the outward pleasure of the ear and vain recrea-'tion, than to the inward comfort of the heart and 'mind with good devotion.'

Thus also in Roy's satire upon Wolsey a man who is speaking of the choir complains to his friend,—

'I understand not what they say.'

To which his friend replies,

'By my sooth no more do they.'

As time went on the murmurs of disapprobation became louder and they were expressed in stronger language. In fact the whole system of choral and musical services was assailed with clamour and abuse; and even the 'playing on organs' was set down as 'foolish vanity.'

But there was fortunately a party, and that a powerful one, who made it their aim not to destroy but to reform: to correct whatever was faulty and

excessive, but to preserve the worship itself. This
was the course recommended by Erasmus. He says
that in regard to the sacred vestments and the vessels
of the Church there is a certain dignity due to solemn
worship, and that the edifice itself ought to possess
all due stateliness and majesty. But, he goes on to
ask, to what purpose are so many holy water vessels,
so many candlesticks, so many statues, so many
organs as they call them? To what purpose is the
din of music and singing—that sound which resembles
nothing so much as the neighing of horses—and which
cannot be hired but at an immense cost? Erasmus
comes to the serious conclusion that in regard to these
mere accessories and appliances they were running to
an inordinate excess.

And the common sense of the people in the end
prevailed. It was agreed that 'singing, music, and
' playing with organs, provided that it be sober, dis-
' creet, and devout, is profitable in exciting people to
' prayer and devotion and to the receiving the sweet-
' ness of God's Word.' Such a form of worship was
in due time established. The choir was no longer
suffered to have the pre-eminence, and fitting regard
was paid both to the saying of prayer and the preaching of God's Word.

This compromise however between music in excess
and a scantiness of music did not prove of long dura-
tion. One party thought that the departure from
the Romish ritual had been carried too far, and the
opposite party thought that it had not been carried far
enough. Any attempt made by the one to retrace
their steps produced an outcry of indignation from
the other side.

Butler gives us an idea of the clamour raised by the party then in the ascendant by those lines of his Hudibras:—

'What makes the Church a den of thieves?
A Dean and Chapter and white sleeves.'

And this cry prevailed. The choirs for a time were put to silence. An extreme on the side towards Rome is followed by a movement on the other side towards Geneva, as surely and as regularly as the pendulum which has been overdrawn on the one side oscillates over an equal space on the other side when it is set at liberty.

The position which our reformed Church of England ought to occupy is that of equidistance from excess on the one side and meagreness on the other side. She ought to retain that amount of decent ceremonial and that moderate admixture of choral music which by their influence on the imagination add to the effect of her grand and pathetic liturgy; at the same time rejecting those theatrical exhibitions and that inordinate display of musical performance which prevailed in the time of Sir Thomas More, and which are still employed among the seductions and decoys of the Church of Rome.[1]

[1] In a leading London newspaper of May 14, 1877, among other attractions intended more particularly for 'the British contingent of the 'world-wide pilgrimage' then assembled in Rome, it is stated that at the church of Santa Croce the festival of the Cross was celebrated 'with much splendour and musical effect, the gem of the choir being 'the renowned Capuchin tenor, Father Giovanni.'

CHAPTER IX.

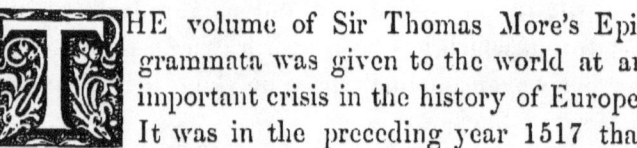

HE volume of Sir Thomas More's Epigrammata was given to the world at an important crisis in the history of Europe. It was in the preceding year 1517 that Luther placed upon the door of the church at Wittenberg his memorable protest against indulgences. In 1518, the year of the publication of the volume, Luther was summoned before the Pope's Legate Cajetan and refused to retract. In 1519 he held a disputation with Eck on the Papal supremacy, and in the year following he burned the Pope's bull in the presence of a large concourse of the citizens of Wittenberg. This was the consummation of the first period in the history of the Reformation, Luther and his followers having now publicly separated themselves from the Church of Rome.

More could not shut his eyes to the signs of the times. The whole nation was roused, and the cry for reform in the Church had become a loud and popular cry. Many of the clergy led immoral lives, many were ignorant men, and most of them were intolerably self-sufficient, furnishing ample food for More's satire. Of theology many of them knew but little,

and of other branches of learning they knew even
less. Of religion spiritual and vital they seem to
have known nothing, their souls being deadened by a
mere routine of ritual. Many of the laity were wiser
men than their teachers. In short the bands by which
the Church in England had been so long held as an
appendage to the Romish Church were gradually
giving way. The system was breaking up. Attempts
were vainly made to stave off that which had become
inevitable. Wolsey advocated measures for correct-
ing some of the more flagrant abuses; and Fox the
good bishop of Winchester, who had long been
labouring with the same intent, was beginning to
hope for a successful result. A letter is extant addressed by him to Wolsey in the year 1521, in which
he says that he longs to see a reformation of the
whole body of the clergy as much as Simeon longed
to see the advent of the Messiah, and that after
receiving a certain letter from Wolsey he had begun
to hope for better days. He says that in his own
diocese he had done all that lay in his power by cor-
recting and punishing the clergy, and more particularly the monks:—but they are so 'depraved, licen-
'tious, and corrupt,' that after labouring in vain for
the space of three years he had begun to despair.
Now that Wolsey, however, has taken the matter in
hand he looks forward to a better result. For he
knows that Wolsey has great influence both with the
King and with the Pope, and that he will assuredly
carry out whatever he undertakes.

Thoughtful and far-seeing men began to give proof
that they were in earnest. Monasteries were purged
of some of their worst corruptions, and there was a

general movement in the way of building churches and founding colleges. Bishop Fox himself was induced by the provident advice of his friend Oldham the bishop of Exeter, to abandon the idea of founding a sort of monastic institution which he had been contemplating, and to found a college.

Oldham's counsel was this:—Let us have care to provide for the increase of learning and for such as by their learning may do good to the Church and Commonwealth, rather than build houses and provide livelihood for a company of monks whose end and fall we may ourselves live to see.[1]

Progress of the Reformation.

But the cause of the Reformation continued to make progress. The community at large were already shaken in their attachment to the Church of Rome, and they were pressed on by a body of men not few in number and daily increasing, who would not be satisfied with anything short of an entire separation from it. Their religious knowledge had been increased by a wider diffusion of the Scriptures in the mother tongue, and they became more and more convinced that the service which man ought to render to his Maker does not consist in artificial and transient emotions which may be induced by mere sound and spectacle, but in the offering of a clean heart and a holy life;—remembering always that God is a Spirit and they that worship Him must worship Him in spirit and in truth.

In England these principles made a steady and a

---

[1] Acting upon the principle which is here enforced Oldham himself founded in 1515 the School at Manchester, and in 1516 Fox followed his advice and his example by founding the college of Corpus Christi in Oxford.

peaceable progress, but in some parts of Europe it was far otherwise. In Germany the insurgents proceeded to acts of violence and outrage, and More, like his friend Erasmus and many others who were Reformers at heart, began to fall back. He saw before him a sea of troubles and he thought it prudent to keep near the shore. In Bohemia the religious houses were plundered and their inmates were murdered; and Erasmus declared his belief that if these men who call themselves Reformers are suffered to get the upper hand there will soon be a general irruption into the cellars and strong boxes of the wealthy, and that every one will be called a Papist who has anything to lose.

There seems to have been in the mind of Sir Thomas More a settled conviction that he must decide upon either a persistent and loyal adherence to the Church of Rome or an entire separation from it. An entire separation he deemed a schism, and upon this he was not prepared to venture. The idea of ecclesiastical unity founded upon long tradition was deeply rooted in his mind, and he had a strong reverence for authority. In his Utopia the magistrates were very carefully selected, and on the part of the people there was required the strictest possible subordination and submission. As More became attached to the Court this reverence for authority would be strengthened. And when he found authority placed in his own hands for the express purpose of suppressing those heretics who were acting in open defiance of the law, he proceeded, no doubt reluctantly, to put the law into execution. And when it came at last to the simple question whether the supremacy of the Church

Chap. IX.

Maintaining the supremacy of the Pope. of Rome over the English Church should be maintained or subverted, he refused to say that he would agree to its subversion, and thereupon laid down his life. It was the belief of Cardinal Pole that Sir Thomas More was reclaimed from his former doubts and errors by a sort of miracle:—' by a light super- ' natural and a supernatural love given him by the ' mercy of God for his salvation.'

But the Pope's supremacy in England was doomed. And neither force nor argument nor the sacrifice of the precious lives of More and Fisher could save it.

A.D. 1529. More as Chancellor. When Sir Thomas More entered upon the duties of the Chancellorship he was about fifty-one years of age, and from that time he appears before us as a decided opponent of Lutheranism. There were only six more years of life remaining to him, and during Bound to suppress heresy. the former half of this term his official oath bound him to suppress all heresy. Well knowing that such a course would be pleasing to the King, he proceeded to act with some amount of vigour. In the impeach- Wolsey had been lenient. ment of Wolsey his predecessor, one of the articles charged him with having been remiss in the searching out and punishing heretics and with having been the rather disposed to screen them, in consequence of which connivance it was said that Lutheranism had been gaining ground. And with this plain warning before his eyes the new Chancellor entered upon his career as the Prime Minister to an arbitrary monarch, who had himself written against Luther, and who was so Catholic a Prince, as Roper said, that no heretic dared to show his face.

In any examination of the records of Sir Thomas More's Chancellorship the grave question arises—how far was he a persecutor of the Lutherans? What ground is there for that sweeping condemnation pronounced by Burnet, that he became 'a persecutor 'even to blood, and defiled those hands which were 'never polluted with bribes'? Sir James Mackintosh, after carefully examining the evidence and remarking upon the extenuating circumstances, absolves him from the charge of persecution altogether: and Lord Campbell says that he neither strained nor even rigorously enforced the laws against Lollardy. Mr. Froude speaks not so leniently. He thinks that Sir Thomas More was urged on in his judicial dealings with the Lutherans by a sort of fanaticism, and he sets the humanity of Wolsey in contrast with what he terms ironically the philosophic mercies of Sir Thomas More.

In dealing with this charge it must be borne in mind that the province of a Judge is to administer the law as he finds it, whatever may be his convictions as to the reasonableness or unreasonableness of any particular law. It is quite possible too that the sentiments of humanity in a man who is not otherwise than kindly disposed by nature may be stifled by the prejudices of education and habit, and by a rather loose but convenient way of thinking that those who made the law were wiser men than himself. In our own day a Judge may in the course of his duty be required to sentence a man to death, although in his conscience he is not satisfied that the Legislature is justified in retaining in its code the extreme punishment of death. Scarcely two centuries have elapsed since Sir Matthew Hale, one of the most virtuous and high-minded of Judges, passed the sentence of death upon persons accused of witch-craft: and he was supported by the countenance and advice of the philosophic Sir Thomas Browne, who laboured much by his writings to put down what he deemed 'vulgar errors.'

By this time the Reformation although primarily a religious movement had doubtless come to be re-garded in some respects as political, and in this aspect it would present itself to all persons of high position, especially if they were connected with the Government and the Court. And if Sir Thomas More who was not exempt from the weaknesses of human nature failed to cherish and retain that for-bearance and kindness of heart and sound sense which naturally belonged to his character, it can scarcely excite surprise.

> Rarus enim fermè sensus communis in illâ
> Fortunâ.

More desirous to please the clergy. It must also be remembered that in this phase of his career Sir Thomas More would be desirous to please not only the King but also the great body of the clergy. The clergy with Wolsey at their head,—with Tunstall and Pace in close connection with the King as his secretaries and ambassadors,—with an array of rich and almost princely prelates and mitred abbots in their several positions over the whole face of the country,—these formed a great and powerful body: and although in the bold exuberance of his early wit he had made some of them the subject of his epigrammatic satire, he came at last to fight their battle; writing numerous treatises against the Lu-therans. So strong indeed was the sense of their obligation to him on this score that they contributed to raise a sum of money amounting to 'four or five 'thousand pounds at the least' if his son-in-law Roper remembered right, to recompense him for his pains. This offer however although pressed almost importunately, with characteristic independence of character he refused to accept. And when at last they besought him to be content that it should be bestowed on 'his wife and children,' he told them that he would rather 'see the money cast into the 'Thames than that he or any of his should receive 'thereof the worth of a single penny.'

The time had come at last when the notions that had floated in his mind twenty years before on the subject of toleration would appear to him something like what the world has learned to call 'Utopian.' He had schooled himself to believe that if only one obstinate heretic is allowed to live, it may endanger the salvation of thousands who are as yet sound in the faith. We do our best to stamp out a deadly and infectious disease of the body,— and shall we not do our best to stamp out a deadly and infectious disease of the soul.— Even the gentle Melancthon allowed that for blasphemy a man might be put to death. A century after this the Chancellor Ellesmere gave his sanction to the burning of two men convicted of being Arians. And the Commonwealth Parliament in times still later were saved only by the intervention of one of their wiser members, Bulstrode Whitelocke, from sentencing a man to death because he was a Quaker.

Sir Thomas More had brought himself into the mind of regarding all offences, whether civil or ecclesiastical, as alike amenable to punishment both in a

Pleas argued casts for persecution.

moral and a legal point of view, thereby bringing
heresy into the same category with murder, theft,
sedition, and treason. In the legal administration
of the day, if the Judge found that he could not get
rid of an objectionable person by sentencing him to
death upon a more definite charge, it was convenient
to pronounce him guilty of high treason. In fact
this appears to have been the process by which the
condemnation of More himself was effected a few
years afterwards.

We have a statement of the conclusion at which he
had arrived in reference to the treatment of heretics
in his own words. Any person, he says, 'who is so
' set upon the sowing of seditious heresies that no
' good means can pull that malicious folly out of his
' poisoned, proud, and obstinate heart, I would rather
' be content that he were gone in time than over long
' to tarry to the destruction of others.' And a little
further, after expressing a wish that 'all these here-
' tics were clean gone for ever,' and that the parties
opposing each other ' would labour to make them-
' selves better and bear somewhat charitably with
' their neighbours,' he proceeds to say that according
to his own judgment ' those offences which neither
' the one party nor the other ought in any wise to
' suffer, such as theft, adultery, sacrilege, murder,
' incest, perjury, sedition, insurrection, treason, and
' *heresy*,—both parties in one agreeing, to the honour
' of God and the peace of Christ's Church, and also
' with rest, wealth, and surety of the Prince and the
' realm,—in regard to such they should diligently
' reform and amend in such as are mendable:—and
' those whose corrupt canker no care can heal, should
' cut off in season from corrupting further.'

An exposition of the sentiments of the Court party respecting Luther and his followers may be found in a letter prefixed to Secretary Pace's Latin translation of a sermon which was preached by Bishop Fisher at St. Paul's Cross in the year 1521. The writer expatiates upon Luther's great influence over his followers, who are spoken of as shrewd men and good scholars, but studious of popularity rather than of truth; looking upon themselves as the exclusive possessors of divine truth and despising all others. Luther is a man of learning, and he was well calculated to be an ornament to the Church of Christ. It is his policy to encourage his followers to simulate those virtues without which a teacher cannot usually bring the people to believe that he is in earnest: which virtues are constancy, frugality, earnestness in labour, humility, and zeal in promoting the glory of Christ.

With such men as Sir Thomas More and Bishop Fisher this seems to have been a settled and honest belief. The general character of the Romish clergy at that period formed a rather striking contrast to the character of such men as Tyndale and the other Reformers; and on the principle that the tree is known by its fruits, the logical inference that the corrupt tree was Romanism and Lutheranism the good tree, could not otherwise be evaded than by assuming, as it is here assumed, that the virtues of the Lutherans were merely simulated virtues, and that this species of simulation had been inculcated by Luther himself.

In More's mind Lutheranism became at last little else than another name for rebellion and anarchy. Lutherans were men who attempted to subvert all

rule and authority. The rise of Lutheranism he
deemed to be 'a great token that the world is near at
'an end.' He depicts in fearful colours the outrages
committed in Germany, and he adds that the fear of
such has been the cause that 'princes and people
'have been constrained to punish heretics by terrible
'death.' Another speaker in the same Dialogue
after expressing a wish that all the world were agreed
to 'take away all violence and compulsion upon all
'sides, Christian and heathen, so that no man were
'constrained to believe but as he could by grace,
'wisdom, and good works be induced,'—goes on to
say—'yet as to heretics rising among ourselves, they
'should in no wise be suffered, but are to be oppressed
'and overwhelmed in the beginning.'

More's epitaph
on himself.

In entire accordance with this is that remarkable
expression in the epitaph which More prepared for his
own tomb in Chelsea church. He there represents himself as having passed through a career of honourable
duties in life not altogether without credit. He had
been approved by his sovereign, and something more
than tolerated by the nobles. The people at large had
shown him favour. Nevertheless to certain classes

Styling him-
self 'hereticis
molestus.'

of the community he had been as a magistrate hard
to deal with:—which classes were the thieves, the
murderers, and the heretics.

In one of his letters to Erasmus he repeats this
asseveration, adding that he had acted with more than
ordinary zeal in regard to heretics. 'Quod in epitaphio
'profiteor, hereticis me molestum fuisse, ambitiosè

Tells Erasmus
why he was so.

'feci.'—He adds that such is his hatred of this race of
men that he should desire to be hated by them in return.
The more he sees of the course they are pursuing,

the more anxious he becomes in his look
to the future. He seems to have persua
that the mere fact of a man's fraternizin
disturbers of the public peace, especia'ly as
read his own reply to their arguments, was a to
proof that the heart of that man was fully s
to do evil. 'Sed isti generi hominum quibus n.
'esse libido est nullâ ratione satisfieris.'

In the face of this plain declaration it c...
denied that in a persecuting age Sir Th. as M
suffered himself to be carried along with the s..
and that this man who by nature was tender he...
and full of sympathy, must nevertheless be num...
among the persecutors. Not that he was the foreald
'tyrant' which Luther represented him to be, for was
he guilty of those acts of actual cruelty which have
been laid to his charge by Fox and Burnet. He r
coiled from the sufferings even of brute animals, as
we shall learn from some of his Epigrammata. At
the same time after a careful investigation of the
evidence Mr. Froude finds instances in which h
seems to have acted with what in modern times would
be termed harshness, if not beyond the actual require
ments of the law.

Yet it will be allowed that he was less of a
persecutor than most other men would have been
in the same circumstances. We have the positive
and weighty testimony of Erasmus that while in
France and in Germany and in the Netherlands so
many persons were put to death for holding the
dogmas of Luther, not one was put to death for holding them in England while More was Chancellor.
The Chancellor who set at liberty a supposed heretic

when he found the man bold enough and ready
enough to bandy wit with him, can scarcely be set
down as a relentless persecutor. This man's name
was Silver, and the Chancellor made the remark that
'silver is tried in the fire.' The man replied, 'Aye,
but quicksilver will not abide it.' And in the end
the Chancellor gave orders that he should be set at
liberty. This anecdote is recorded by Strype upon
the authority of an old manuscript.

In reply to charges which were brought against
him on the ground of his having abandoned principles
which he had formerly advocated, More adverts to
the 'Encomium Moriæ' of his friend Erasmus. He
speaks of the 'Encomium Moriæ' as a work in which
'faults and follies in every state and condition spiri-
'tual and temporal are touched upon and reproved.'
And he says that Tyndale, assuming that his opinions
are the same with those enunciated by Erasmus in that
work, asserts that if it were in English the public would
see that at that time he was 'far otherwise minded'
than he is now. And if it be so, More continues,
'the greater reason have I to thank God for amend-
'ment.' He will not allow however that at that
time he was 'otherwise minded' than he is now, and
he makes a show of defending himself on that score.
He argues also that the style of jesting and banter in
which Erasmus wrote his 'Encomium Moriæ' ought
not to be condemned, inasmuch as the object in using
it is to expose the abuse of things which are in themselves good. At the same time if any harm should
accrue to any one from the work itself he agrees
that it ought to be suppressed. For, he says, even the
Holy Scripture itself 'may have its honey turned

'into poison,' and therefore it is that t..
of it in English is forbidden. And h...
declaring that in days like the present w...
'are given to take' harm of that which is
would himself with his own hands 'help...
'Encomium Moriae,' and together with it a...
works of his own, 'rather than that folk... It
'through their own fault take any harm o' it.

Whatever may have been More's treatment of ...
dividual heretics in his judicial capacity, it must b...
allowed that he did not spare heresy in the abstract
when he took up his pen as a polemic. In the year ...
before his elevation to the Chancellorship he wrote
a 'Dialogue' in condemnation of the 'pestilent
'sect of Luther and Tyndale.' And no sooner had
he resigned the Chancellorship than he resumed his
pen and worked so vigorously that in the course of
two years he sent out eight treatises, covering more
than a thousand pages in the volume of his works.
To use the words of Erasmus in his later days, 'ex
'cultore Musarum fit gladiator.' Being intended for
the special edification of the commonalty who were
the readers of Tyndale's works, these treatises are
written in a popular style, and they are enlivened by
many amusing anecdotes together with a seasoning
of More's characteristic humour.[1]

The charge brought against Sir Thomas More of
violence and coarseness of language in his polemical
writings rests mainly upon that attack on Luther[1]

[1] In allusion to the rejecting of Tradition by Tyndale, he charges
him with refusing to trust God 'upon his word,' not being satisfied
'unless he gives him his writing thereupon and his letters patent under
'his great seal.'

under the assumed name of Rossæus, which has already been alluded to.[1] If More was really the author of that work it must have been written at the time when his better self was succumbing to the blandishments of a courtly life, caring not how strong his expressions and how coarse his ideas might be provided only that he could adapt them to the taste and the expectations of those about him, and acquit himself with *éclat* as the King's champion. Passages occur in his English works which cannot be read without pain. In one place he speaks of heretics as 'denounced by the clergy, and condemned 'by the civil power to be burned, and from the fires 'of Smithfield transferred to other fires where the 'wretches burn for ever.' Mr. Brewer remarks very feelingly and truthfully that 'when we find a nature 'so pure and gentle thus soiling its better self, it 'shocks us like the misconduct of a dear friend.'

Burnet does not scruple to attribute the growth and progress of a polemical and persecuting spirit in Sir Thomas More to 'the charms of that religion 'which can darken the cleverest understanding and

'corrupt the best natures.' And Mr. Froude remarks that as the lives of remarkable men usually illustrate some emphatic truth, so Sir Thomas More may be said to have lived to illustrate the tendencies of Romanism in an honest mind convinced that it is the true faith.

It has been already remarked that at least in the latter part of his life Sir Thomas More wrote under

a strong feeling of disquietude and alarm. 'The 'uplandish Lutherans,' he says, 'set upon the tem-'poral lords: they slew 70,000 persons in one sum-

[1] p. 110.

'mer, subduing the remnant in that part of Almagro
'into a right miserable servitude.' In common with
his friend Erasmus he had once looked forward to
a time when through the advancement of learning
and a better knowledge of Scripture there might be
effected a gradual and peaceable reform of abuses, preserving the unity of Christendom under the Bishop
of Rome as its one visible head. But this hope
was now abandoned, and in its place there was
a settled conviction that if the heretics in England
were suffered to take their own course, a result
might be expected no less disastrous than that which
had already taken place on the Continent. A man
of More's gentle temperament would look upon
scenes of internal commotion and bloodshed with
horror. If the danger could be averted by making
an example of a few of the more obstinate heretics he
was content to be classed among the persecutors.
And the pains which he took during the two years
after his resignation to convince the people by his
writings that Luther and Tyndale were false teachers
are a clear evidence that he was in earnest. The King
was alienated from him, all Court favour was at an
end, and he was active now from no other motive
than a desire to uphold the connection with that
Church which he believed to have been through the
Middle Ages the embodiment and preservative of
much that is grand and chivalrous; and although he
was quite aware that she had fallen from her high
estate and that a reformation was needed, more
especially in regard to the lives and characters and
qualifications of her priests, he refused to trust the
work of reformation to such men as Luther and his
followers.

CHAP. IX.

Similar
change in
Burke.

It was remarked by Lord Macaulay that the violence of the Democratic party in France in the last
century made Burke a Tory and Alfieri a courtier:
and that in like manner the violence of the chiefs of
the German schism made Erasmus a defender of
abuses and turned Sir Thomas More into a persecutor. Throughout the respective lives of Burke and
Sir Thomas More there are several remarkable points
of coincidence. Each in early life wrote a work in
which social and political questions were treated of
in a style and manner that puzzled some of his
readers: the one writing as it would appear in imitation of Lord Bolingbroke, the other borrowing his
plan from Plato and Lucian. Each took alarm at
excesses committed under the name of reform; mis-
taking, as it has been said, the turbulence by which
the tempest clears the stream for a permanent defile-
ment of the water. And each employed the later
portion of his life in resisting measures intended to
remove those identical abuses which in early life he
had himself endeavoured notably to expose.

More's fore-
cast of the
future.

It appears however that Sir Thomas More had a
sagacious presentiment that the party who called out
for reform would prevail in the end. At a time when
his son-in-law was expatiating upon ' the happy estate
' of the realm with so Catholic a Prince that no
' heretic dared to show his face,' More's reply was,
' Truth indeed it is, son Roper; and yet I pray God
' that some of us, as high as we seem to sit upon the
' mountains, treading heretics under our feet like
' ants, live not to the day that we would gladly be at
' league and composition with them, to let them have
' their churches quietly to themselves so that they

'would be contented to let us have our-
'ourselves.'

It happens occasionally in public life that
who comes to discover that his long oppos-
certain measure or movement is ineffectual.
gradually turn round and place himself at th....
of the party which he formerly opposed. Th...
chine is framed for mischief, and it is pleas... to
think that by taking it in hand he may p... to
succeed in checking its precipitancy. A... ... ...t
is one thing, and expediency or the doing of ...
that seems practicable under the circumsta... is
another thing; yet the attempt is made to ...
them. And there is no doubt that an ambitious ...
is strongly tempted to make a sacrifice of principle if
he can thereby place himself on the winning side.

But Sir Thomas More did not desert his colours.
For some time past he had been acting and writ...
against the Lutherans, and in this course he continued to the end. If he had set himself to play the
part in England which was played by Luther
Germany it would have furthered the progress of
the Reformation, but it would doubtless have cost
him his life. This however would be to him a matter
of small concern. And it cost him his life to remain
as he was.

In that ingenious work by Southey which is entitled
'Colloquies upon the Progress of Society' he gives
a series of imaginary dialogues between himself and
Sir Thomas More's disembodied spirit a fanciful device upon which it was quaintly remarked by Charles
Lamb that great as may be the merits of the work
itself there was no need to call up a ghost to hold

conversation with, and that it was making too free
with a defunct Chancellor and martyr.—Southey gives
it as his opinion that if More had been a younger man
by twenty years he would have joined the Reformers.
It seems likely enough that if he had lived in Elizabeth's reign the example and the influence of Henry's
daughter would have told upon him as her father's
did.   And if he had lived in our own times with the
experience of three centuries to show what Protestantism really is, we cannot suppose for a moment
that he would have held on to the Church of Rome.

The imagi-
nary More
lauds the
Church of
England.
Southey puts into Sir Thomas More's mouth an
admission that the Church of England is ' positively
' good and comparatively excellent; if not the best
' that might be conceived, incomparably the best the
' world has ever seen.'   Such was Southey's idea of
the judgment that would have been pronounced by
Sir Thomas More if he could have lived to compare
the Church of England as it now is with the Church
of Rome as he knew it in his own times.

On the other hand, in a work published about the
same time with Southey's Colloquies, and bearing
the somewhat similar title of ' Morus,' the author
indignantly repudiates the assertion made by Dr.
Knight that Sir Thomas More was a leading Reformer until 'human fears and worldly policy turned
' him out of the way which he saw to be right.'   He
treats this assertion as utterly unfair and unfounded.
He would hold that Sir Thomas More having been
brought over from his early opinions to the true faith
by a pure love of the truth, and having also ' a super-
' natural light given to him for his salvation,' could not
under any circumstances be in danger of falling away.

In times nearer to our own we have on the one hand a Life of Sir Thomas More in which he is represented as having been throughout life a faithful and devoted member of the Church of Rome.[1] And on the other hand Mr. Seebohm represents him as one of the three 'Oxford Reformers;' the other two being his friends John Colet and Erasmus. He thinks that Colet, Erasmus, and Sir Thomas More were no less instrumental in bringing about a revival of religion in the University of Oxford and eventually throughout the country at large, than John Wesley and his few compeers were in the same University some centuries afterwards.[2]

Thus we see that a man of mark who has been connected with each of two opposing parties in his lifetime comes at last to be claimed by them both; and there is as warm a contest to secure for themselves the sanction of his name as there was between the Greeks and the Trojans of old to gain possession of the body of the hero Patroclus.

It is to be observed that the early and original biographies of Sir Thomas More were written by his son-in-law and his great-grandson, both of them being members of the Church of Rome; and the bias with which they were written is manifest throughout. His strict and punctilious observance of the ordinances of the Church, and his hair-shirt together with his 'discipline of knotted cords,' are prominently brought forward. The difficulty which is found by

More's biographers were Romanists.

---

[1] The Life and Letters of Sir Thomas More, by Agnes M. Stewart. 1876.

[2] The Oxford Reformers: John Colet, Erasmus, and Sir Thomas More. By Frederic Seebohm. Second edition. 1869.

experienced lawyers in ascertaining clearly and positively the charge upon which he was pronounced
guilty is altogether ignored, and it is assumed as a
fact that he died a martyr to the Catholic faith. It is
also worthy of remark that while his early biographers although they were members of the Church
of Rome have not placed upon record any incident of
a miraculous character, several of that character are
recorded by Stapleton, who wrote his book after a
long interval and at a great distance from the scene
of action. And when we come down to a still later
period we find Cresacre More, who wrote in the reign
of Charles I., introducing grave statements of what

Miracles attri-
buted.
he believed to be genuine and unquestionable miracles. A sum of money was supplied by a miracle to
provide the winding-sheet for Sir Thomas More's
burial. And one of his teeth which was claimed by
each of the brothers Heywood,—' suddenly to the
' admiration of them all parted in two.'

Bearing in mind that all the early and in any sense
original biographers of Sir Thomas More were devoted members of the Church of Rome, we shall agree
that if any one of Sir Thomas More's three grandsons
who were Protestants had undertaken the writing of
his life, we should have been better able between the
two to arrive at the truth.

CHAPTER X.

HE common incidents in domestic life supplying ready subjects for such attempts, it was More's custom to amuse himself in his leisure moments,—perhaps while passing to and fro between his own house and the Courts at Westminster,—by exercising himself in Latin versification. Like most persons of a kindly disposition he was fond of animals, and we are told by Erasmus that he took pleasure in watching their ways and habits;—a taste which was inherited in a remarkable degree by his descendant Charles Waterton. He had at Chelsea an extensive and well stocked aviary. And when he came home to his children he would throw off all the cares of his busy life and join them in their amusements;—taking as much interest as they took themselves in all their pet animals, the rabbits, the fox, the ferrets, the weasel, and the monkey. This is stated by Erasmus in one of his letters.

In one of the Colloquies of Erasmus an amusing description is given of the clever tactics employed by this monkey in his attempt to defeat certain evil designs of the weasel upon the rabbits. The same little animal is represented as playing under a cushion before

Fondness for animals.

The monkey mentioned by Erasmus.

Painted by Holbein.

Chap. X.

Dame Alice in Holbein's famous picture of the More household. And inasmuch as the cats of Montaigne and Jortin and Cowper's hares are allowed a certain sort of celebrity, some portion of the same may perhaps be extended to Dame Alice More's marmoset, whose strategic exploits are commemorated in one of the most popular works of Erasmus, and whose actual portrait is introduced into one of the most remarkable paintings of Hans Holbein.

Present of dogs to Budæus.

The interest which Sir Thomas More took in dogs may be inferred from the fact of his having presented two valuable dogs, supposed to have been greyhounds, to his learned friend Budæus the secretary of Francis I. The safe arrival of these dogs in Paris was announced by Budæus in a letter which is still extant. The polite French secretary concludes his expression of thanks by assuring Sir Thomas More that the obligation would have been still greater and the present still more acceptable if one of the donor's witty letters had accompanied it. The greyhound had long been held in high estimation by the French, and a certain breed of these ' lords of dogs ' had the privilege of being admitted with their masters into the presence of the Emperor Charlemagne. Cavendish saw greyhounds in the hunt at Compiègne wearing richly damasked plates of armour upon the back and upon the chest to protect them from the tusks of the wild boar.

Verses on the cat and the spider.

After having watched at one time the attitudes and antics of a cat playing with a mouse which is making unsuccessful attempts to escape,—and at another time the entanglement of a vagrant fly in the web of a spider,—More set himself to describe what he had

seen in spirited and not inelegant Latin ve... ...,
there is something characteristic in his r...
the intended victim in each case as succeed... ...t
in extricating itself, although apparently in th
jaws of death.

It is evident that any infliction of un... ... y
pain and any wanton destruction of life was revolting
to his nature. The people of his ideal Utopia maintained the belief that it cannot be suitable to th
Deity by whose bounty animals have received the
gift of life, to take pleasure in their death or in th
offering of their blood. They held also the ...
that the souls of beasts are immortal. They accounted
it more decent to put animals to a speedy death when
required for man's food and assistance, than to take
pleasure in the spectacle of a timorous and helpless
hare torn to pieces by a pack of hounds.

It will be remembered that Cowper in one of his
shorter pieces remonstrates rather pathetically with
his favourite spaniel for having killed a young bird.
In stronger language More denounces the cruelty of
a certain sportsman who seized upon a rabbit which
was making its escape from the teeth of a weasel and
threw it to be torn limb from limb by his dogs. The
man, he says, who can stand by and enjoy such sport
as this, is more of a brute than the brutes themselves.

To show how much these sentiments of More were in
advance of the age in which he lived, it is only necessary to observe, that Ascham, his junior by nearly
half a century, a man whose rare attainments in
classical learning have gained for him a distinguished
place among the early scholars of his country, while

his unaffected kindness of disposition has been scarcely less applauded than his scholarship, was from his own confession an admirer of the inhuman practice of cock-

fighting. His apologists indeed have gone so far as to assert, that few if any in the sixteenth century condemned such amusements merely on the ground of their involving the misery and destruction of animals. To this sweeping charge More is a splendid exception; his gentle spirit would have acquiesced in the poet's counsel,

Never to blend our pleasure or our pride
With sorrow of the meanest thing that lives.

The same feeling of compassion for all animal suffering was a trait in the character of Sir William Jones, upon whose mind was indelibly impressed a couplet of the Persian poet Ferdusi,—

Ah! spare yon emmet, rich in hoarded grain:
He lives with pleasure, and he dies with pain.

It is evident from the number of pieces in this collection of which death is directly or indirectly the subject, that the writer's thoughts were often dwelling upon death. There is throughout the whole a tone of melancholy, making itself heard in the midst of those sportive and satirical effusions which form the staple of the work. He was accustomed to contemplate death in its most solemn aspect:—the certainty of its coming and the uncertainty of the time when it may come.

With but one month to live, thy soul
Would sink to earth.
To-morrow thou may'st die, and yet
Thou'rt full of mirth.

In his own person no one contemplated pl.
pain and the ordinary terrors of death with mo un-
flinching firmness.   Addison has remarked 'that I
' looked upon the severing of his head from his body,
' as a circumstance which ought not to produce any
' change in the disposition of his mind;' and in these
poems we find many proofs that he had disciplined
himself to this conviction from his earliest youth.   In
one place he expatiates on the folly of promising to ourselves a long life, or even wishing to arrive at old age.
In another, he compares life to a vast prison-house,
containing a multitude of wretched inmates all sentenced to death; a sentiment, which might well have
been expressed at that latter period of his life, when
he was confined for the space of a whole year in the
Tower, and removed from his dungeon only to be
conveyed to the block.   In another piece, written probably about the year 1516, on the occasion of an escape
from shipwreck, he mournfully remarks that the joy
felt upon such a deliverance is nothing more than the
momentary intermission from pain in a fever.   With
something like an unconscious presage of futurity, he
observes that on land there are more dangers than
on the sea; and that steel, or some malady more to be
dreaded than death itself, will be its precursor.   In
another place he speaks of life itself as nothing better
than a gradual process of dying.   The oil in the lamp
is continually wasting away; we are dying even while
we speak.   By constant discipline he had acquired
this settled habit and conviction of mind; and at last,
when reminded by the Duke of Norfolk that the
King's displeasure might probably deprive him of life,
he replied, ' Is that all, my Lord?   why then there is

' no more difference between your Grace and me, but ' that I shall die to-day, and you to-morrow.'

The age in which Sir Thomas More lived and indeed the whole of the preceding century had been

to men of high position a season of peril and vicissitude. The Pope himself having been driven to extremities by famine was kept for many months a prisoner in the castle of St. Angelo. In England it was no unusual thing for the highest and mightiest in the land to find themselves sinking into unforeseen troubles and disasters, the end of which was often upon the scaffold. Such was the fate of Fisher, Cromwell, the Earl of Surrey, and of More himself: and such would probably have been the end of Wolsey if that fatal disease at Leicester Abbey had not intervened.

The slipperiness of Fortune, her blindness, the constant revolution of her wheel, and her proneness to bring down the man of high degree and to exalt the lowly, form the subject of one of More's Epigrammata. And he has left several English pieces upon the same subject, administering wholesome advice to those who seek Fortune and also caution to those who trust in her. These were written in early youth, and they evince a thoughtfulness in advance of his years. If he had been gifted with the power of looking into futurity he could not have delineated with more preciseness the transmission of the Chancellorship from Wolsey to himself, and from himself to the next of Fortune's favourites, than in a passage which with a slight modification of obsolete orthography will run thus :—

' And when she robbeth one, down goeth his pride,
' He weeping wailing curseth her full sore.

> ' While he, receiving it on t'other . . .,
>   ' Is glad, and blesseth her oft'me . . . . . r
> ' But in a while she loveth him no more,
>   ' And glideth from him.'

And presently follow the ominous lines:

> ' The head that late laid easily and soft
> ' Instead of pillows lieth on the block.'

It seems not at all improbable that Holbein took . . p from these lines of his friend and patron Sir Thomas More, an idea which was afterwards developed in a remarkable picture of Fortune and her wheel, bearing the date of 1533 which was the year after More ceased to be Chancellor.[1] Fortune is represented as standing upon a globe, and she holds a rope which is attached to her wheel. On the top of the wheel is seated a man wearing a crown, who says in German something to this effect:--

> ' Now hold I rule and sway,
>   How long 'twill last I cannot say.'

On the right a man who is falling down from the wheel clutches it with his hands and exclaims:

> ' My day is o'er, no more I reign,
>   Say, God and Earth, what shall I gain?'

On the other side a man is climbing the wheel, who says:--

> ' Now shall I soon a ruler be
>   If death do not lay hold of me.'

At the bottom of the wheel lies a fourth man, who says:--

> ' I bide the hour.'

[1] This picture is in the possession of the Duke of Devonshire.

Over the wheel are three figures hovering in the air, which are intended to represent the Almighty Father and two angels.

The same sentiment was adopted by Philip Earl of Arundel who died after a long imprisonment in the Tower in the reign of Elizabeth, and who, as we may suppose, was not unacquainted with the writings of More and the paintings of Holbein. On his death-bed he addressed Blount the Lieutenant of the Tower, who had treated him harshly, in these words,—

The Earl of Arundel's allusion.

' Remember, good Mr. Lieutenant, that God who ' with his finger turneth the unstable wheel of this ' variable world, can in the revolution of a few days ' bring you to be a prisoner also, and to be kept in ' the same place where you now keep others.' Which actually took place in the course of seven weeks. Blount fell into disgrace and was kept a close prisoner in the Tower under another Lieutenant who, as we read,—' carried as hard a hand over him as he had ' done over others.'[1]

In those days besides the more summary process on the scaffold there was an amount of wear and tear in public life which operated much in contracting the allotted span. Wolsey was a worn out old man

Life speedily worn out.

before he had reached the age of sixty. Erasmus struggled on through accumulating infirmities until he died at the age of sixty-nine. More himself at the time when those solemn reflections upon the un-certainty of life were noted down had scarcely arrived at that turning-point which has been styled the keystone of life's arch. And when he resigned his office at the age of fifty-four, he said to the King

[1] See a Life of the Earl of Arundel edited by the Duke of Norfolk.

that he felt the time had come for him to 'bestow the
' residue of his life about the provision of his soul in
' the service of God.' At fifty-five he had ' left off
' all earthly pursuits, having nothing to seek or desire
' but the life to come.' And at the time of his execution he was suffering under painful and fatal maladies,
although his age was not more than fifty-seven.

That very striking remark made by Sir Thomas More's pre-
sentiment.
More to the Duke of Norfolk which has been already
alluded to will show that he felt a sort of presentiment that it would be the King's policy to remove
him in order to act as a warning to others. Being reminded by the Duke that—' Principis indignatio mors
' est;' and warned that his refusal to acquiesce in
the divorce of Katharine and the abrogation of the
Pope's supremacy in England might cost him his life ;
he told the Duke that neither his own life nor the
Duke's life was worth much. ' There is no more
' difference between us than that I shall die to-day
' and you to-morrow.' A prediction which was very
nearly being fulfilled. The Duke was formally sentenced to be beheaded, and if the King had lived one
day longer that sentence would have been carried out.

Among other pieces in the volume which are of a Lines on
prayer.
character more serious than the rest may be placed
a distich which is headed by the scriptural injunction respecting prayer,—' Let thy words be few.' Although it is not here introduced as a translation, the
idea occurs among the sayings which have been
ascribed to Socrates, and it occurs also in a well-
known couplet from the Greek Anthologia.

> O God, each blessing true bestow
> Whether we ask for it or no.

And every ill for which we pray
In thy great mercy turn away.

The same sentiment occurs also in a letter which
More addressed to his wife at home when he was informed that his barns and all the produce of his land
had been consumed by fire. After giving instructions
that their poor neighbours and dependents should
suffer no loss, he adds,—'peradventure we have often
'more cause to thank God for our loss than for our
'winning, for his wisdom better seeth what is good
'for us than we do ourselves.'

It is also introduced by Johnson in his Vanity of
human Wishes.

'Still raise to Heaven the supplicating voice,
'But leave to Heaven the measure and the choice;
'Implore his aid, in his decisions rest,
'Secure whate'er he gives, he gives the best.'

We find it recorded that in an argument entered
into by Henry VIII. with a learned theologian, the
King maintained the thesis that in the case of laymen it is not necessary that words should be used in
the offering of prayer, all that is required being inward prayer, the prayer of the mind. Doubtless at
a time when all public prayer was offered in Latin,
which language very few of the worshippers under-
stood, the King might plausibly maintain his thesis.

Sir Thomas seems to have endeavoured to impress
upon his mind various maxims of morality by putting
them into Latin verse. Of one of such the following
is a contemporaneous translation:—

'Bear grief with patience. Fortune will amend.
'If Fortune mend not, death will soon it end.'

Another of the same date runs thus:—

'Let no vexations trouble make thee *a la mort.*
'If long, it is but light :   if burdensome, but short.'

He gives very profitable advice to those persons who *Anticipation* make themselves miserable by the anticipation of evils *of evil.* which may never come.

> Fool! thy bosom thus to fill
> With boding fears of future ill.
> If it cometh not, 'tis plain
> Thou hast suffer'd needless pain,
> If it come, however sore
> Troubles press'd on thee before,
> Thou hast added one grief more.

In another place he says :—

> I grieve not for the dead :
>   I grieve for some I see,
> Living men tortured with the dread
>   Of evil yet to be.

This corresponds so exactly with a passage in Comus *Milton's* as to render it probable that Milton may have had *Comus.* More's lines in his mind when he wrote it :—

> 'Be not over exquisite
> 'To cast the fashion of uncertain evils.
> 'For, grant they be so ;—while they rest unknown,
> 'What need a man forestall his date of grief,
> 'And run to meet what he would most avoid!'

The same may be said of the anonymous author of the following distich :—

> 'If evils come not, then our fears are vain :
> 'And if they do, fear but augments the pain.'

The emptiness of popular applause, and the folly *Popular* of being anxious about the fame which it lies within *applause.* the power of the unwashed artisan,—'cerdo,'—to give or take away at his pleasure, is gravely dilated upon. What will such honour do for you—he asks—

as if anticipating a well-known passage of Shakespeare,[1]—if your finger aches? In one of his recorded
apophthegms we have a sentiment not very dissimilar
to this :—' To aim at honour here is to set up a coat
' of arms at the prison-gate.'

Another piece on the emptiness of all earthly
things,—' Ad contemptum hujus vitæ,'—has been thus
translated :—

> By the wind the reeds are shaken,—
> Daily troubles man do shake :
> Anger, fear, and hope and sorrow
> Cause his very soul to quake.
> Trifles light as air they be,—
> Shame if such should ruffle thee.

A considerable number of the Epigrammata have for
their subject the perfections and the imperfections of
the female character, to describe which was a favourite
occupation with writers of poetry in England from
an early period, having its origin perhaps in the
writings of Boccaccio.

Chaucer on
the female
sex.

Chaucer represents woman in one passage as a
creature almost if not quite angelic. In early life we
are cherished and fostered by her. In time of sickness she cheers us and comforts us, and oftentimes
she suffers sore for our distress. In adversity she
is true as steel. And therefore we ought not to speak
harm of woman carelessly, but rather—

> ' In reverence of the heaven's queen
> ' We ought to worship all women that been.'

And as to those ' janglers or praters ' who speak
evil of woman, Chaucer prays devoutly that they may

---

[1] Can honour set to a leg? No ;—or an arm ?—No. Or take away
the grief of a wound?—No.

Henry IV., Part i. Act v.

come to an untimely end; suggesting specially that
it may please heaven they break their necks.

On the other side of the question however we find
a passage in which, after solemnly professing to a
certain lady the most devoted admiration of her
beauty, he concludes and crowns the whole by quoting what he gives her to understand is a wise and
much approved adage :—

> 'In principio mulier est hominis confusio.'

Adding what he rather impudently avouches to be a
true translation of the same :—

> 'The sentence of the Latin is
> 'Woman is mannes joy and mannes bliss.'

Gower says that there is for man no solace if
woman is absent. In her absence the world's joy is
away. Her presence inspires knighthood, fosters
chivalry, causes men to be jealous of their honour, and
to make it their aim to be 'sans peur et sans reproche.'
And Lydgate argues that the failings of a few should
not be allowed to bring rebuke upon the good and
perfect. The ruby and the sapphire are not thought
the worse of because there are counterfeits in the
world; the lily and the rose and the violet are not
the less lovely because the soil produces weeds also;
nor are the herbs in the garden of the less virtue because out of the earth there grow also many 'crooked
'sticks and briers.'

Every medal however has its reverse :—in another
place Lydgate expatiates upon the deceitfulness of a
certain portion of the sex,—those 'serpents of silver
'sheen,'—those heavenly ones 'with their golden
'tresses' who are very lionesses when brought to the

proof.   Here however prudence interposes and he
checks himself.—'Of this matter I dare to speak
' no more.'

In coming down to the sixteenth century we find
popular tracts written on both sides of the question,
and in one instance by the same author, Edward
Gosynhyll.[1]   In the following century the heroines
as depicted by Sir Philip Sidney are faultless per-
sonifications of virtue, grace, and loveliness.

Among the Epigrammata we find a few in which
the female sex, both wedded and unwedded, are
treated with much tenderness and respect: in others
they are treated much the reverse.

One lady whom he calls Gellia is addressed thus :—

> Gellia, thy looking-glass is all a snare :—
>   If it told true,
> A second time therein thou would'st not dare
>   Thyself to view.

She is reminded that her complexion is not such as
to place her among the ' fair ' sex.

> Gellia, the man is wrong who calls thee dark :
> Who calls thee black, is nearer to the mark.

In another place he humorously dilates upon her
practice of spending half the day in bed.   And he
also amuses himself by exposing certain artificial con-
trivances for preserving the graces of youth, with
which the ancient belles of the reign of Henry VIII.
seem to have been sufficiently well acquainted.

Sir James Mackintosh remarks, that More's
daughter Margaret seems to have been the only
female whom he regarded with positive respect;

---

[1] In his ' Scole House of women,' and his ' Praise of all women.'

looking upon the sex in general as better qualified to
relish a jest, than to take part in more serious conversation. At a period when all education was
extremely meagre and defective, this is easily accounted for; and More was the first to find a remedy
for it. The system of education adopted by him in
his own family was calculated to exalt the female
character to an unprecedented degree of excellence.
His daughters indeed were the admiration of all
learned men. Leland compares them to the three
Graces, addressing them in complimentary lines as
'Charitæa corona.' He says that they did not employ
their fair and dextrous fingers like others of their sex
at the spinning-wheel, but rather in turning over the
pages of Roman eloquence or in writing out their
comments upon Homer and Aristotle; and that in
these nobler pursuits the manly sex are in danger of
being outstripped. Erasmus also in one of his
dialogues represents a learned lady as warning an
Abbot that if his fraternity do not give better heed to
their learning, they will soon find the women preaching to the people and presiding in the Divinity schools
and even wearing the mitre. In another place Erasmus says that the generality of young women when they
come home from hearing a sermon are quite ready to
tell you in their way something about the capabilities
of the preacher, and to describe his features and his
person: but when you ask them what subject he
treated upon and how he handled it, they become silent.
Not so the daughters of Sir Thomas More. They will
give you an epitome of the whole discourse. And if
it happens that the preacher has said anything rather
foolish, anything unsound, anything foreign to his

Sir Thomas
More's
daughters.

How educated.

Their report
of sermons.

O

subject, as preachers are sometimes apt to do, they
will pronounce upon it the judgment which it deserves.
Erasmus thought that this is beyond question the
right way in which we should hear sermons. And it
was his belief that to enjoy the social intercourse of
accomplished females such as these were, cannot fail
to increase a man's happiness and to give an additional charm to life.

Erasmus goes on to say that while he was in conversation with More on this subject he happened to
remark, that to lose a child upon whom so much
loving care has been bestowed in the training must
on that account entail the greater amount of sorrow
upon the parent. To which More replied that if it
should ever be his lot to part with one of his daughters,
he would rather that she should die an intelligent and
accomplished woman than an ignorant one.

In dealing with the trials and misfortunes of wedded
life he allows unlimited scope to his satirical pleasantry,
and to a worthless wife he gives no quarter. When
he says, in one place, that nature has produced nothing, 'quod tristius sit, ac magis viros gravet,' than
a wife;—and again that she who is permitted to tread
on her husband's foot to-day will trample upon his
head to-morrow;—there is a seriousness about it
which hints that he was in earnest.

The fate of an unlucky fortune-teller, who read in
the stars everything except the misdeeds of his own
spouse at home, is descanted upon in every variety of
form. To a friend, whose choice in matrimony had
been unfortunate, he says:—'If you treat her well,
' she becomes worse, and if you treat her ill, she is
' worst of all: she will become a good wife when she

Marginal notes:

A striking
remark.

Severe re-
marks on
wedded life.

' dies; better if she dies before her husband; and less '
' of all if she dies speedily.'

From this Francis Thynne takes his epigram.

> My friend, if that my judgment do not fail,
> As one well taught by long experience skill,
> Thy wife always is but a needful ill,
> And best is bad, though fair she bear her sail.
> But used not well, she worser is to thee;
> And worst of all when best she seems to be.
>
> Thy wife is good, when she forsakes this light,
> And yields by force to nature's destiny;
> She better is, than living, if she die,
> And best when she doth soonest take her flight.
> For so to thee thine ease she doth restore,
> Which soonest had, doth comfort thee the more.

It is quite possible that More may have been made
familiar with hard sayings against women in his early
youth. His father the Judge was accustomed to
say that when a man took to himself a wife it was
like putting his hand into a vessel containing a hundred
snakes and one eel: - possibly he might draw out the
eel: but the chances are a hundred to one that he is
stung by a snake.

The same idea is found in one of More's English
pieces.

> ' Lo in this pond be fish and frogs they both,
> 'Cast in your net, but be you lief or loath,
> ' Hold you content, as Fortune list assign,
> ' For it is your own fishing and not mine.'

And Fortune acts as a sort of Nemesis, distributing
her gifts on the whole impartially.

> ' To some she sendeth children, riches, wealth,
> ' Honour, worship, and reverence all his life:
> ' But yet she pincheth him with a shrewd wife.'

Sir Thomas More's friend Erasmus after spending
some time in England with his patron Lord Mountjoy, writes an amusing account of his reception in
England, and of his admiration of the English ladies ;—
so fair, so beautiful, and so affable that if his Parisian
friend were to see them he would prefer them even to
the Muses, and would desire to spend his life among
them.   On the subject of matrimony however Erasmus was cool and cautious.   He wrote two pieces,
one in its praise and the other against it.   Lord
Mountjoy having read the former told Erasmus that
it had entirely convinced him and that he had resolved
to marry without delay.   Erasmus replied,—'but you
' have not read the second!'—'No; I leave that to
' you,'—said Lord Mountjoy.   Erasmus, who died
unmarried, seems to have thought the adverse argument the more conclusive of the two.

In connection with this subject it may be remarked
that in one of More's Dialogues allusion being made
to the superstitious manner of worshipping saints and
the preferring to them unlawful petitions, a special
reference is made to a practice then in vogue among
married women of presenting an offering at St.
Paul's to a certain Saint Wilgefort—better known as
Saint Uncumber,—' in trust that she shall uncumber
' them of their husbands.'   More undertakes to say
something in defence or rather in extenuation of the
practice.   In the first place he says that the offering
consists of nothing more than a few grains of oats, and
that it is allowed that the offerings of a whole year
' would not feed three geese and a gander for a week : '
—it is not therefore maintained for the sake of any
profit accruing thereby to the Church.   But to the

women themselves who made the offering prof[...] [...] accrue in various ways. They may be [...] [...] if their husbands change their 'cumberous conditions' towards them. And they may be [...] bered, if they themselves 'change their [...] 'tongues,' which in fact may perhaps be 'the cause 'of all this cumberance.' And lastly, if they cannot be uncumbered but by death, yet it may happen to be ' by their own death,' in which case ' their husbands will be safe enough.'—' Nay, nay,' says More's respondent in the Dialogue, 'ye find them not such fools, I warrant you!'

At a time when marriages were often brought about without much regard to the feelings of the contracting parties, we cannot be surprised at the great number of unhappy marriages. It appears from a letter written by Sir Thomas More to Wolsey that a certain Mr. Broke was desirous to obtain the King's sanction to a marriage which he contemplated. At Wolsey's request More laid the matter before the King;—who ' answered that he would take a breath ' therein,' and that he would ' first speak with the ' young man himself.' The truth of the matter was that the King had got a promise from Mr. Broke that he would not marry without his advice;—' because the ' King intended to marry him to one of the Queen's ' maidens.'

In another of these pre-arranged marriages Sir Thomas More appears to have been employed by the King as a sort of official negotiator. He writes to Wolsey that Sir William Tyler an alderman of London is desirous to marry a certain widow who in some sense is a ward in Chancery: and that he is

instructed by the King to represent to Wolsey, being
the Chancellor, that 'for special favour which he bears
' to Tyler he greatly desires that he should have the
' widow.'   And the King requires Wolsey to pursue
the most effectual means by which 'his Highness'
' desire ' may be carried out;—so will he be 'right
' specially pleased,' and the fortunate Sir William
will be bound to pray for the Cardinal's 'good Grace'
during the remainder of his life.

Whether the lady herself is likely to be 'right
' specially pleased,'—indeed whether she has herself
been consulted in the matter at all,—is a question upon
which 'his Highness' does not appear to have bestowed a thought.

The following English epigram illustrative of that
good old proverb which gives a caution against
marrying in haste lest you should have to repent at
leisure, is ascribed by Warton to Sir Thomas More.
He states it also to be the first printed epigram in
the language.

An epigram
attributed to
More.

> A student at his book so placed
> That wealth he might have won,
> From book to wife did flit in haste,
> From wealth to woe to run.
>
> Now who hath played a feater cast
> Since juggling first begun ;—
> In *knitting* of himself so fast,
> He hath himself *undone !*

The writer of the Epigrammata however makes
ample amends for his satirical remarks upon married
life by introducing certain longer and more studied
pieces in which there is displayed such a courteous
delicacy of feeling, as will remove in some degree

the imputations which lie upon his gallantry. The first of these is the recommendation to his friend Candidus of a wife;—a certain lady whom he describes as worthy to be classed with all the illustrious matrons of antiquity;—although portionless, she will be a treasure more precious to her husband than all the wealth of Crœsus.

It has been thus translated by Archdeacon Wrangham:—

TO CANDIDUS.

Enough by vagrant love
    Dear youth, you've been misled,
O rise these joys above,
    And quit the lawless bed.

Some consort in your arms,
    Heart linked to heart, embrace,
Who with transmitted charms
    Your lengthening line may grace.

So did for you your sire:
    The debt with interest due
Posterity require,
    My Candidus, from you.

Nor be it chief your aim
    Fortune or face to seek,
Slight love attends the dame
    Sought for her purse or cheek.

No purer love can bear
    The flame which fortune fires:
It vanishes in air,
    And ere it lives, expires.

Nay, fortune's courted charms
    Fade in the miser's grasp,
When doomed within his arms
    An unloved spouse to clasp.

And beauty's vaunted power
 By fever's tooth decays,
Or time-struck, like a flower
 Beneath the solar blaze.

Then vows are urged in vain ;--
 With beauty's passing hue,
Bound singly by that chain,
 Affection passes too.

But genuine is the love
 Which reason, virtue, rears :
All fever's force above,
 Above the assault of years.

First, scrutinize her birth :
 Be sure her mother's mild.
Oft with her mother's milk
 The mother fires her child.

Next, in herself be seen
 Good temper's gentlest tone.
Still placid be her mien,
 Unruffled by a frown.

And still her cheek's best charm
 Be her's—sweet modesty.
No lover-clasping arm,
 No love-provoking eye.

Far from her lip's soft door
 Be noise, be silence stern,
And her's be learning's store,
 On her's the power to learn.

With books she'll time beguile,
 And make true bliss her own,
Unbnoyed by Fortune's smile,
 Unburthened by her frown.

So still, thy heart's delight,
 And partner of thy way,
She'll guide thy children right,—
 And their's—as dear as they.

So, left all meaner things,
　　Thou'lt on her breast recline;
While notes of love she'll sing
　　As Philomel's divine.

While still thy raptured gaze
　　Is on her accents hung,
As words of honied grace
　　Steal from her honied tongue—

Words they, of power to soothe
　　All idle joy or woe,
With learning's varied truth,
　　With eloquence's glow.

Such Orpheus' wife, whose fate
　　With tears old fables tell,
Or never would her mate
　　Have fetched her back from hell.

Such Naso's daughter—she
　　Whose Muse with Naso vied:
And such might Tullia be,
　　Her learned father's pride.

The Gracchi's mother such,
　　Who trained the sons she bore:
Famed as their mother much,
　　And as their tutoress more.

But what to distant days
　　My lingering glance confines?—
One girl, of equal grace,
　　E'en in this rude age shines.

Single, worth all, she stands—
　　By fame through Britain flown,
Hail'd—gaze of other lands,
　　Cassandra of her own.

Say—would a maid so rare
　　Within thy arms repose;
Were she nor rich nor fair,
　　Could'st thou decline her vows?

Enough of beauty her's,
   With whom a husband's blest:
Enough of wealth she shares,
   To whom enough's a feast.

So loved, were she—I swear—
   Than soot of darker die;
I'd think her far more fair
   Than e'er met mortal eye.

So loved, were she, I swear—
   Than poverty more poor,
I'd think her richer far
   Than kings with all their store.

In another of these poems we find a graceful and earnest apology offered for an unintentional act of discourtesy to a lady. It appears that the lady in question had accompanied a certain dignified ecclesiastic when making a call at Sir Thomas More's house, and that she entered the room at a moment when the two were engaged in close conversation together. Although she stood at the very elbow of the master of the house, he was so attentive to his episcopal friend and so wrapped up in the conversation as never to notice her or even become aware of her presence. She was a French lady of high distinction and character, richly apparelled, and of a comely person. She admired his pictures, examined his cabinet of coins, and partook of the simple refreshment which was on the table. Yet More himself,—strange and almost incredible as it may appear,—knew nothing of all this until he was informed of it by his servants some days afterwards.

He then writes to the bishop an epistle in Latin verse giving a very interesting account of the whole affair, and making an earnest request that he will

offer to the lady that explanation and apology which
in consequence of his imperfect knowledge of her
language he feels unequal to make for himself. He
prays very devoutly that the earth may swallow him
up alive rather than that he should intentionally
commit such an act of barbarism. Diverging into
the classical style he likens the bishop's conversation to the music of the lyre of Orpheus which is
said to have charmed even the wild beasts: and he
intimates that as the spear of Achilles cured the
wound of Telephus which it had itself inflicted, so
should the bishop's all-prevailing tongue be employed
to remove that displeasure which may have been
caused by this apparent lack of courtesy to a lady
and a stranger.

Imagination may be employed to fill up the detail
of a rather interesting scene. The earnest and ex-
pressive countenance of More, the graver assumption
of dignity in the ecclesiastic, the uneasy look of the
lady who felt herself overlooked by these important
personages, the contrast between her showy costume
and the sombre habiliments of the others, the quaint
fittings and furniture of the apartment itself, the portraits on the wall, probably Holbein's work, and the
antique cabinet of coins, combine to form a picture
which is here presented to us in the words of Sir
Thomas More himself.

CHAPTER XI.

HE notices of contemporary literature, although somewhat scanty, are quite as numerous as we can expect at a period when literature itself was at so low an ebb. Three separate pieces are written in commendation of the celebrated edition of the New Testament published by Erasmus in 1516. Under the title of

'Novum Instrumentum' we have the Greek text together with a new translation into Latin:—a work in virtue of which Erasmus ranks among the great men of his day as the father of Biblical criticism. It is indeed as it has been well designated, a noble monument of genius, erudition, and industry. The object which Erasmus had in view, as he states in an epistle to Wolsey, was to produce the original Greek as it was written by the Apostles themselves. In his preface to the Latin version he says that it may reasonably be deemed a safe thing for earthly kings to conceal their state secrets, but that with regard to the mysteries of Christ an injunction was left by Christ Himself that His mysteries should be published as widely as possible. And in an epistle to Pope Leo X. he says that inasmuch as the waters of divine truth when drawn from the fountain head are more likely to be pure than when taken out of artificial tanks, so by placing before readers the 'ipsissima 'verba' of the Apostles and Evangelists you lay a foundation for the hope of a restoration of Christ's true religion.

These words of Erasmus thus spoken according to the dictates of reason and common sense were literally fulfilled;—more literally perhaps than the Pope himself expected. It was from this book that Bilney and Latimer and the early Reformers derived their enlightened ideas as to the errors and corruptions of the Church of Rome.

The Reformation furthered by it.

But Leo X. was too much occupied in the pleasant society of elegant scholars and clever artists in that luxurious Court of his, to think further about any call for reformation; and after a few words in commendation of a work of so much learning and so well calculated to advance the orthodox faith,—as he is pleased to say,—he gives to Erasmus the assurance that besides the praise awarded to him by all the faithful in Christ he will have his reward hereafter: —this assurance being given 'sub annulo Piscatoris.'

Approved by Pope Leo X.

Cardinal Ximenes, who was engaged at the time on the Complutensian Polyglot, expressed his approval of the work, as did also several other foreign ecclesiastics. In England Archbishop Warham and Fox the Bishop of Winchester among the more moderate and enlightened dignitaries of the Church, did the same. Fox indeed declared before a large concourse of people that he found the Latin translation to be of more value to him in giving the true meaning of the original than ten of the ordinary

Also by Ximenes, Warham, and Fox.

CHAP. XI. commentators. Melancthon who was at that time a
student at Tubingen sent to Erasmus a copy of Greek
verses in praise of the work.

In many quarters however the 'Novum Instru-
'mentum' was received with suspicion, and by one
Anathema- of the colleges in Cambridge it was strictly prohibited.
tized at Cam- They have been told,—Erasmus writes,—either over
bridge. their cups or in the gossip of the market-place, that
a book is come out which will put all the old theo-
logians out of the field. And he adds in his characteristic style that they have issued a solemn decree
that neither carrier, nor waggon, nor beast of burden,
nor barge shall be allowed to bring this proscribed
book within the walls of the college.

Opposed by The Scotists opposed the book because they pro-
the Scotists. fessed to believe that when Erasmus amends the
errors of the Vulgate by referring to the Greek original, he is assuming to correct the Holy Spirit itself.
In that defence of Erasmus which has been already
Defended by alluded to, Sir Thomas More quotes the approval of
Sir Thomas Dean Colet and Bishop Fisher, of whom he speaks in
More. the most laudatory terms. Fisher he says is a man
of high distinction both on account of his learning
and his virtues: and it is a long time since there has
lived in England a man of erudition more profound
and of a holier life than Colet. Both of them have
recommended a diligent study of the book as tending
to great profit. He states also that it has been distinctly and repeatedly approved by the Pope himself,
the Vicar of Christ. And he proceeds to apostrophize
his opponent thus.—From that work, which the
supreme Prince of the Christian world speaking as
an oracle from the citadel as it were of our religion has

pronounced to be profitable, you a mere boy-prophet set up yourself to prognosticate evil:—that work to the value of which he has affixed the seal of his testimony, you, a 'monachulus,' unlearned and unknown, out of the obscurity of your cell presume to defile with the utterances of a corrupt and filthy tongue.

From a letter addressed by Erasmus to his learned and lively young friend Peter Mosellanus the Greek Professor at Leipsic, we learn that a certain divine preaching at Court before the King,—Sir Thomas More and Richard Pace the Secretary being present,—thought fit to launch out in the most absurd and offensive manner against the Greek language in general, and also against all new-fangled interpreters.[1] Attacked in a sermon at Court. Pace fixed his eyes upon the King, wondering what would be the effect of this tirade. After awhile the King looked at Pace and smiled. When the sermon was ended he desired that the preacher should be summoned; and he assigned to More the office of making a reply to these attacks and invectives, which he did thoroughly and with considerable eloquence. All present were on the *qui vive* to hear what the Defended by More before the King. preacher would say in reply;—when, to their surprise, he fell down upon his knees and pleaded for pardon, alleging in extenuation of his folly that what he had said was said under the influence of a spirit. The King remarked that it could not have been the Spirit of Christ. And then he asked him whether he had ever read any of the works of Erasmus;—well knowing that what he had said about new-fangled

---

[1] Henry Standish, whose name frequently appears in the annals of that period, and who afterwards became the Bishop of St. Asaph, applied to Erasmus the contemptuous appellation of ' Græculus iste.'

Chap. XI.

The preacher rebuked.

interpreters was levelled at the 'Novum Instrumen-
'tum.' The man replied that he had not. Upon
which the King told him in plain terms that any man
who condemns a book which he has never read is
little better than a fool. The preacher then said that
he had read one book written by Erasmus, 'which
' is called Moria.' Upon this Pace observed that the
preacher's argument and 'Moria' the book's title seem
to be well suited to each other. The preacher
ventured upon a further attempt to clear himself, by
saying that his aversion to the Greek language had
become less decided since it was brought to his recollection that the Greek was derived from the Hebrew.
The King, growing more and more amazed by the
man's egregious folly, bade him depart, and take
away with him the assurance that after this he
would never again be appointed to preach at Court.
Erasmus concludes his narrative of this affair with
the expression of a wish that it had fallen to his own
lot to live under such a Prince as the King of England.

Erasmus pre-
sents it to
the Bishop of
Liege.

Erasmus states in one of his letters that he had
presented a copy of his 'Novum Instrumentum'
printed upon vellum, in a costly and elegant binding,
to the Bishop of Liege who afterwards became a
Cardinal; at the same time offering thanks to the
Bishop for certain promises which had been made
repeatedly but had never been fulfilled. In return
for this he says that the Bishop presented him with

What he re-
ceived in re-
turn.

a sum of money,—which sum of money if it were to
fall into an eye however tender, would not cause the
very slightest amount of pain. And this,—he adds,
—the Bishop of Liege himself cannot deny.

Among the Epigrammata we find three separate

pieces written in commendation of the 'Novum
'Instrumentum.' In the first of these, which is
addressed to the reader, he extols the judgment of
the translator and the usefulness of the work itself.
The old version, he says, never remarkable for its
correctness, was rendered still more objectionable by
the blunders of copyists; and although restored by
Jerome to some degree of purity, it had again become
faulty and corrupt. The present translation, however, is entirely new and free from errors.

Atque nova Christi lex nova luce nitet.

On giving it a hasty inspection you might think
perhaps that what has been done amounts to very
little; but you will be satisfied after a careful
perusal that it is really one of the most important
works ever published.

The other two of these brief epistles are addressed
to Wolsey and Warham; the one rapidly advancing
in his career of ambition, having just before been
elevated to the dignity of Chancellor; and the other,
by whose resignation it had become vacant, having
retired into a life of comparative privacy. The address to Wolsey is replete with flattery. He is extolled as the great patron of literature,

Pieridum pendet cujus ab ore chorus;

and he is entreated to look favourably upon the work
for two reasons: first, because the author is one of his
admirers; and secondly, because the work itself is the
source of that wisdom which enables him to administer justice with so much satisfaction to all parties, that
even the unsuccessful suitor leaves the court without
murmuring. He is pronounced to be such a personi-

P

fication of all that is great and good that the honours
and distinctions which have been heaped upon him
are below his deserts.—Yet at this moment he was
Archbishop, Cardinal, and Chancellor.

It has been remarked by Jortin that never were
Nero and Domitian flattered more obsequiously by
the Roman courtiers than Wolsey was by his numerous parasites: and that as Augustus was a 'præsens
'Divus' to Horace, so Wolsey was installed as a
'præsens Numen' by certain admirers at Cambridge.
After this More's eulogium will read rather tame.

In addressing Warham More ascribes to him the
honour of having originated the work, by supplying
the pecuniary aid of which those early scholars were
too frequently destitute. This volume, he says, shows
in an especial manner with regard to the author,—

Quàm non ducat iners quæ tu facis otia :—

and he desires no other reward of his labour than
this;—that the world may have cause to love you
for the sake of this book, and you also to love Erasmus :—

Hanc petit ille sui fructum, Pater Alme, laboris,
Charus ut hôc tu sis omnibus, ille tibi.

Erasmus himself has left it upon record that Warham's
treatment of him was that of a father or a brother.
And a letter is extant from Warham to Erasmus,
thanking him in the most courteous manner for conferring upon him by this book a more lasting glory
than that of princes and emperors.

The fact that Warham took means to suppress Tyndale's translation of the New Testament into English
while he thus encouraged the Latin translation by

Erasmus, arose doubtless from an unwillingness to place a weapon in the hands of those by whom it would be used on the adverse side. He would give the New Testament to men of learning, but not to the community at large. He thought it dangerous to supply the body of English Lutherans,—who as he feared were already disposed to follow the example of the Lutherans on the Continent,—with the means of satisfying themselves and proving to others how far the Church and the Clergy had departed from the plain truth of Scripture.

If history had left us no other means to judge of the opposite characters of Warham and Wolsey than such as are furnished in these lines, we should be able to form a tolerably correct estimate. More was quite aware of the kind of address which would suit each of them. The somewhat fulsome panegyric upon Wolsey's patronage of men of letters and his popularity as Chancellor, indicates his ambition and love of power: while the simple intimation on the other hand, that Erasmus desires nothing so much as that his work may secure for his patron the affections of those who may profit by it, and for Erasmus himself the affection of the Archbishop, leads us at once to conclude that simple piety and singleness of heart were prominent features in that patron's character. And such in truth was the case. After expending the whole of his vast revenues upon the suitable hospitalities of his station and the improvement of his see, Warham when on his death-bed was informed by his steward, that all the money left in his hands amounted to no more than thirty pounds; to which he calmly replied,—' satis viatici ad cœlum.'

Opposite characters of Warham and Wolsey.

Erasmus says of Warham that there was in his character a remarkable combination of ability, erudition, and gentleness. He was a faithful friend, and no one ever parted from him without sorrow. His humility of soul was correspondent to his elevation of character, and of that elevation of character no one was so little conscious as himself.

From this time the Archbishop sent to Erasmus an annual pension, which was generally conveyed to him by the hands of More. Wolsey gave him a prebend in the Church of Tournay of which see he was the Bishop. Erasmus spoke of it as δῶρον ἄδωρον, and he never gave to Wolsey a good word afterwards.

Thus at one view are placed before us three of the chief historical characters of the reign of Henry.VIII. in the respective stages of their public and official life. When these lines were written, Warham, undermined by Wolsey, had resigned the Great Seal, and was retiring to the duties of his diocese and his favourite pursuits of literature. Wolsey,—the son of ' an honest ' poor man ' at Ipswich whose calling was said to be

that of a butcher,—had now ' touched the highest ' point of all his greatness.' After this he more than once aspired to the Popedom, but it proved beyond his reach. In England however he was a greater man than any subject had ever been before him. The Crown was absolute, and Wolsey was thought on some occasions to set himself before the Crown. More, the youngest man of the three, and destined in process of time to fill the same office of Chancellor in succession after the other two, had already set his foot

upon the ladder of promotion, being Master of the Requests, a Privy Councillor, and acting occasionally as the King's representative in embassies to the Netherlands, which at that time formed a part of the dominions of the Emperor Charles V.

Vicissitudes in life.

No apter illustration of More's favourite allusion to the wheel of Fortune could be produced than that which is here presented to us. After the lapse of only fourteen years from the present time we have to contemplate the scene at Leicester Abbey.

> 'O father Abbot,
> 'An old man broken with the storms of state,
> 'Is come to lay his weary bones among ye.
> 'Give him a little earth for charity.'

And the high office which Wolsey had vacated was filled by the writer of those complimentary lines which he now lays as it were at the Cardinal's feet. And after six or seven years more had elapsed, there was placed over London Bridge and exposed to the gaze of the passing multitudes, a blood-stained and disfigured head,—being the same from the busy brain of which those lines had been produced just twenty years before.

Subsequent intercourse between More and Wolsey.

During this interval Wolsey and More were frequently associated with each other in the discharge of their public duties, and for some time More seems to have treated the Cardinal with a considerable amount of deference. This is stated by Pace the King's secretary in a letter to Erasmus. And in a letter from More himself to Wolsey which is now extant he subscribes himself—'your humble orator and most 'bounden bedesman.'

Wolsey's over-bearance.

We are informed however by Erasmus that Wolsey's feeling towards Sir Thomas More was that of fear rather than regard. It is said that Wolsey told him that he wished he had been at Rome when they made him Speaker of the House of Commons:—to which More replied that it would have pleased him well, inasmuch as Rome was a city which he had long had a wish to see. And on another occasion when More suggested an amendment in certain conditions of peace which Wolsey had laid before the Council board, Wolsey told him that he was the veriest fool in all the Council:—to which More replied with a smile that

More's retort. thanks were due to God that 'the King our master 'hath but one fool in his Council.'

A.D. 1529.
More's speech before Parliament.

From these not over-courteous remarks and retorts we pass on to the speech delivered by Sir Thomas More as Chancellor on the opening of the parliament which had been summoned for Wolsey's impeachment:—a speech which certainly is not remarkable either for generosity or good taste. After speaking of the King as a shepherd—a comparison which he had made long before in these Epigrammata—he said that in a great flock there 'be some rotten and faulty,'

Invective on Wolsey.

and that in the King's flock there is a certain 'great 'wether' whom they all knew, and who 'had juggled 'with the King so craftily, so scabbedly, yea so un-'truly,' that he must have persuaded himself either that the King 'had not wit enough to perceive his 'crafty doings,' or else that he 'did not choose to see 'and know them.' But herein he was deceived. For 'his Grace's sight was so quick and penetrable that 'he saw him,—yea and saw through him both within 'and without. And according to his desert he hath 'had a gentle correction as a warning to others.'

After reading all this, and still more after setting in contrast with it the elaborate series of compliments

conveyed in the Latin lines, we are sadly reminded of
the words put into Wolsey's mouth by Shakespeare

'How eagerly ye follow my disgrace!'

Among other notices of contemporary literature it
may be placed an ode addressed to his friend Busleiden, with a view of persuading him to bring out his
Muse from her retirement, or in other words to pub-
lish his poems. The style which he uses is figurative,
and the personification of the Muse is ingeniously
maintained. She is said to be chaste as Diana and wise
as Minerva, and well able not only to take care of
herself but to acquire distinction by her elegance and
wit, if he will only allow her to present herself to an
admiring world.

In another place we find mention made of a collection of sacred poems, consisting of a kind of versification of the legends of the Saints. The author, a
man of little erudition but considerable talents for
poetry, had given his book to the world without pretension; declaring in his preface that it was composed
offhand, and that the ordinary rules of verse were
disregarded. In proportion however to the author's
modesty, so is More's encomium. To be fettered, he
says, by the rules of prosody, would be degrading
to the dignity of the subject; and another person after
long study would not have written so well as this
author has written on the spur of the moment. The
unlettered reader will be pleased with the piety of the
work; while all those who have been accustomed to
drink at the Castalian spring will acknowledge that it
affords them as much pleasure as any book they ever
met with.

We have More's Latin translation of two songs or sonnets which were probably among the popular pieces of the day. One of these is a tragi-comic effusion upon a lover's dream. The other is an invocation to Death, calling upon him to release a desponding lover from his burden of woes.

Mors ades et tantis horrida solve malis.

It bears some resemblance to those plaintive lines beginning,

'Death, death, rock me to sleep':[1]—

which some critics have assigned to Thomas Lord Vaux, others to Anne Boleyn, and others to her brother Viscount Rochford. But if they did in fact suggest to More the Latin lines before us, they could not have been written by any one of the three persons thus mentioned, who were mere children when this volume of Epigrammata was published.

A certain poetaster—'stultus poeta'—who has made an unfortunate attempt to adopt the phraseology of Virgil and to apply it to the King—and another who professes to have written his verses impromptu—are animadverted upon rather severely. A certain French writer is told that he is undoubtedly animated by the spirit of the ancients, inasmuch as he frequently hits upon the selfsame lines which have been composed by the ancients long before. A Spaniard who had adopted an unlucky expression in reference to the 'genius' of his poetry, is assured that it will be an 'evil genius;'

---

[1] They are quoted by Pistol in Henry IV. pt. ii.

' What! shall we have incision? shall we imbrue ?—
Then Death rock me asleep—abridge my doleful days!'

Act ii. sc. 4.

and that the immortality which he anticipates will be
an immortality of shame.

Of More's taste and fondness for pictures there is
abundant evidence. He was the first patron of
Holbein; and it was through More's introduction that
this artist obtained the royal patronage of Henry VIII.
Among the numerous works of Holbein none are
more noted than his group of More's family; and the
portraits we have of the Chancellor himself are from
the same pencil. More was acquainted too with Quintin Matsys, the celebrated painter of Antwerp: and in
one of his letters he describes both in prose and verse
a piece executed by this artist at his own express
desire. It represented two of his most intimate
friends, Erasmus and Ægidius: the former being
depicted in the act of commencing his paraphrase on
the Epistle to the Romans; and the latter holding in
his hand a letter from More, addressed to him in an
exact representation of More's handwriting.

It appears that while Matsys was engaged upon
this portrait it happened that Erasmus fell sick, in
consequence of which the work was for a time suspended: and when Erasmus presented himself again
after his recovery the painter declared that the face
was no longer the same face, and for several days he
refused to proceed with the portrait. In one of his
epistles More describes this painting, and in a string
of Latin lines which are appended to that epistle he
extols the skill of the artist, the correctness of the
portraits, and the illustrious character of the individuals; all of which, he says, deserve a more
durable material of preservation than the panel of
the picture. If future ages retain any love of litera-

ture, and if the horrors of war do not obliterate the works of Minerva; how highly, he says, will this painting be prized—how fortunate will be accounted its possessor!

It is to be observed that Matsys painted this very interesting picture at the request of More himself, who was much struck with the close imitation of his own handwriting in the address of the letter which Ægidius held in his hand;—styling him a ' mirificus ' falsarius' as well as a ' mirificus pictor.' And he asks that if that letter is still in existence it may be returned to him, in order that he may place the reality side by side with the representation. The comparing of the two together ' duplicabit mira- ' culum.'

Allusion to St. Luke as a painter.

In one of his Dialogues, among other statements referring to the question of the worshipping of images, Sir Thomas More adopts the tradition that the Evangelist St. Luke was a painter. He says that—' Christ ' taught his holy Evangelist to have another mind ' with regard to images than these heretics have, ' when he put it in his mind to counterfeit and express ' in a table the lovely visage of our blessed Lady his ' mother.'

Head of John the Baptist.

In the Epigrammata he alludes more than once to a painting of the head of St. John the Baptist on a charger; the lines however contain little more than a comparison of Herod to some monster of classical antiquity, without any particular reference to the painter's skill. He delights to exercise his wit at the expense of certain contemporary artists, whose attempts, especially in portrait painting, were pre-eminently unsuccessful. When it is considered that at this time, and for a long period afterwards, there was not in the country a single native artist of any reputation, it will account for More's admiration of what he saw in Flanders, as well as his ridicule of the miserable caricatures alluded to in these epigrams.

One portrait painter however has been more fortunate, and the lines upon his picture both Kendall and Pecke have undertaken to translate.

By Kendall they are translated thus:—

> So well this table doth express
> The countenance of thee,
> As, sure it seems no table, but
> A glass thyself to see.

Pecke's translation runs thus:—

> Your shadow for yourself might almost pass,
> 'Tis not your picture, but your looking-glass.

An anecdote is recorded of an interview between Sir Thomas More and Hans Holbein which affords evidence at the same time of the ready skill of the one in striking off a likeness, and the quickness of the other in recognizing it. Holbein happened to mention in the course of conversation the fact of his having met with at Basle an English nobleman whose name he was unable to recollect; and although he described his person More failed to recognize the man. But when Holbein took out his pencil and produced a sketch, More recognized him at once as the Earl of Arundel.

The engraved portraits of Sir Thomas More himself amount to nearly fifty in number, and on the whole the artists appear to have been scarcely more successful than the portrait painters whom he ridicules in these Epigrammata. In fact Dibdin remarks that no human features have ever been so tortured and per-verted. In one print the countenance is long and bony;—in another it is rotund and plump. In one it is stern and morose;—in another there is an un-meaning softness. In one we see a man large-featured and athletic;—in another he is exactly the reverse. At the same time there are certain accessories in the attitude and the drapery, the high-pointed cap and the gold chain, which identify the individual at once.

The genuine prototype is found in two of Holbein's drawings;—the one being the preliminary sketch for his great picture of the More household, which is at Basle,—and the other a single head, which is at Hampton Court. In these the thin prominent nose, the keen retiring eye, and the general expression of quiet shrewdness and sagacity, are too distinctly marked to be easily forgotten. Mr. Brewer has made the rather striking observation that there is ‘ an anxious peering look as of a man endeavouring ‘ to penetrate into, and yet dreading, the future.’

That well-known painting of the assembled family which Holbein painted about 1529 is identified by repeated reference made to it in the letters of Erasmus. In one written at Friburg in that year to Margaret Roper, he says that he had long cherished a wish to see once more the family which was to him the dearest of all families, and that now his wish had been in some sort gratified. When contemplating the picture he seems to himself to be actually present in the midst of them. He recognizes each individual in the group. In Margaret Roper herself he sees the fair form which is the lodging place and domicile of a still fairer mind. And he tells her that if any distinction in life has been his lot, he owes it all to the companionship of her father and her father's family; and that there is no one upon earth to whom he would owe this with more satisfaction.

Like many of the distinguished men in Italy who were his contemporaries, Sir Thomas More had a full appreciation of the interest attached to works of ancient art, and more especially coins. Pomponius More an admirer of ancient coins. Lætus was distinguished by an almost insatiable passion for medals and manuscripts, Lorenzo de' Medici had a museum of gems and antique vases, and Bembo was ranked among the most scientific collectors of classical antiquities of his day. The collections of Busleiden at Mechlin have already been mentioned as the subject of one of these pieces, and his Roman medals as the subject of another. So precious were these relics in the eyes of men of taste and learning, that two medals,—the one of the Roman emperor Augustus and the other of Tiberius,—were deemed worthy by Sir Thomas More to be offered as a special present to Nicolas Perrenot de Granvelle the favourite Chancellor of the emperor Charles V. This is stated in a letter to Erasmus by Granvelle himself.

CHAPTER XII.

MONG the miscellaneous pieces in this volume one of the longer and more amusing is an enumeration of the absurdities practised by a certain Lalus, who having lately returned from his travels on the Continent, had brought home with him a variety of French fashions. Although the two countries about this period were often in a state of warfare with each other, it was a favourite pastime with young Englishmen to make a journey to Paris whenever they had an opportunity. In Shakespeare's time there was a complaint of—

The imitator of French fashions.

> 'Our travelled gallants
> 'Who fill the Court with quarrels, talk, and tailors.'

And when some one asks,—

> 'Is 't possible the spells of France should juggle
> 'Men into such strange mimicries?'

It is replied,—

> 'New customs,
> 'Though they be never so ridiculous,—
> 'Nay, let them be unmanly,—yet are followed.'

Sir Thomas More was a thorough Englishman; and in a vein of patriotic indignation against this affectation of foreign fashions he wrote thus:—

A friend and chum I have, called Lalus, who
Was born in Britain and in Britain bred.
And though by seas, by manners, and by speech,
We islanders are sever'd from the French,
Lalus holds British ways and fashions cheap,
Doting upon the French.

                                He struts about
In cloaks of fashion French.   His girdle, purse,
And sword are French.   His hat is French.
His nether limbs are cased in French costume.
His shoes are French.   In short, from top to toe
He stands the Frenchman.

                                Furthermore, he keeps
One only servant.—This man, too, is French;
And could not, as I think, e'en by the French,
Be treated more in fashion of the French.
Lalus ne'er pays him wages,—that is French:
He clothes him meanly,—that again is French;
Stints him with meagre victuals,—that is French;
Works him to death,—and this again is French;
Belabours him full oft,—and that is French.
And in the street, the market, every place
Where men resort, delights in sorry French
To chide the knave; knowing as much of French
As parrots know of Latin.   If he speak
Though but three little words in French, he swells
And plumes himself on his proficiency.
And his French failing, then he utters words
Coin'd by himself, with widely-gaping mouth
And sound acute, thinking to make at least
The accent French.   *   *   *
With accent French he speaks the Latin tongue,
With accent French the tongue of Lombardy,
To Spanish words he gives an accent French,
German he speaks with the same accent French.
In truth, he seems to speak with accent French
All but the French itself.   The French he speaks
With accent British.   *   *   *
In short, of all the fopperies of France
He is an Ape,—a very Ape.

CHAP. XII.

More's lines attacked by De Brie.

More's defence.

More's abstemiousness.

Lines upon wine-bibbers.

At the time when Sir Thomas More was engaged in that warm controversy with the French scholar Germain de Brie which has been already referred to, these lines were brought forward as evidence of an acrimonious feeling against the French people in general. More said in self-defence that the worst charge which he had brought against the French was that of being 'in ministros paulo duriusculi;' at the same time he acknowledged that the lines were written 'parum tempestivè—non admodum feli-'liciter.'

In his mode of living Sir Thomas More was temperate if not abstemious, and he seems to enjoy a fling at the excesses of others. In Harpsfield's biography it is stated on the authority of 'those who best knew 'him,' that in his youth he drank only water, and in after life his 'common drink was very small ale,' and 'as for wine he did but sip of it, and that only for 'company's sake or for pledging his friends.' Widely different from this were the habits of two men whom he describes in these Epigrammata under the names of Fuscus and Marullus. Fuscus had been warned by his physician that he must either abandon his habits of wine-bibbing, or lose his eyesight. To this he replied, that all the objects of nature around him, the earth, the sea, and the stars, had been viewed by him times without number; that there remained nothing which he had not *seen*, while there were many kinds of wine which he had not yet *tasted*. He had *seen* enough, but he had not *tasted* enough; and therefore he bids his eyes farewell. 'Better,' he says in another piece, 'to part with one's eyes in the 'pleasant process of drinking wine, than to keep them

' for worms to feast upon.' Of a like character is the
story told of Marullus, who for two days abstained
from wine altogether; but finding it impossible to
keep his resolution . pathetically exclaimed :—' Ye
' faithful guides, by whose aid I have been conducted
' hither, now must I part with you for ever!' He then
sips his wine, and inhales its fragrance; the mellow
tint gradually fades before him, and he is involved in
darkness. Reflecting, however, that of all the qualities which the wine possesses, that which he loses is
the least valuable, he thus reconciles himself to the
loss.[1]

Among the Latin verse compositions of Erasmus
there is one upon a veteran wine-bibber who after
spending his whole life in tippling sank at last into
the deep sleep of death.

Lines by Eras-
mus upon a
wine-bibber.

> Idem bibendi finis atque virendi
> Fuit.

If you disturb him this sweet sleep in which he lies
will come to an end, and he will begin to feel his accustomed thirst. Therefore depart in silence. Read
these lines ;—but not aloud :—

> Vale, viator :—jam silenter abscede.

The spendthrift and the miser both come in for
their share of ridicule. The man whose fortune had
been lavished upon his wardrobe is laughed at for in-
commoding himself by carrying about on his back
several acres of land. The miser is disquieted on his

The spend-
thrift.

The miser.

[1] Something like this is found in a song of modern date :—

> 'Tis better with wine to extinguish the light
> Than live always in darkness without it.

Q

death-bed by the thought of the cost of his funeral. The lines have been thus translated by Kendall:—

> Rich Chrysalus at point of death
> Doth moan, complain, and cry:
> Was never man as he, so loth
> To leave his life and die.
> Not for because he dies,—he cries—
> His death he doth not force:—
> This cuts: his grave must cost a groat,
> To shroud his carrion corse.

To the same purport with this is an apophthegm of Sir Thomas More preserved in Lloyd's State Worthies. ' A man who is covetous when he is old is like a thief who steals when he is on his way to the gallows.'

Another of the Epigrammata upon misers has been translated thus:—

> Avarus, chuckling o'er his pelf,
> His days in dreaming passed.
> Death woke him up:—he found himself
> How poor a man at last!

The subject of one train of reflection in which Sir Thomas More often indulged was the effect which sleep produces in placing the rich man and the poor man upon the same level; and he has embodied his thoughts in several of these Epigrammata. Supposing that neither of the two dreams at all in his sleep, the poor man is on an equality with the rich man. And supposing that the rich man has a dream which is uneasy and wearisome—as is frequently the case—while the poor man dreams upon subjects which give him pleasure, although both the pleasure of the one and the discomfort of the other are unrealities, the poor man for the time is unquestionably the happier man of the two.

One of these pieces, entitled 'Aristotelis sententia
' de somno,' has been thus translated by Pecke :—

> Half of our lives to grateful sleep we spare,
> Thus half their time Rich and Poor equal are.
> Crœsus and Irus rich alike are found,
> When silken slumbers have their senses bound.

Sir Thomas More had a delicate constitution, and
he was subject to occasional illnesses. Erasmus mentions one illness of a very serious character which
seems to have been brought on by over-anxiety at
the time when he was detained by his diplomatic
duties in the insalubrious climate of the Low
Countries. We are told that at one time he suffered
from ' an ague fit so marvellous that the physicians
' said it could not be :'—the cold shiver and the burning
heat coming on at the same moment. On hearing the
dictum of the physicians a young damsel in More's
family who had been educated with his daughters remarked that Galen in his treatise De differentiis Fe-
brium, 'avoucheth that such agues are sometimes
' met with.' This lady became afterwards the congenial
wife of a physician by name Clement, who was a friend
of Sir Thomas More and ' famous for his skill both in
' physic and in Greek.' [1]

It is evident that certain members of the medical
profession were held by Sir Thomas More in rather
low estimation; both the 'medicus' and the 'chirur-
' gus' being satirized very freely. Only two of those
whom he mentions are treated with respect: the one

Marginal notes: More's delicacy of constitution. An ague. Margaret Gigs quotes Galen.

---

[1] In Holbein's well-known painting of the family, she is represented
as holding in her left hand an open book, and with her right hand
pointing to a passage with much apparent earnestness. The painter
evidently knew the lady's character.

being the 'medicus' who honestly told his patient
that unless he would give up his wine he must lose
his eyesight, and the other being Hippocrates himself,
whose epitaph More has translated from the Greek.

Of the rest, a 'medicus' of small repute, and small
practice, and small means, is told that he is something more than a 'medicus;'—that he should add a
letter and style himself 'mendicus.'—Adopting a conceit of which many instances are to be found in the
Greek Anthologia More likens the 'medicus' in his
power of killing to the general of an army. Sir John
Harington, who wrote in the reign of Queen Elizabeth, in one of his epigrams gives a new turn to this
worn out idea. He tells the story of a 'paltry leech'
who must needs give up his profession and become a
priest. But he succeeded so ill—

In patching sermons with a sorry shift,
As needs they must, that ere they learn, will teach—

that he fell into disgrace and was removed from
his office. In departing—

He shut up all with this shrewd muttering speech:
' Well, though,' said he, ' my living I have lost,
' Yet many a good man's life this loss shall cost.'

Being summoned to appear before the Justices for
having uttered this 'heinous threat,' he pleaded that
if the course which he was about to take is a 'vicious'
course, he is driven to it under ' curst constraint.'

' For, of my Living having lost possession,
' I must,' said he, ' turn to my first profession :
' In which I know too well, for want of skill,
' My medicines will many a good man kill.' [1]

[1] Of another of these Epigrammata Sir John Harington gives a literal

In another of More's Epigrammata we are told of a certain physician who when called in to a case of fever, asks for a goblet of wine and immediately drinks it off. He then directs a like draught to be administered to the patient, remarking that there is much heat in the system that requires to be carried away. Another story is told of a certain quack,—'impostor'—who sold his specific balsam at the price of ten pounds,—a very considerable sum in those days,—for one single drop:—the patient being required to lay down five pounds at the time, and to pay the other five when cured. If he should chance to die the second drop will not be asked for. The balsam is produced in a very small phial carefully wrapped in linen; and one drop, exhibited on the point of a sword for the greater effect, is mixed with wine. The 'medicus' declares that the small quantity still remaining upon the point of the sword is of the value of twenty pounds, and he will not allow it to be touched. The patient takes the dose, and presently he expires. By this unlucky compact the precious drop of balsam and the precious life of the patient are both gone at one stroke.—A certain 'chirurgus' undertakes to restore the sight of a purblind old female within the space of five days. He applies an ointment to her eyes and orders that a bandage be kept over them until the end of three days. In the meantime he purloins at each visit certain articles of furniture and ornament which were in the room. The five days being ended he removes the bandage

translation. But although he addresses his translation to a lady, it is of a character which modern refinement would not tolerate for a moment.

and asks for his fee.   This the patient refuses to pay. She tells him that he had promised to restore her eyesight, whereas her eyesight is now worse than it was before.   Before this she was able to see certain objects around her in the room;—but now she can see nothing.

From a letter which was written soon after the execution of Bishop Fisher, by a physician who had attended him during an illness in the Tower, it appears that even in matters relating to their own

grave profession they could occasionally be facetious. This letter is addressed to the Lord Privy Seal, and the purport of it is a petition for the usual physician's fee.   The writer states that for twelve days' labour and four nights' watching he had as yet received no fee whatever; the Bishop's goods having been seized and 'converted to the King's coffers.'   He is therefore in danger of losing both his labour and his physic, as well as his friend the patient.   He urges that if physicians were not entitled to receive a fee for the patients whom they lose, as well as for those whom they cure, they would have but a sorry living.   He says that from those who escape death 'we may take ' the less amount in money, there being a hope that ' they may in due time fall again into our hands.'   He therefore asks in the present instance for a more liberal remuneration on the ground that this payment will be the last.   And he prays in conclusion that the health of the Lord Privy Seal may be 'long main-' tained and kept in all honour and felicity.'   The name of the writer of this singular epistle is Jonathan Fryer.

The military profession also comes in for its share

of satire and ridicule. At the time when the young King of England was eager to win his spurs and was avowedly emulous of the military renown of his predecessors who had conquered France, there were wise and prudent men who raised their voices as advocates for peace. Such were More's friends and advisers Colet and Erasmus. Colet preached boldly against war in the presence of Henry himself, who was at the time preparing for an invasion of France. Erasmus in his ' Encomium Moriæ,' his ' Enchiridion,' his ' Pacis Querela,' and in other of his works, argued that war is not justifiable except in self-defence. More himself represents this as a principle adopted by his favourite Utopians. And in conversation with King Henry he made a remark bearing upon this question which is worthy of being recorded. It was his duty when acting as the King's secretary to lay before him for signature a certain document which had been sent over from France by Wolsey, who was there acting as the King's representative. The King, being otherwise engaged at the moment, laughed and said,—' Nay, by ' my soul, that will not be; for this day is my re-' moving day soon to New Hall: I will read the ' remnant at night.'—After the King had dined More came again to submit to him his papers. Among them he read to the King a letter from the Earl of Surrey the Admiral of the Fleet, in which it was said that the French King would now be ' toward a ' Tutor, and his realm to have a Governor.' Upon which the King said that he ' trusted in God to be ' their Governor himself, and that they should by this ' means make a way for him, as King Richard did for ' his father.' Sir Thomas More well knew that King

Colet preached against aggressive war.

Erasmus wrote against it.

Henry's designs upon France.

Richard did not make way for Henry VII. until after the shedding of much blood in the battle of Bosworth field; and while he expressed his acquiescence in the ambitious schemes of the young monarch so far as they might be for his good and the good of his subjects, he did not omit to say as much as he dared to say in favour of peace. ' I pray God that if it be good ' for your Grace and this realm, in such case it may ' prove so:—and else I pray God send your Grace an ' honourable peace.' To say this to such a King as Henry VIII., and at such a moment, argues no small amount of moral courage, and perhaps none of his courtiers excepting Sir Thomas More would have ventured to say it.

More speaks in favour of peace.

On another occasion when it fell to More as the Secretary to acknowledge the arrival of certain dispatches from Wolsey in which the King was informed that his army in France had been so far successful as to give reason for expecting ' an unresisted entrance ' into the bowels of the country, with likelihood of ' the King's obtaining his ancient right to the French ' crown,'—he was instructed to inform Wolsey in reply, that the King much applauded his industry and zeal in providing for the reinforcement of the army. With the King in this humour it would have been useless and perhaps dangerous to say a word suggestive of peace.

Wolsey in favour of conquest.

In touching upon members of the military profession the Epigrammata are by no means complimentary. The soldier whose legs had saved him on the field of battle is told that the rings by which his hand is adorned ought rather to have been worn upon his foot:—

Jests upon soldiers.

Why should those rings thy finger grace?
The foot would be their rightful place.
One of thy feet, mid war's alarms,
Hath done more service than both arms.

A certain cavalry officer whom he calls Riscus provides himself with two horses for the war,—the one slow and sluggish, the other high-mettled and fleet. The former is to carry him when he goes into the fight, and the other to bring him out of the fight.

In another piece a rencontre is described as taking place between a military braggadocio and a clown who had insulted his wife :—

He stopped the man—his sword he drew—
His sword the man defies :
Didst thou insult my wife—thou wretch?
I did—the man replies.

Thraso rejoins,—thou own'st it then!
'Tis well thou'st told me true.
This sword, I swear,—if thou had'st lied,—
Had pierced thee through and through!

No class of men come more frequently under the lash than the pretenders to astrology. Many years ago More had exposed their notorious failure in his elegy upon the death of Elizabeth of York, who died in the very year in which they had predicted for her all manner of prosperity.

Astrology in repute.

Yet was I lately promised otherwise,
This year to live in welthe and delice.

Henry's divorce from Katharine of Arragon was said to have had its origin in a prediction made by an astrologer to Cardinal Wolsey. The Cardinal patronized men of learning, and took pleasure in their society. And it was a current story among the gossips of the Court that a certain astrologer who passed as a learned man among the rest, gave him to understand that it would be his fate to come to grief through a woman. Wolsey thought that the only woman whom he had occasion to fear was the Queen;—he knew that she took it ill that a man so low born as himself should be in so lofty a position. He therefore determined to effect her overthrow. For this purpose he put it into the King's head that his marriage was unlawful: and there being already on the King's part a latent inclination towards Anne Boleyn, the scheme of the divorce was decided upon at once.[1]

The pretended powers of the astrologers obtained credit in quarters where we should have least expected to find it. The authorities at Oxford consulted an astrologer in order to obtain a clue to the route taken by one Garret, a heretic, who had made his escape from them: and they were informed that he had ' fled in a tawny coat, toward the South East, ' and is now in London, whence he will shortly make ' for the coast.'

Ridicule of the astrologers.

More however makes the astrologer the butt of his ridicule. A certain astrologer who consults the planets respecting the fidelity of his own wife is informed that planets cannot tell tales. The following More addresses to an astrologer whom he calls Fabianus :—

[1] This anecdote is found in a Spanish work entitled,—' Cronica del ' Rey Enrico Otavo de Ingalterra. Escrita por un autor coëtaneo. ' Madrid. 1874.' The work is a record of the gossip of the English Court at this period as jotted down by a Spaniard. The original manuscript is in the possession of a Spanish family, and it has been published under the authority of the Academy of History in Spain.

The crowd proclaims thee wondrous wise,
  If out of all thy prophecies
    One only proveth true. —
  Be, Fabianus, *always wrong*,
  Then will I join the gaping throng,
    And call thee prophet too.

The remonstrance of a creditor with his friend Appeal to a slippery debtor.
Tyndale who was slow in refunding the money which
he had borrowed, contains some touches of quiet
humour very characteristic of the writer:—

O Tyndale, there was once a time, Tyndale.
  A pleasant time of old,
Before thou cam'st a-borrowing,
  Before I lent thee gold;

When scarce a single day did close
  But thou and I, my friend,
Were wont, as often as I chose,
  A social hour to spend.

But now, if e'er perchance we meet,
  Anon I see thee take
Quick to thy heels adown the street,
  Like one who sees a snake.

Believe me, for the dirty pelf
  I never did intend
To ask; and yet, spite of myself,
  I must, or lose my friend.[1]

To lose my money I consent,
  So that I lose not thee:
And thee to lose I am content,
  If safe the money be.

With or without the gold return,
  I take thee nothing loth;
But, sooth, it makes my spirit yearn
  Thus to resign you both.

[1] For loan oft loses both itself and friend.—*Hamlet*, act i. sc. 6.

If thou returnest not, at least
Return the money due ;
And I to thee shall then return
A long and last adieu.

An anecdote is told in one of Latimer's sermons of a certain rich merchant in London who is known to have been a friend and benefactor of William Tyndale the Reformer, so similar in its circumstances to those related in More's verses, as to give rise to a conjecture that the stories relate to the same persons.

A certain rich merchant ' loved his poor neighbour ' very well, and lent him money.' But certain differences having occurred between them, the poor neighbour ' would come no more to the other's ' house nor borrow money from him.' The rich man ' offered many times to talk with him and set ' him quiet, but it could not be.' If he met the rich man in the street ' he would go out of his way.' One time it happened that ' he met him in so narrow ' a street that he could not avoid but come near him.' Yet ' for all this the poor man was minded to go ' forward and not to speak.'

This rich merchant in London was one Humphrey Monmouth an alderman, who is known to have

especially befriended William Tyndale the Reformer, and to have lent him money at a time when he was living in London and hard pressed for the means of subsistence. This fact would be well known to Latimer. And inasmuch as Humphrey Monmouth was the Sheriff of London at the time when Sir Thomas More was the Under-sheriff, it seems extremely probable that More may have heard the detail of the story from the mouth of Monmouth

himself. More would then appropriate as a convenient subject for Latin verse: identify
man by the introduction of the name of Tyne.

When Sir Thomas More held the office of Under-
sheriff in the City of London he would know something of the city banquets. Hence an epigram
which is thus translated by Kendall:

> When Eutiches doth run a race
> He seems to stand, perdy!
> But when he runs unto a feast,
> Then sure he seems to fly.

The well-known story of a shrewd compact entered
into between two beggars, the one being blind and
the other lame, the blind man undertaking to carry
the lame man on his back, is singularly worked out
in no fewer than seven different forms. The great
number of beggars swarming over the land, many of
whom counterfeited all manner of ailments and infirmities in order to excite pity, is set in contrast by
More himself with the better state of things which
he describes as existing in Utopia. It forms the
groundwork also of that smart satire upon the
clergy by Simon Fish, entitled 'A Supplication for
' the Beggars,' in which he attributes the poverty of
the people at large and their consequent inability to
succour ' the poor lepers,—the blind, sore, and lame,'
— to the absorption of so large a portion of the wealth
of the country by the Church.

Peeke's translation of an epitaph upon a waiting
maid, although rather clumsy, will give some idea of
what More intended to express:

> She served in body, but her soul was free:
> Her body now Death sets at liberty.

Like the Greek epigrammatists More turns certain personal peculiarities into exaggerated and rather absurd ridicule; as when he speaks of a man whose nose was of magnitude so portentous that when it required blowing it was beyond his reach, and when he sneezed it was beyond his hearing.—More was not himself a tall man, yet he looked down upon men of small stature and enjoyed his good-natured fling at them. He says that Epicurus held that the world was composed of atoms,—not being aware that there exists anything in the world smaller than atoms:— but that if he had lived to see a certain man called Diophantus he would have said that the world was made up of Diophantuses.

Another small person is recommended never to go outside the walls of his city, lest some Pigmy-devouring crane should get hold of him. Another, bent upon suicide, is said to have made his exit thus:—

> Weary of life, the tiny elf
> A cobweb took—and hung himself.

The last of the miscellaneous pieces which we notice will serve to show—like another which has been given in page 127,—that Sir Thomas More was wont to treat the practice of auricular confession with very little reverence. It is in fact the Latin version of a story told in one of his Dialogues. A man whom he calls Hesperus when at Confession was asked by the Priest, whether he meddled at all in witchcraft or necromancy, or had any belief in the devil. The man warmly disclaimed anything like a belief in the devil, and added that he ' had work enough to be- ' lieve in God.' In the same Dialogue we have a story

of a man who declared that he would not for twenty
pounds hear a certain double-tongued hypocrite repeat
the Creed; inasmuch as he thought that he should
' never believe his Creed after, if he heard it once
' come out of that man's mouth.'

It must be allowed that these stories do not tend
to make good Cresacre More's assertion that his quips
are ' full of pleasantry and very proper;—he scoffeth
' but without contumely.' Very different from these
are the Sacred Hymns of John Picus of Mirandola,
whom More is said to have proposed to himself in
early life as a pattern. Although rather overlaid with
classical allusions those hymns have a grandeur and
a profoundly devotional feeling which in More's Latin
poems we look for in vain, however devotedly in early
life he may have admired them. He dearly loved a
jest, and we know that his jests were sometimes introduced inopportunely.

The following lines are taken from the first Hymn
of Picus:—

> En nova lux:—jam mente feror super ardua cœli
> Culmina, et empyreos tractus felicibus alis
> Transcendisse juvat. * * *
> Te colo, te veneror, te supplex semper adoro.
> Te genetrix natura colit, te pontus et aer.
> Quæque imam nimio sortita est pondere sedem
> Terra parens. * * *
> Errantes variis te observant sedibus ignes.
> Te Dominum, Regem, Moderatoremque fatentur
> Omnia ;—te summis affectant viribus omnes
> Cœlicolæ, affectant terrestres, tartara nomen
> Formidant, celerique fugâ mandata capessunt.

CHAPTER XIII.

T was in the month of May, 1532, that Sir Thomas More ceased to be Chancellor. He had incurred the King's displeasure by refusing to acquiesce in the divorce of Queen Katharine, and this displeasure was further aggravated by his declining to be present at the coronation of her successor. An endeavour was made to implicate him in the affair of the Nun of Kent, and paltry charges were brought against him in connection with his office as Chancellor. As he now draws nearer to the decline of life, there is forced upon him the reality of what he had imagined in the poetry of his earlier years, when he set himself to describe the freaks of Fortune, and to warn those who trust in her that although she may for the present 'beck and 'smile' upon a man, and help him to reach the height of his ambition, yet the time comes inevitably when—

> She whips her wheel around—and there he lies.[1]

---

[1] In Holbein's picture there is attached to the wheel a rope, which Fortune is supposed to use precisely for the purpose here described. Having recently had an opportunity of examining this remarkable painting for myself, I find that the description of it given in page 185 is

We learn from a letter addressed to Secretary Cromwell by Sir William Fitzwilliam the Treasurer of the King's household, that about this time Sir Thomas More,—who, being altogether out of favour at Court was living in a sort of seclusion at his house in Chelsea,—sent to desire an interview with Fitzwilliam; and that Fitzwilliam took Chelsea in his way to his own residence in Surrey, going up the river by boat and sending his horses forward to meet him. More's principal object in seeking this interview was to beg that the Treasurer would stand his friend in advocating a petition he was then making to Cromwell, who was now rapidly approaching to the zenith of his greatness;—being already Master of the Rolls and a principal Secretary of State. More at the same time made a complaint of the uncourteous treatment which he had met with from a certain person whose name is not mentioned. And Fitzwilliam states in the letter that this person had certainly behaved to Sir Thomas More otherwise 'than one gentleman ' should do to another;'—which he undertakes to show to Cromwell more fully when next they meet.[1]

More a suppliant to Cromwell.

It will not be out of place to introduce here a few passages from a letter addressed about this time by Sir Thomas More to the King. He refers to his having received from the King a gracious licence—

A touching letter to the King.

in one respect inaccurate. The Being who appears over the wheel in the clouds is the Salvator mundi, and the two others, although perhaps superhuman, do not at all accord with the conventional type of angels.

[1] So true to the life are Johnson's well-known lines: -

> At length his sovereign frowns. The train of state
> Mark the keen glance and watch the sign to hate.
> Where'er he turns he meets a stranger's eye,
> His suppliants scorn him, and his followers fly.

R

'that I should bestow the residue of my life about
' the provision of my soul in the service of God, and
' be your bedesman and pray for you:'—and also a
promise, that—' I should find your Highness good and
' gracious lord unto me.'—He prays that the King
will not be 'moved by any sinister information' to
distrust his truth. In the matter of 'this wicked
' woman of Canterbury,' he says that if he were 'a
' wretch of such monstrous ingratitude as to digress'
from his allegiance, he should 'desire no further
' favour than to be called upon to give up goods,
' lands, liberty, and life;'—the keeping of which
could never do him 'penny-worth of pleasure.' His
only comfort would then be to look forward to their
joyful meeting in heaven, where 'your Grace should
' surely see that I have ever been your true bedes-
' man.' He prays to be relieved from the 'torment'
of his 'present heaviness' caused by the 'dread and
' fear' of the Bill against him brought into Parliament.
He prays that he may not suffer from any 'sinister
' information,' and that the King will not allow any
man taking occasion from this Bill 'untruly to slander'
him.—He writes this at his 'poor house in Chelcith;'
and it is 'by the known rude hand' of the King's
' most humble and most heavy faithful subject and
' bedesman.' [1]

Very shortly after this, on their refusing to take
an oath of allegiance to the King and to the issue of

---

[1] Doubtless the handwriting of Sir Thomas More was well known
to the King. Like the writer himself it was plain and simple in
character, and by the admirers of the fantastic style of writing which
was in fashion with some persons at that period it might be thought
' rude.'

his marriage with Anne Boleyn, and to abjure the
supremacy of the Pope in England, Sir Thomas More
and Bishop Fisher were committed to the Tower.—
The state of things in England was thus reported to
the ambassador in Spain :—" Papam non agnoscimus.
" Every one now swears 'in verba Regis et Reginæ.'
" —Qui nolunt *turriti* statim fiunt.—Inter quos
" maximus ille Morus, et Roffensis." [1]

CHAP. XIII.

More and Fisher committed to the Tower.

While he was lying in the Tower Sir Thomas More
was repeatedly visited by the Law officers of the
Crown, who endeavoured by their questioning to
inveigle him into a denial of the King's supremacy
with a view to proceed against him ultimately on the
charge of high treason. Fisher put his questioners
to very little trouble in this matter. In fact the
simple refusal to give explicit answers to their inter-
rogatories was held sufficient by the State lawyers
to convict a man without any evidence of positive guilt.

More is urged to deny the King's supremacy.

Something similar to this occurred in the case of
Philip the nineteenth Earl of Arundel in the reign of
Elizabeth. While he lay a prisoner in the Tower, the
question was put to him by the Law officers of the
Crown, whether he held that it lay in the power of
the Pope to dethrone the Queen. And when it was
found that no explicit answer could be got from him
upon this point, the Chancellor proposed that he
should signify in writing that he refused to answer the

A refusal to answer is set down as guilt.

[1] Such was the singular and summary report of news brought from
England. In early life this ambassador—whose name was John Mason
—had been much befriended and assisted by Sir Thomas More; and
the fact of his using the term ' maximus ' may be taken as a pleasing
proof that he was not afraid to express his admiration of the character
of his former patron, although now lying as a criminal in the Tower.

question. This he declined to do. Shortly afterwards he was publicly arraigned, and condemned as
it would appear to perpetual imprisonment. He died
in the Tower in 1595.

Henry had fully made up his mind to carry two
points. He was determined that the legality of his
divorce, and also that the abrogation of the Pope's
authority in England, temporal and spiritual, should
be acknowledged by the nation at large. Upon the
first of these would depend the validity of his
marriage with Anne Boleyn; and the latter consti-
Henry's rea-
sons for super-
seding the
Pope. tuted his title to those large revenues which the
Pope had hitherto abstracted from the English people,
and to the temporal powers which he had hitherto
exercised over the English Church. All these were
transferred from the Pope to the King by the act of
his investing himself with the Pope's supremacy.

These events have been recorded by that Spanish
chronicler alluded to in page 234, with an amusing simplicity of narrative. He states that the King sent to
assemble all the great men of the kingdom and made
a speech to them, having told them at the outset that
he would have no one contradict him. You know—
he said—the great tyranny exercised year by year in
this kingdom, and the large sums of money which
the Pope extracts from us. It is my will that from
this day forward he shall extract no more. For this
I will that a Parliament shall be held, and that by
this Parliament he—the Pope—shall be abolished
forthwith. The assemblage answered with one voice
that it should be done. And it was done—for he had
already declared that no one should contradict him.
They even declared that it was done very well.

Henry had now fairly crossed the Rubicon in his march against Rome, and it was not in his Tudor nature to recede. He found however two embarrassing obstructions in the way. The venerable Bishop of Rochester and Sir Thomas More,—men of high position and spotless character, whose example would go far in influencing the people at large, were obstinate recusants, now lying in the Tower. By way of intimidating these two men, certain Carthusian monks who refused to take the oaths, were conducted to Tower Hill before the eyes of More and Fisher and put to death there by a most barbarous mode of execution.

These warnings however did not produce the effect which Henry desired; and he then determined that the two prisoners in the Tower should themselves be brought out to execution as a warning to the whole nation. The one a venerable bishop, who had been the confessor of the Countess of Richmond and Derby, the mother of his own father;—and the other one of his old and well tried servants, who had been raised by him to the Chancellorship only six years before, and with whom he had taken sweet counsel as they walked together like familiar friends in the garden by the riverside at Chelsea, his own arm being placed round the other's neck:—these two men were doomed to die. And it became a question how the law might be stretched so as to sentence them to death with at least the semblance of legality.

Sir Thomas More's legal knowledge and his natural acuteness enabled him to fence so adroitly with the Crown lawyers and others who were sent to examine him, as to baffle them in their attempts to manipulate

Chap. XIII.

Obstructions in the way.

Attempts to intimidate.

Henry's final resolve.

Difficulty in concocting a capital charge.

out of his answers anything that would constitute a capital charge.

At length Rich the King's solicitor came with two clerks as attendants to fetch away his materials for writing and his books. And while the two others were employed in 'trussing up' the books Rich drew him into a familiar conversation under the pretence of ancient friendship; and he stated at the trial that in this conversation More declared that it was not in the power of the Parliament to make the King supreme head of the Church.

During the interval between this visit and the trial, being forbidden the use of writing materials and being deprived of his books, he gave himself—we are told —entirely to meditation, 'keeping his chamber windows ' shut and his room very dark.' He said that now the wares were gone out of the shop, the windows must be closed.

There is a tradition that after the carrying away of Sir Thomas More's books a devotional work was sent to him by Bishop Fisher containing certain lines in English verse written with the Bishop's own hand;— the purport of the lines being to the effect that whoever desires to attain to the bliss of heaven must remain within the unity of the Church. The work itself is a treatise on the seven Penitential Psalms composed by Fisher at the suggestion of the Lady Margaret, and it is now in the library of the college at Douay.[1]

The trial came on in Westminster Hall before a

---

[1] Printed by Wynkyn de Worde in 1508. On the same page with the English lines is written :—

'Thomas Morus, dns Cancellarius Angliæ.
'Joh. Fisher, Epus Roffensis.'

special commission on July 1, 1535. There were
several charges in the indictment, to which charges
he gave answers at length; and it is remarked by
Mackintosh that the specific charge under which he
was actually convicted is not easily ascertained. It
being however a foregone conclusion that he must be
found guilty of a capital offence, the Commissioners
pronounced him to be guilty of high treason. a charge
at once ambiguous and comprehensive, resolving itself virtually into an opposition to the arbitrary will
of the Sovereign. The charge upon which Wolsey
had been arrested at York was a charge of high treason:
but he died at Leicester Abbey when on his way to
London for trial, and the precise nature of the charges
against him has never been ascertained. Wolsey
however knew with whom he had to deal, and he
prepared himself for the worst. When he found that
the Constable of the Tower had been sent by the
King to convey him thither, he said at once—I know
what is provided for me.

It was upon the evidence of the solicitor Rich
already alluded to,—the truth of which however Sir
Thomas More stoutly denied,—that the Court found
him guilty of treason. He boldly told the solicitor
to his face that he had perjured himself in giving that
evidence, and argued strongly upon the extreme
improbability of it. The Chancellor however pronounced in due form the frightful judgment of the
law upon persons found guilty of treason, and More
was taken back to the Tower. After four days a
message was brought from the King and Council
directing that before nine o'clock of the same morning Sir Thomas More should suffer death by behead-

ing. In consideration of his having filled the office of Chancellor, the more barbarous part of the sentence upon traitors was remitted by a special act of mercy —as he was told—on the part of the King. On receiving this intelligence he made the characteristic remark, that it was to be hoped that none of his friends would ever meet with the like act of mercy on the part of the King.

In Secretary Cromwell's private list of agenda the following significant entry is found:—'to learn the 'King's pleasure when Master More shall go to his 'execution.' Doubtless in a certain sense King Henry may be supposed to have taken pleasure in the execution even of those with whom he had once been familiarly associated. And in the period of exactly five years from the date of Cromwell's very business-like memorandum, it was Henry's pleasure that the secretary himself—having been created in the interim Earl of Essex—should suffer in the same manner and also in the same place whither 'Master More' went to his execution.[1]

In that Spanish 'Cronica' which has been already quoted a circumstance appears in connection with the execution which is not found in any of the biogra-

A statement made in the Spanish 'Cronica.' phies. It is stated that Sir Thomas More said to the executioner,—'Brother, give me five blows, in honour 'of the five wounds of Christ:'—and that he also desired the people to call upon the name of Christ

---

[1] It is remarked by the learned Thomas Jackson that on the same day of the same month, exactly twenty years after this, King Edward VI. died:—'as if that day were inserted in the everlasting calendar of the 'Righteous Judge to be after signed with the untimely death of King 'Henry's only son.'

while the five blows were given. It is stated that all
this was done;—the writer himself being an eye-
witness.

But while we give to the writer of this statement
all due credit for having faithfully recorded what he
actually saw, and what he actually heard, it cannot
for a moment be supposed that he heard those words
which he states to have been addressed by Sir Thomas
More to the executioner. Doubtless this Spanish
gentleman would hear the half-stifled murmur of the
irrepressible lamentations and prayers of the multitude at the moment when the axe fell, and for this
part of his story he was able to vouch. But for the
more important part he must have been indebted
either to imagination or to hearsay. If it was a fact
that any such request was made by Sir Thomas More
to the executioner, it was a striking and memorable
fact, and by persons of a religious turn of mind this
request would never be forgotten. It could not fail
to be handed down as a family tradition. Roper would
have known it; Cresacre More would have known it;
it would have been known to all those familiar friends
of Sir Thomas More who were about Stapleton at
Douay when he wrote his ' Tres Thomae : '—and if it
had been known to these persons or to any one among
them, it would certainly not have been left unrecorded
in the biographies.

Among other quaint stories told by this Spanish From the Spanish 'Cronica.'
chronicler of Court gossip, whose familiar and homely
style of narrative is almost Herodotean, there are
several conversations in which he represents Sir
Thomas More as having been one of the interlocu-
tors. After the manner of those ancient historians

he professes to give reports verbatim of speeches made and conversations held at which we cannot suppose him to have been actually present. He tells us that after the oath of supremacy had been taken by all the high personages of the realm both ecclesiastics and laymen, Sir Thomas More addressed the peers in his place as Chancellor, and warned them of approaching sorrow; at the same time declaring for himself that he would never bring his soul into condemnation through the fear of death. The peers in reply told him that he was setting his own opinion above that of all the prelates, and also assuming that his own soul was of more value than theirs. After further remarks made on both sides Sir Thomas More was committed to the Tower. This was a subject of great concern to the King, who had much affection for him, regarding him as one of the most learned men in the kingdom; and he resolved to pay him a visit in the Tower. He began the interview by asking ' good Thomas Mur ' what delusion had taken possession of his mind. He reminded him who it was that had lifted him up as it were from nothing and had made him Chancellor, and who holds at his disposal all the dignities of the realm. He asked More why he should refuse to do what all the others had done. The ' good Thomas Mur ' replied very deliberately but without the slightest symptom of fear, that he well knew how great a benefactor to him the King had been, at the same time he declared that all the world would never induce him to risk his soul which had been redeemed by our Lord Jesus Christ. There being two lords set over him, the one upon earth who has power over the body, and the other in heaven,

who has power over the soul, he cannot hesitate in $\qquad$
fixing upon the one whom he ought to obey.

The Chronicler goes on to say that after the
execution of Fisher the King decided that a few days'
respite should be allowed to 'the good Mur,' in
the hope that he might change his mind; but that
having the Holy Spirit in him he remained firm to
his resolution and braved the terrors of death. And
he adds that if the other great men had resisted the
King's persuasion as stoutly as 'the blessed Mur' resisted it, heresy would not have been so rampant over
England as it then was.

It will scarcely be doubted that such a culprit as
Sir Thomas More had never stood at any European
tribunal for a thousand years. These are the words
More on his
of Sir James Mackintosh. And he questions whether
trial compared
in any moral respect even Socrates could claim a
to Socrates.
superiority.[1] The Emperor Charles V.—in whose
presence at the ceremonial of his public entrance into
London some years before, Sir Thomas More had
Declaration
delivered a complimentary oration,—declared to the
made by
Charles V.
English ambassador that if it had been his own good
fortune to possess such a servant and councillor, he
would rather have lost the best city in his dominions
than have lost Sir Thomas More. The Pope, Paul III.
in the first outbreak of his anger prepared a Bull of
excommunication with a succession of formidable
anathemas against Henry VIII., but for the moment
he suspended it through the intervention of Francis I.

[1] In this remark Mackintosh was anticipated by Hieronymus Gebui-
lerus, a German scholar, who spoke of Sir Thomas More as —'non
'minorem constantiam in judicio et supplicio præ se ferentem quam
'iniquissimo Atheniensium senatus-consulto condemnatus Socrates.'

and it was not actually issued until three years afterwards.

Immediately after Sir Thomas More's execution certain tracts or brief narratives in Latin, styled 'Expositiones,' were circulated in manuscript, chiefly on the Continent:—into England they were introduced by stealth and very sparingly.   One of these manuscript 'Expositiones'[1] is in the form of a Latin epistle written to Jacobus Godrandus a senator of Dijon by his son who was afterwards President of the Senate of Burgundy.   It is illustrated by a singular device after the manner of the mediæval illuminations.   The ex-Chancellor, arrayed in his robes of office, is about to be decapitated with the sword as in the martyrdom of certain saints.   He kneels to receive the stroke, with hands clasped together and head bowed down reverently in prayer.   King Henry—who stands by, wearing an ample robe of royal purple and having upon his head a golden crown, with the sceptre in his right hand,—raises his left hand as if in the act of speaking. The headsman is clad in showy attire, and the sword which he holds uplifted is of large and ponderous dimensions.[2]

One of these 'Expositiones' was printed in Paris, being compiled as the writer states partly from manuscript narratives in French and partly from hearsay.   A similar narrative in German is also in print.

---

[1] Sold in the library of Mr. Corser.

[2] In Henry's own Psalter, which is in the British Museum, there is a representation of him as King David singing to the harp; while Somers his jester stands a little way apart with clasped hands in a sort of solemn rapture.

These 'Expositiones' were followed by pieces in Latin verse, dirges, and elegies; a 'Carmen Heroi-
'cum' printed at Hagenau, and a 'Naenia' at Lou-
vain. Both of these were at first attributed to Eras-
mus. But the latter was avowedly the composition of
Joannes Secundus; and of the former Jortin ventures
to deny utterly that it could have been written by
Erasmus, who was now an old man in declining health
and not at all 'likely to be in a versifying humour.'
The editor however pronounces it to be 'tam elegans
'quam lectu dignissimum,' although he rather hesi-
tates to vouch for its being the actual composition of
Erasmus.

CHAPTER XIV.

HE Pope having been now stripped of his supremacy in England, and the King's title being established by Act of Parliament to those powers and temporalities in England which had been usurped by the Pope,— specified in the Act of Supremacy as 'immunities, 'profits, and commodities,'—Henry took active measures to make this fact known to his subjects at large.   Preachers were sent over the country to proclaim it in the churches.   Bishops were required to see that their clergy impressed it upon the people in their respective dioceses.   And the civil authorities had orders to apprehend and commit to prison all persons who should so much as speak against the King's supremacy.

Proclamation made over the land.

A letter is extant in which Lee the Archbishop of York informs the Secretary Cromwell that he had committed to prison a certain priest in Holderness who had spoken words ' sounding towards the advancement ' of the Bishop of Rome :' the words alleged to have been uttered being these ;—' They say there is no ' Pope :—I know well that there was a Pope.'   And Sir Piers Dutton from his residence in Cheshire writes to

Gainsayers committed to prison.

the Lord Privy Seal that he has committed to the
Castle of Chester, there to await the King's pleasure,
one John Heseham, who had spoken divers 'traitorous
' and seditious words:'—to wit that 'if the spiritual
' men had holden together the King could not have
' been the Head of the Church, and that the Bishop
' of Rochester and Sir Thomas More had died
' martyrs.'

The following passage is taken from a sermon
which was preached before the King on Palm Sunday,
1539, by Cuthbert Tunstall Bishop of Durham, and
for some time Master of the Rolls. In the title the
King is styled ' in earth next under Christ Supreme
' Head of the Church of England.'

' But the Bishop of Rome because he cannot longer
' in this realm wrongfully use his usurped power in
' all things as he was wont to do, and suck out of this
' realm by avarice insatiable innumerable sums of
' money yearly, to the great exhausting of the same,—
' he therefore, moved and replete with furious ire and
' pestilent malice, goeth about to stir all Christian
' nations that will give ear to his devilish enchant-
' ments, to move war against this realm of England,
' giving it in prey to all those who by his devilish
' instigation will invade it. Which few words,—to
' give it in prey,—how great mischief they do contain
' I shall open to thee, thou true Englishman. * * *
' But for all this take courage unto thee, and be
' nothing afraid. Thou hast God on thy side, who
' hath given this realm to the generation of English-
' men, to every man in his degree, after the laws of
' the same. Thou hast a noble, virtuous, and victo-
' rious King, hardy as a lion, who will not suffer thee

' to be so devoured by such wild beasts. Only take
' an English heart unto thee, and mistrust not God,
' but trust in him firmly.'

In short, so long as the Pope was invested with the
supremacy, it was simply by the Pope's permission

Power of the
Pope to de-
throne sove-
reigns.

that Henry held the Crown itself; inasmuch as the
Pope claimed the power of depriving the King of his
sovereignty and absolving his subjects from their
allegiance. It has already been stated that the Earl
of Arundel was kept in the Tower until his death
after an imprisonment of six years, simply because he
refused to say that the Pope did not possess the
power to depose Queen Elizabeth.

Richard Croke, one of the Canons of Wolsey's
recently founded college in Oxford, wrote to inform
the Secretary Cromwell that he had ' preached six
' score sermons ' upon this subject, some of them in
Oxford: 'not failing in every one of them to speak
' effectually against the usurped power of the Bishop
' of Rome; and some time as the matter gave occasion
' against the abomination of him, his Cardinals, and
' his cloistered hypocrites.' He states that he had
proved by Scripture, and by the authority of the
ancient doctors,—and also 'by the sayings of More[1]
' and other Papists themselves,'—that the assumed
power of the Bishop of Rome in England was an
usurped power; and that ' for maintenance of their
' pomps and fruitless ceremonies they have always

[1] Croke's allusion to Sir Thomas More, who had been his patron in
early life, is much less respectful than that made by the ambassador
Mason, which was quoted in a former page. Sir Thomas More and
his friend Richard Pace, by their influence with the King, had materially
promoted Croke's advancement in the Church.

'been cause of all the greatest schisms that have been
'in Christ's Church.' He says that in order to adapt
his discourses to the level of his audience he had used
'similitudes meet to make them perceive the force'
of his arguments, and that he often found them 'in-
'clinable to the truth.'

Lee the Archbishop of York was supposed to have
been remiss in enforcing the publication of the King's
supremacy among his clergy, and several letters are
extant,—one to the King and two to Cromwell,—in
which he labours to exonerate himself from the charge.
To the King,—'in most humble manner prostrate,'—
he represents, that he has himself ' taught and caused
' to be taught' throughout his diocese that the King
has been declared 'as well by Convocations of the
' clergy as by the High Court of Parliament to be the
' Supreme Head in earth of the Church of England.'
He states also that he has caused 'all collects and
' places of the mass book wherein any mention is
' made of the Bishop of Rome, to be rased out.'
He enters into the detail of all this, and most humbly
entreats the King not to believe any complaints
against him before hearing him in self-defence.

In writing to Cromwell he dilates upon the low
condition of the clergy of his diocese with regard to
learning. In the whole diocese he does 'not know
' that there are more than twelve secular priests who
' are preachers; and to put learning and cunning to
' preach into the heads of such as have it not already,'
is beyond his power. Many of the benefices being
only four or five or six pounds a year are 'so exile'
that no learned man will take them, and they are
' fain to take such as are presented, provided that

S

     'they are honest of conversation and can competently 'understand what they read, and can in due form and 'rite minister sacraments and sacramentals.'

     At this crisis and for some time after this many thoughtful people in England became dumb, and all who were adherents of the Pope dared not to

Latin verses on Sir Thomas More's execution. open their mouths. But on the Continent the execution of Sir Thomas More was frequently taken as a subject for Latin verse by foreign scholars and Englishmen in foreign parts who thought themselves out of reach of the summary vengeance of King Henry VIII. According to the prevailing fashion of the day comparisons are drawn in these compositions with the great classical worthies and personages of

Holland. antiquity. Henry is another Nero, while More is the wise and philosophic Seneca. Henry like Nero puts to death his mother the Church, and he causes Sir Thomas More to be beheaded for endeavouring to save her. In another piece this writer places More in the same category with Aristides, Socrates, and Boethius. And in another he introduces the favourite conceit of placing him on a par with Cicero in point of eloquence, and in poetry superior; while Anne

Hervetus. Boleyn is another Fulvia.[1] A learned French scholar says that as the people of Rome looked up at the head of Cicero upon the rostra with feelings of sorrowful indignation, so would the English people look up at the head of Sir Thomas More upon London

Joannes Secundus. Bridge, lamenting over the loss of the best and most learned of their citizens.[2] Another throws out ominous hints of the approach of an avenging

---

[1] Henry Holland, a Roman Catholic divine at Douay.

[2] Hervetus, a friend of Linacre and Lupset.

Nemesis.[1] Another compares Sir Thomas More to
Cato, and taunts the people of England with their
effrontery in calling him their countryman. He does
not belong to England: he has created a native land
for himself—

Ipse sibi patriam condidit Utopiam.[2]

A similar attempt to play upon the word Utopia
occurs in a piece by an English divine who became
eventually a bishop. He says that perhaps you may
find another man like More,—or even better than
More;—but you must look for him in Utopia.[3]
Another writer gives us to understand that it had
struck him as he was contemplating Sir Thomas
More's portrait that the biographer who should be
able to portray in all its fulness the noble character
of Sir Thomas More would be among biographers an
Apelles.[4]

Stapleton the Jesuit of Douay commemorates his
virtues in one set of verses and his attainments in
another. He is represented as having possessed an
entire 'encyclopædia' of virtues: and in literature
he is said to have been at once an orator, a poet, a
classical scholar, a lawyer, an historian, and a philo-
sopher. Now that More and Fisher who were the
great luminaries of England have been extinguished

---

[1] Joannes Secundus.

[2] Latomus, a Professor at Louvain.

[3] White, appointed Bishop of Winchester by Queen Mary.

[4] John Fowler of Bristol, a learned printer, who left England at the
Reformation, and printed at Antwerp and elsewhere many treatises
against the Lutherans. He printed in 1573 Sir Thomas More's Dialogue of Comfort in tribulation.

by the impious Henry, the whole realm is plunged into darkness.

The following lines have a quaint epigrammatic turn, though far-fetched:

Cope.

> Quis vivente velit Thomâ non vivere Moro?
> Quis Moro nolit sic moriente mori ? [1]

Owen.

The same may be said of Owen's lines written half a century afterwards:

> Abscindi passus caput est a corpore Morus.
> Abscindi crines noluit a capite.

Joco-seria.

The following belongs to a class of epitaphs which have been styled 'Joco-seria':

> Mori memento—quisquis nunc tumulum vides :
> Ille, ille gentis tanta lux Britannicæ—
> Charitum voluptas—dulce Musarum decus—
> Virtutis ara—terminus constantiæ—
> Hic ille Morus—ille divisus jacet,
> Irâ furentis immolatus Principis.
> Pœnâ quid istâ fecerit dignum, rogas ?
> Age—arrige aures,—Ipse, quamvis mortuus
> Tibi dicit ipse.—Nempe quid dicit ?—Nihil.

But while in other countries so many eulogistic effusions were circulated after Sir Thomas More's execution, there was at least one virulent detractor at home. His memory was reviled in a series of Latin epigrams by Nicolas Bourbon a French scholar who was at the time a resident in England, being engaged in the tuition of several youths in

Latin verses by Borbonius.

---

[1] Alan Cope, who wrote against the Lutherans, and also affixed his name to certain Dialogues written by his friend Harpsfield at that time in prison.

families of distinction. He had acquired some
facility in writing Epigrammata of passable merit,
and he seems to have amused himself by 'spinning a
' thousand such a day.' Having caught the ear of the
Court he made the most of his opportunities by
flattering the great, and reviling those who were
obnoxious to the great. The reforming party was
now in the ascendant, and to that party he administers fair words and flattery. When Cromwell is
placed at the head of ecclesiastical affairs as the
King's Vicar General, the poet's heart is said to leap
with joy. When Cranmer is made Archbishop of
Canterbury, Britain is congratulated on her good
fortune in possessing such a paragon of all that is
good and great; and this is followed by a sort of
deification of Cranmer. The preaching of Latimer is
the sound of the trumpet of the Eternal Father.

The Queen seems to have been the special
patroness of Borbonius. She had interested herself
to procure his release from imprisonment, and she
had also procured for him certain pupils:—the names
of Hervey, Carew, and H. Norris being specially
mentioned. It is to be remarked that Sir Henry
Norris was connected with some of the charges
brought against Anne Boleyn at her trial.

There seems no doubt that Anne Boleyn had
reason to believe that if it had been in his power Sir
Thomas More would have prevented her marriage
with the King;—and if so, she would be tempted to
'indulge a sort of revenge by encouraging Borbonius
to traduce his memory.

The reflections made by Borbonius upon More's
character and memory are extremely bitter and

CHAP. XIV.

Scurrilous lines on Sir Thomas More.

On the imputation of low birth.

utterly devoid of wit. He makes several awkward attempts to play upon the Greek word ' μωρός '— which is assumed as the Græcized form of the name ' More.'[1] More is also represented as a man of low birth—' earth-born '—capriciously raised by Fortune to a false position of wealth and dignity. In that position he is represented as having demeaned himself both towards the people and towards the King in the spirit of a tyrant and in a manner hateful in the sight of God. In his presumption he dared to say that he was beyond the reach of fate. But the neck of the wretched man has lately come under the stroke of the axe. The bubble was not long in bursting.

Borbonius was probably quite aware that in reality Sir Thomas More was no tyrant towards his fellowmen, nor—as Borbonius puts it,—hateful in the sight of God. But he saw that it would please the party who were dominant to have his memory thus stigmatized. Neither was Sir Thomas More a man of low birth. To his contemporaries Wolsey and Cromwell this term was applied, and doubtless with sufficient reason. But More, although not of noble extraction, was unquestionably of gentle blood. His family were entitled to wear arms, a privilege and distinction which at that period was real. It was well known however to the parasites about Court that these scornful imputations of ignoble origin would sound sweetly in the ears of the proud old nobility, who had been elbowed out of some of the great offices of State by

---

[1] To an ill-natured punster the Greek word would be tempting. On the other hand it suggested to Erasmus the idea of paying his friend a compliment by entitling his famous work—Μωρίας Ἐγκώμιον.

men who did not belong to their own grade, which was uppermost and had been hitherto exclusive.

It has been already stated[1] that the early and more original Lives of Sir Thomas More were written by members of his own family and that the writers belonged to the Church of Rome. In the elaborate account of the family and descendants of Sir Thomas More which is given by Hunter in his edition of the Life by Cresacre More, it is stated that only two out of five grandsons—they being the sons of Sir Thomas More's only son John More—continued to be members of the Church of Rome. Edward and Bartholomew joined the Reformed Church, and Thomas became a clergyman in that Church.

Many of his descendants became Protestants.

Another of Sir Thomas More's descendants by name George More is mentioned by Philip Camerarius as having accompanied Sir Philip Sidney in his embassy to the German emperor Rudolf II. in the year 1575. Camerarius speaks of this George More as a man distinguished for his abilities, his sweetness of manner, and his singular modesty, and he says that the pleasant conversations which they had together will not easily be effaced from his memory. This George More must also have been a Protestant. The fact of his being associated with Sir Philip Sidney in a mission the object of which was to negotiate a coalition of the Protestant States against the Pope and Philip of Spain speaks for itself.

Although we now find Lives of Sir Thomas More in almost all the languages of Europe, it does not appear that any Life in the English language existed even in manuscript until the reign of Queen Mary, nor was

No one ventures to write his Life.

---

[1] P. 177.

CHAP. XIV. any published in England until the reign of Charles I.
To have ventured upon making Sir Thomas More the
subject of any published work,—unless it were after
the manner of Borbonius,—so long as Henry VIII.
lived, would have amounted to treason.   During the
brief period of Queen Mary's reign the admirers
of Bishop Fisher and Sir Thomas More began to
breathe more freely.   Mary herself would reverence
the memory of one who stood out against the King in
More's English
works : 1557. the question of her mother's divorce.   She caused his
English works to be collected and published by his
nephew William Rastall in the year 1557, and to her
the volume was dedicated.   About the same time there
was published at Florence an interesting little work
in Italian containing reminiscences of conversations
which had taken place at More's house in Chelsea
nearly a quarter of a century before.   It was published by Ellis Heywood the son of John Heywood
Il Moro. the epigrammatist, with the title of ' Il Moro.'   It is
dedicated to Cardinal Pole who at that time was the
Archbishop of Canterbury.   In Mary's reign also was
Roper's Life,
written circa
1557. written Roper's Life, which must be regarded as the
fountain-head of all the biographies ; Roper being the
son-in-law of Sir Thomas More and for some years
an inmate in his house.   Although the first written
of all the Lives, for many years it existed only in
scattered manuscript copies.   About this time a Life
was written by Nicolas Harpsfield a divine of the
Church of Rome :—this Life has never been printed,
but at least two copies are said to exist in manuscript, the one in the Lambeth library and the other
in the library of Emmanuel College, Cambridge.[1]   In

---

[1] See Wordsworth's Ecclesiastical Biography, ii. 45.

the year 1588,—the Spanish Armada being sent out under the auspices of the Pope, and there being on the Continent a general expectation that the supremacy of the Pope over the English Church would be re-established,—Thomas Stapleton an English Jesuit at Douay gave to the world a Life of More in Latin, which forms one portion of his work entitled 'Tres Thomæ,' the other two being St. Thomas the Apostle and Archbishop Thomas à Becket. This was the first Life actually printed, although Sir Thomas More had now been dead nearly a quarter of a century.

Stapleton derived his materials partly from Roper's manuscript, partly from More's own writings, and partly from information communicated by Englishmen who were Stapleton's fellow exiles. Among these were Dr. Clement, whose clever wife had been brought up in More's house with his daughters;—John Harris, More's secretary;—John Heywood the epigrammatist;—and William Rastall, More's nephew.

He introduces his work with a rather affected and turgid preamble. He says that for a long time past many most learned, most distinguished, and most estimable persons have desired to see an account of the life and actions of Thomas More, to whose name he appends another like string of superlative epithets, as well as a reference to his noble martyrdom for the orthodox Catholic, Apostolic, Roman faith. And whereas not a few persons have attempted to write such a work, but have not carried it into effect, Stapleton himself undertakes to supply that which is so much to be desired: having a full reliance upon the Divine aid, and also a confidence that he shall be furthered in the work by the prayers and intercession of the martyr himself.

About ten years after this, there being the prospect of a disputed succession after the death of Elizabeth in 1599, a somewhat enlarged Life was written by an unknown author, who derived his materials in part from the manuscript Lives of Roper and Harpsfield, and partly from Stapleton's Life which was in print. This work remained in manuscript until it was published by Dr. Wordsworth in his Ecclesiastical Biography from a copy in the library at Lambeth. In the list of what may be termed the early Lives of More this brings up the rear: and as each successive writer had the materials of his predecessor to make use of, it may be regarded as the fullest and most complete of the list.

At length in the year 1627, being the second year after the accession of Charles I., the Life of Sir Thomas More by his son-in-law Roper was actually published. Nearly seventy years had passed since it was written, and Roper himself had now been dead fifty years. The editor, who is nameless, states that by 'good hap' he had lighted upon a copy in a friend's house, and that he 'deemed it an error to 'permit so great a treasure to remain buried as it 'were within the walls of one private family.' He therefore committed it to the press, 'to the end that 'the whole world might receive comfort and profit by 'reading the same.' Charles I. had recently married a Roman Catholic queen, and it might be thought that better prospects were now dawning upon the Romish Church in England.

Soon after this another Life came out which was

written by one of the great-grandsons of Sir Thomas
More,—either Thomas, a priest, or Cresacre who
succeeded to the family estate at Barnborough.
This work was for two centuries ascribed to the
former; but in 1828 the Rev. Joseph Hunter who
published an edition of it, adduced strong reasons for
believing that the real author was Cresacre More.
It seems possible that Cresacre may have edited and
added to a memoir originally written by his elder
brother and founded upon the two Lives already
existing. This Life is dedicated to Queen Hen-
rietta Maria, who is reminded that Thomas More
the ecclesiastic had been instrumental in procuring
the Pope's sanction to her marriage with King
Charles.

In more recent times Lives of Sir Thomas More
have been written by Warner, Cayley, Macdiarmid,
Mackintosh, Lord Campbell, and several other biographers. In staple and substance each of these is
of course derived from those early biographies, and
primarily from Roper; supplementary memoranda
being gleaned from the various extant letters of Sir
Thomas More and some of his learned friends, among
which none are so valuable as the letters of Erasmus.
The fact is noted in a recent number of the Quar-
terly Review, that out of the number of fifteen
biographers of Sir Thomas More there is not one
that had a manuscript to work from.

The Life of Sir Thomas More by Sir James
Mackintosh has been pronounced by one admiring
critic to be among the most charming pieces of
biography in any language. Another critic condemns the author for showing in the work a tendency

to idealism;—a professing to deal with thoughts rather than with things. No such imputation as this can be thrown upon Lord Campbell's Life. It is full of facts. The author's remarks are always pleasantly made:—and they are generally much to the point.

APPENDIX.

ESIDES several historical works Pirckheimer wrote a humorous piece entitled 'Laus Po-'dagræ' in imitation of the Encomium Moriæ. Podagra is represented as boasting that the greatest warriors have succumbed to her, and that she had slackened the speed of the swift-footed Achilles. It was not Briseis, but Podagra who caused him to keep aloof from the fight.

Rhenanus was a scholar, a theologian, and an antiquary. Like Erasmus he thought it possible to devise a system of concord in religious matters which might include all parties. Erasmus presented to him a Commentary on the first Psalm with a laudatory dedication.

———————

APPENDIX.

See page 22. Tho following aro translations from the lighter compositions of Hieronymus Amaltheus and Politian:

THE HOUR-GLASS.

Amaltheus.

The dust that trickles through this glass,
Marking tho moments as thoy pass,
Was onco Alcippus;—who, combust
By Galla's lightning, shrank to dust.
Ill-fated dust,—thus doomed to prove
No rest remains for those who love!

THE FUNERAL OBSEQUIES OF THE POPE.

Politian.

Stretched for the tomb the Pontiff lay,—
Crowds flocked to kiss the lifeless clay.
Matrons with maidens fair and meek
Touched with warm lips the livid cheek.—
Our Pontiff next—if he be wise—
Will lie in state before he dies.

See page 23. From one of tho epigrammata of Philip Melancthon,
entitled " Jocus in importunum januæ pulsatorem."

Melancthon.

In his attic, all divine,
Poet sits in phrensy fine:
Far above tho vulgar ken,
Verses trickling from his pen.
In furious haste a rustic boor .
Comes up thundering at tho door,
And cries,—there's nought—and this doth show it,—
Between an ass and such a poet!—
Poet answers, short and sore,
Nought between them,—but a door!

The following translation of Sir Thomas More's piece,— APPENDIX.

See page 12. 'De nautis ejicientibus monachum cui fuerant confessi,'—is taken from a manuscript of miscellaneous verses by Sir Nicholas Bacon, entitled,—'The Recreations of his age.' The measure is the same with that of Sir Thomas More's early production,—'A merry jest, how a Serjeant would learn to play the Friar.'

A FRIAR AND THE MARINERS.

Once in storms great
  A ship was beat
So strong with tempest's rage,
  That naught was able,
  Anchor nor cable,
The danger to assuage.

Sir Nicholas
Bacon.

The shipmen were
  Stricken by fear
With fervent devotion ;
  They cried—alas—
  Their ill life was
The cause of God's motion.

Amongst this sort
  To their comfort
A friar there was within,
  Who willed them all
  On knees to fall,
And straight confess their sin.

For, as he said—
  Heavier than lead
The Prophet calleth sin.
  A cork unmeet
  While tempests beat
To carry when we swim.

To bo confessed
Each man straight pressed :—
The friar was thoroughly wrought ;—
Confessing men,—
Absolving them,—
So much a calm they sought.

But when they spied,—
And had well tried,—
No calm thereby to grow :
But surges high
So ragingly
Their ship did overflow :—

Straightway quoth one,—
Marvel is none,
Though water come herein ;
While we forget
The ship as yet
Is laden with all our sin.

This friar our mate,
Within whose pate
Our sins remain this day,
Take and cast out,—
Who without doubt
Shall carry them clean away.

This they agree,
And in the sea
The friar straight is cast.
Then in their sight
The ship sailed light
And through the danger passed.

Sir Nicholas Bacon found amusement in versifying also one of More's recorded ' Witty sayings.'

On a Glorious Man and a Plain Friend.

In wanton rhyme a great grave matter
   A glorious man showed to his friend one time,
Who said straightway,—being loth to flatter—
   The body grave was marred with too fond rhyme.
This man then all his labour loth to lose
Mad metre turneth straight into sad prose.
And—to be glorified above the stars
Again to his friend's judgment he refers.—
   Oh, quoth his friend—thou seemest at this season,
   Out of good rhyme t' have made nor rhyme nor reason.

The following is told as a ' merry tale ' of a visit paid by John Skelton the poet to the Bishop of Norwich his diocesan. See page 133

The Bishop and Skelton had been at variance, and the Bishop's porter had been strictly charged to refuse him admission at the gates. He contrived however to cross the moat by means of a tree which had been blown down, and presented himself suddenly before the Bishop who was just rising from dinner. The Bishop addressing him as,—' thou caitiff'—demanded to know how he had gained admission. Skelton replied that he had crossed the moat, and had nearly been drowned therein: and that he had encountered these difficulties in order to present the Bishop with a couple of pheasants for his supper. The Bishop ' defied ' both him and his pheasants, and ordered him—wretch as he was—to pack out of the house. Skelton mused for a while, and then said that if his Lordship knew the names of the two pheasants he would be ' content ' to take them. The Bishop hastily Skelton's visit
to Bishop Nix

T

and angrily asked,—' what bo their names?' This one,—
said Skelton,—is called ' Alpha,' and the other is called
' Omega :'—and if it please your Lordship to take them, I
promise you that as ' Alpha' is the first I ever brought you,
so ' Omega' shall be the last.

The company who were present begged the Bishop to bo
' good lord ' to him for the sake of his ' merry conceit;' and
in the end Skelton was taken into favour again.

In another of the popular stories of the day John Skelton
is brought into immediate contact with Sir Thomas More
himself.   It is said that a certain Amazonian female who was
employed as a servant in a tavern in Westminster, dressed
herself in male habiliments and fought a duel with a Spaniard
in St. George's Fields.   Having disarmed her antagonist,
she granted him his life on condition that he should wait
upon her at supper in the evening and own himself van-
quished.   It was arranged by Skelton that Sir Thomas
More and certain others should be invited to this supper.
Before supper-time the Spaniard took an opportunity of
making Sir Thomas More acquainted with his own version
of the late encounter, representing his opponent as ' a des-
' perate gentleman of the Court;' upon which Sir Thomas
assured him that to be foiled by any gentleman of England
was no dishonour to him, inasmuch as the great ' Cæsar
' himself was beaten back by their valour.'   At length the
heroine herself made her appearance before the company ;
and the Spaniard said,—addressing himself to Sir Thomas
More,—' this is that gentleman of the Court whose prowess
' I do so highly commend, and to whom in all valour I
' acknowledge myself so inferior.'   Then she also addressed
Sir Thomas More, and taking off her hat, with her hair
falling about her ears, exclaimed amid much laughter of the
company,—' and, Sir, he that hath so worsted the gentleman

'to-day is none other than Long Meg of Westminster:[1]—
'and so you are all welcome.'

Then they all 'made good cheer' with no small merriment; and 'the Spanish Knight waited on her trencher,—
'she sitting in her majesty.'

[1] Such was the heroine's sobriquet. The place of her birth is said to have been in Lancashire, a county famous in those early days for the great stature and strength of its natives.

THE END.

www.ingramcontent.com/pod-product-compliance
Lightning Source LLC
Chambersburg PA
CBHW031343070726
47496CB00017B/1640